# SUFFER THE CHILDREN

## James R. Olson

**Erian Press**

*To Katherine, the daughter I always wanted, but never had. You are in my heart always.*

# CHAPTER ONE

Our footsteps echoed off the tiled walls of the basement corridor as I followed the morgue attendant through double, swinging doors into a room where too many fluorescent lights cast a blinding glare off sterile surfaces. Everything was white and stainless steel, with an overpowering odor of antiseptic and strong detergent. Frigid air blasted from the air conditioner, chilling the room for the dead that resided behind the rows of stainless steel doors.

I was shivering, but only partially from the cold air. This was my first visit to a morgue and I had a queasy feeling in the pit of my stomach. Standing in the presence of death was causing me to sense my own mortality in a way that was making me very uncomfortable. If I didn't feel a strong obligation, I would have gotten out of that room as quickly as possible.

The jaded attendant stopped in front of one of the numbered doors and pulled out the shelf-like slab. He turned back the sheet, exposing the head and shoulders of a naked female corpse. "Here she is."

This was the first time I had ever seen a dead body that had not yet been prepared by morticians. When I gathered enough courage to look at the body there was a momentary sense of relief, and then confusion. This emaciated woman, with sunken cheeks and long, snarled hair, couldn't possibly be my younger sister. Yet this couldn't be a case of mistaken identity. The cops, who had contacted me after finding my name and address in the dead woman's purse, had already positively identified the body from fingerprint files. Confirming the identification was merely a formality.

Even though it had been years since I'd seen Jenny, it didn't seem conceivable she had changed so drastically. I would have passed this woman on the street without even looking twice. However there was one sure way to satisfy myself this was really my sister.

"Could I see her left hand?" I asked.

"She ain't gonna care." The attendant lifted the sheet to display the left arm.

It required an effort of will to touch the cold, waxy flesh as I turned the hand to examine the little finger. My heard skipped a beat when I saw the tiny knob on the second knuckle of the deformed finger. When Jenny had been five years old she had fallen off her bike and broken the finger. The injury had never healed properly, and the distinct abnormality had always embarrassed her.

*"Jenny, Jenny,"* I thought. *"How the hell did it come to this?"*

I should have felt shock or grief, but none of this seemed real —not the body or the morgue or that my little sister was dead.

"Hey buddy, have you seen enough?" the attendant asked. "I can't stand around here all day, you know. I've gotta get this one ready for an autopsy."

"I've seen enough," I replied, wondering whether my feeling of sadness was because of Jenny's wasted life, or because I hadn't done anything to prevent her death, or because the last of my family was gone. "The police asked me to make a positive identification. Do I have to sign a form or something?"

"I don't know nothing about forms," the attendant said as he covered Jenny's body and slid it back into the cooler. "If the cops told you to ID the body, I suppose you need to tell them. Far as I'm concerned this one's already been identified. The toe tag says Jennifer Wilson, and that's good enough for me."

I bit my tongue to keep from making a caustic comment. "What was the cause of death?" I asked.

"Beats me." The morgue obviously didn't care how Jenny died. "She was probably an addict. We get 'em in here all the time. They overdose and go off on a one way trip to some fantasy world. If you want more information, you'll have to ask the cops."

"I'll do that. Thanks for your concern."

"No problem," he said, not recognizing my sarcasm—or maybe he just didn't give a damn.

I followed the morgue attendant's directions and drove across town to the Campbell police station. The bright, clean lobby, about the size of a large living room, still had the smell of new construction. There was no one in the waiting area when I stepped up to the window where a uniformed female officer was talking on the phone.

"May I help you?" she asked when she disconnected the call.

"Good Morning. I'm Jonathon Wilson. An Officer Ryan contacted me concerning my sister, Jennifer Wilson. I've just come from the hospital where I identified the body and would like to speak to someone concerning the details of Jennifer's death."

"Please have a seat. I'll see if Officer Ryan is available this morning."

I sat on one of the Naugahyde and chrome chairs, positioned so I could see out the large, floor-to-ceiling windows along the front wall. There were several tattered magazines on a table, but I didn't feel like reading.

It had been nine years since I'd seen Jenny, and there hadn't been any contact at all during the four years since the auto accident that killed our parents. I had sent a telegram to her last known address, but she hadn't bothered to reply or attend the funeral. She never answered the few letters I sent, and my last attempt, three years ago, had been returned marked, 'Not at this address'. A sense of guilt flooded over me because I hadn't made a greater effort to locate her. If I had tried harder, maybe I could have done something to prevent this tragedy.

Jenny and I never had much in common. I was four years older, which is a wide gulf when you're young. Mostly she had gone her way and I'd gone mine. In my memory she was still a beautiful teenager, with the long brown hair and laughing hazel eyes.

Because I was attending college at Madison, I hadn't been home when Jenny began her downhill spiral. I'd never met Justin, the young man our parents considered the cause of Jenny's deterioration. I didn't even remember his last name. All I knew about him was what Mom had told me, and she had vehemently disapproved. Justin, two years older than Jenny, was a high school dropout working a minimum wage job at Johnson's Hardware. Mom had complained that he drank too much and had a wild streak that had gotten him into occasional trouble with the law. However Jenny fancied herself wildly in love and Mom worried the relationship would lead to a broken heart. It would have been better for everyone concerned if it had only resulted in a broken heart.

According to Mom, Jenny had started drinking, had quit the girl's basketball team, and had begun neglecting her studies. Maybe that's when I should have acted like a big brother, but I had been engrossed in my own life and easily convinced myself Mom had been overreacting. Having just finished my own teen years, I was familiar with adolescent rebellion, certain in my twenty-year-old wisdom that Justin was only a temporary distraction.

Then, just a few weeks past her sixteenth birthday, Jenny and Justin had run away to parts unknown.

Eventually Mom and Dad learned the two runaways had been in Chicago for several months, and then had lived in Cleveland for a short time before settling in Milwaukee. Nine years ago, Jenny had called Mom and Dad collect. She had managed to get herself pregnant and had given birth to a baby girl. Apparently when she had experienced labor pains and entered the welfare ward of Milwaukee County General Hospital, Justin had abdicated his parental responsibilities, leaving her without money or a place to live. Alone and frightened, she had asked Dad to wire enough cash for a bus ticket so she could return to Westport with her daughter.

Mom and Dad had been overjoyed to have Jenny home again,

and had doted on Marie, their only granddaughter. They did everything they could to provide a happy haven for them both. It just hadn't worked out.

Although my schedule had been crowded with classes and a part time job, I had managed to get home for a few days between semesters. Even nine years ago, I had been shocked at the change in Jenny's appearance. She had lost so much weight she looked sick. Her once beautiful hair was dull and lifeless. There was a haunted, dead look in her eyes.

While Jenny had been with Justin, her drinking had escalated into drug usage, and she had become addicted. Prostitution had paid for both her and Justin's habits until she was too pregnant to turn tricks.

Mom and Dad paid for counseling and treatment—anything to rescue their daughter from drugs. I had to give Jenny credit for trying to straighten out and be a good mother, but she hadn't been able to shake the addiction.

One morning, after only a couple of months in Westport, Jenny had taken all the money she could find in the house, and with her baby had caught a bus for parts unknown. Occasionally she had called collect to ask for money, which our parents had always sent. Mom and Dad had begged her to let them take care of Marie, but Jenny had refused. She had been stubbornly convinced she could take care of her own child.

"Mr. Wilson?"

The summons snapped me back to the real world. I turned away from the window and walked across the waiting area to where a pretty, blond policewoman was standing in the open doorway.

"I'm Officer Ryan," she said, briefly shaking hands before leading me down a short corridor to what I assumed was an interview room.

The area wasn't very large, maybe ten feet by ten feet, with a long table and accompanying chairs taking up most of the space. "Please have a seat," Officer Ryan said, sitting on the far side of the table as I selected a chair opposite her. She opened the file folder she had been carrying and smiled at me. "What can I do for you?" she asked.

"I've just come from the hospital morgue," I said, suddenly finding it difficult to speak.

"I'm sure it was an ordeal for you," Ryan said when I hesitated. "Were you able to positively identify the body?"

"Yes, it was my sister, Jennifer Wilson."

"I'm so sorry for your loss," she said. "Seeing your dead sister must have been a terrible shock." I suppose cops were used to dealing with grieving relatives, but Ryan sounded genuinely sympathetic.

"Yes, it was."

She made a notation in the file. "Thank you for driving in from Westport and confirming the identification. We appreciate your help."

"Jenny and I hadn't been in contact for several years," I said. "She was only twenty-six, but she looked like an old woman. God, but she must have been living a hard life. I'd appreciate anything you could tell me concerning her death."

Ryan scanned the file a moment as if she were trying to decide how much information to divulge. "We don't have many details. Your sister was living in an apartment on Harris Street, which is a very rough part of town. The building manager called to report a body and the paramedics pronounced your sister dead at the scene. Preliminary indications were that she'd been dead for at least two days."

The thought of Jenny dying alone and friendless, then not even being discovered for two days made me feel worse. It didn't seem right that no one had known or cared.

Obviously my guilt showed because Ryan reached across the table and touched my hand. "Are you all right, Mr. Wilson?"

"I'm okay. It's just that this whole thing is so...so overwhelming. No one expects to see their younger sister dead."

"I understand."

"How did Jenny die?" I asked.

"We won't know for certain until the autopsy, but most likely

Jennifer died from a drug overdose. Were you aware your sister used drugs?"

I nodded. "When I lost contact with her, she had already been addicted for several years." There was a moment of awkward silence. "This is all a new experience for me. As far as I know I'm Jenny's only living relative. Is the proper procedure for me to make funeral arrangements?"

"State law requires an autopsy in all cases of unattended death. When the autopsy is completed, we can release Jennifer to the funeral home of your choice. It should only take a couple of days. I'd suggest you make arrangements with a local mortuary in Westport and they'll handle the details."

"I just can't get over how old and sick she looked," I said, almost to myself. "It seems like such a waste of a potentially beautiful life."

"A tragic death is always a waste." Ryan stood and handed me a business card. Obviously she considered the interview ended. "Thank you for coming in. If there's anything further we can do, please don't hesitate to call."

"There is one more thing," I said. "Do you know where they've taken Jennifer's daughter? I wasn't much help to Jenny while she was alive, but maybe I can do something for Marie."

Ryan looked surprised. "I wasn't aware a child was involved. The official report doesn't mention a daughter."

"Marie would be about nine-years-old," I explained, wondering how anyone could miss the evidence of a child in Jenny's apartment. It didn't seem reasonable that the police would simply leave a nine-year-old to fend for herself.

"Can you give me a description of the girl?" Ryan asked, her pencil poised over the form.

"I'm sorry, but I can't." I remembered Marie as I had seen her briefly during Jenny's short stay in Westport, a beautiful baby with Jenny's large hazel eyes. As an infant her toothless smile had already been able to break hearts, but I had no idea what she would look like as a nine-year-old. "I haven't seen Marie since she was a baby."

Ryan shrugged and shook her head. "Like I said, no one saw a child, or any indication a child had been living in the apartment. However, considering the circumstances, the responding officers didn't do a thorough search of the premises. If you'd like, I can contact Child Protective Services and have them investigate."

Perhaps there wasn't any valid reason to get involved further, but I felt guilty for ignoring Jenny and Marie all these years. "Would it be alright if I looked around the apartment? Maybe I can find some clue concerning Marie."

"That probably isn't a good idea. The apartment has been sealed. In the unlikely event the autopsy indicates foul play, we don't want any evidence lost or destroyed."

"It wouldn't be right for me to leave Campbell without knowing what happened to my niece," I insisted. Suddenly it was important that I do this one last thing for Jenny and Marie.

"If there is a daughter, she'd fall under the jurisdiction of Child Protective Services. It'd be best if you left it to them."

"I ignored Jenny and her daughter all these years. Now that Jenny is dead I can't just walk away and forget about Marie. After all, she's family and I've an obligation. She's only nine and someone should care."

"I understand your concern," Ryan said. "Hold on a moment and I'll speak to my supervisor." She picked up the phone on the table and tapped in a few numbers. "Hello Matt, it's Liz. Do you remember the body we picked up on Harris Street yesterday—Jennifer Wilson?" There was a brief pause while she listened to the reply.

"I'm with her brother right now. He just told me his sister had a nine-year-old daughter. He wants to visit the apartment to see whether there's any indication what happened to the child." Another pause.

"Yes, I know the apartment is sealed and I've already explained the little girl is a problem for CPS. I don't think it would hurt if Mr. Wilson satisfied his curiosity, do you? Maybe it'd help him have closure. I can accompany him to make certain he doesn't disturb any possible evidence." A pause.

"No, the autopsy isn't completed. But the paramedics and the admitting doctor are all certain it was a drug overdose. The body had needle tracks everywhere." A pause.

"Okay. If Sam is free, maybe he'd go with us." A pause. "Thanks. I'll let you know what happens." Ryan hung up and turned to me. "Lieutenant Thomas gave permission for you to visit the apartment, but a detective will accompany us to protect evidence."

"Thank you."

"Don't thank me yet, it isn't a pretty place."

"That doesn't make any difference. If I don't check this out, it'll haunt me the rest of my life."

"I understand." Ryan stood. "We'll go in my car. I have some paperwork I have to complete, so if you'll wait out front I'll pick you up in about ten minutes."

I didn't feel much like sitting in the waiting area, so I went outside and began walking up and down the sidewalk. It was almost exactly ten minutes when an unmarked police car pulled to the curb beside me. Ryan motioned to me and I slid into the back seat.

"Mr. Wilson, this is Detective Kincaid. He's going with us to the apartment."

The plain clothed detective turned in his seat and we shook hands. His brown hair was thinning on top and there was a weariness around his eyes, like he had seen too much of life's seamier side.

"You can call me Sam," he said. "I hope you know what you're doing. Your sister didn't exactly live in luxury."

I didn't have the faintest idea what I was doing or what I hoped to find, just that this was something I had to do. I certainly didn't realize my life was about to be changed forever.

JAMES R. OLSON

# CHAPTER TWO

"Were you one of the officers who found my sister?" I asked Detective Kincaid as we pulled away from the station.

"A patrol unit responded to the call," he replied. "Whenever there's a body involved the uniforms request backup from Criminal Investigation. Detective Anderson handled the call, but I'm familiar with the case. I've had previous dealings with your sister."

"What sort of dealings?"

"Nothing serious. She was picked up a few times for prostitution, and I believe she spent a stretch or two in county jail for possession. She was on probation when she died."

Officer Ryan frowned at her partner. "I don't think it's appropriate to discuss this with Mr. Wilson. After all, Jennifer was his sister."

"No, please," I insisted. "I've been out of touch with Jenny for several years. I really want to know about her life."

"Jennifer didn't have a very nice life—at least for the last few years," Kincaid continued. "She wasn't a bad person. It's more like she was the victim of her life style. The only way she could support her drug habit was by working the streets. The last time I arrested her, she was living with a real scumbag and hooking to support them both."

"Then you know about her daughter," I suggested.

"A daughter?" Kincaid sounded just as surprised as Ryan had been. "A lot of the hookers have kids, but this is the first I've heard that Jennifer had a daughter."

"If no one found her daughter in the apartment, what could've happened to her?" I asked.

"I don't know," Kincaid said. "Maybe Child Protective Services can locate her. I'm not saying this happened with your sister, but addicts have been known to sell their children for drug money."

"Sell their children!" I was shocked. Maybe I'd led a sheltered life, because it was impossible to imagine Jenny being so depraved. "This is twenty-first century America. No one can be so hard up they'd buy and sell children?"

"There are a lot of creeps out there," Kincaid said. "After a while drugs become the focus of their lives and they'll do anything to get their next fix. Unfortunately there are also plenty of pedophiles who would buy a kid."

"Not Jenny! She wouldn't sell her daughter to some pervert!"

"That's enough, Sam," Ryan scolded. "You know better than to speculate. As far as we know Jennifer's daughter is perfectly safe with friends." She turned to face me. "Working girls look out for each other."

"You're probably right," Kincaid agreed, sounding embarrassed. "I didn't mean to sound like Jennifer actually sold her daughter—just that it's a possibility."

An ugly thought nagged at the back of my mind. Jenny had become a stranger, living with pressures I couldn't begin to imagine. Could I really be certain she wasn't capable of selling her daughter for a fix?

"Here we are," Ryan said as Kincaid pulled to the curb in front of Jenny's apartment building.

Even in the bright sunlight the large, two-story brick structure looked shabby and worn. The wooden trim around the doors and windows hadn't been maintained for years and large chips of paint were flaking off. The surrounding neighborhood probably wouldn't have been classified a slum, but it didn't have far to go. Most of the houses were visibly in need of repair. The lawns had gone to seed, with large dead patches where the dirt showed through. Everywhere was a scattering of beer cans, broken bottles, and assorted debris.

The building had no lobby, only a small foyer, with a stairway to the right, and a trash littered hallway to the left. The stench of urine and vomit and spoiled garbage was so thick I had an almost overpowering urge to step back outside into the fresh air.

"If you think this is bad," Ryan said, "you should smell it on a really hot day."

"My sister lived in this dump?" I asked, completely shocked. "This building should be condemned."

"It's better than living on the streets," Ryan said. "When addicts can afford a roof over their heads, they generally live in a series of communes or flophouses or rundown apartment buildings like this. It isn't a pretty life, but food and shelter become secondary when your first priority is drugs."

"Like most buildings in the neighborhood, this joint is owned by an absentee landlord," Kincaid said. "Fortunately this one has a resident manager. He may know something about Jennifer's daughter." He approached the first door on the left and banged on it with the side of his fist.

"Okay. Okay. I'm coming. Don't knock the fuckin' door down."

The man who answered the summons could have been anywhere between thirty and fifty. He was barefoot, unshaven, and wore a stained T-shirt that barely covered his bulging stomach.

"What's the beef this time?" he asked when Kincaid flashed his badge.

"No beef," Kincaid said. "We have a couple of questions concerning your late tenant, Jennifer Wilson."

"Like what? She only lived here a couple months and I barely knew her. Hookers come and go. They're all pretty much the same as far as I'm concerned."

"Did she have a daughter—nine or ten-years-old?" Ryan asked.

The manager belched, long and loudly, and scratched his

belly. "Not that I'm aware of. As far as I know, except for an occasional John, she lived alone."

"You've never seen any kids around?"

"Of course I've seen kids around. The brats are always running through the halls making noise. I suppose one of them could have belonged to Jennifer, but I doubt it."

"And you would know?" Kincaid asked sarcastically.

"Hey, look, all I do is collect the rents. I don't check on the tenants. They pay their rent and I leave 'em alone. I don't give a shit about anything else."

"Okay," Kincaid said to a closing door. "Thanks for your help."

All I wanted to do was wake up and discover this all was a dream. Jenny must have descended into some personal hell to even consider living is such a place.

"Your sister's apartment is on the second floor," Ryan said. "Are you sure you want to do this?"

"No, I'm not sure," I replied, "but if I ever want peace of mind I have to look for Marie."

"Okay, but don't say we didn't warn you."

Ryan led us up the stairs and stopped in front of a door with the numbers '227' stenciled on the top panel. Yellow crime scene tape was x'd across the frame.

"This is it," she said, unfastening one end of the tape and unlocking the door. "It isn't a very nice place." She pushed the door open and stepped aside. "After you."

I thought I'd grown accustomed to the foul odors of the building, but the smell in the apartment nearly made me gag. It was a thick combination of feces, urine, rotting food, vomit, and a dozen other odors I didn't recognize. When I hesitated, Kincaid put his hand on my shoulder.

"We don't have to do this, you know," he said.

"Yes, I do." I shrugged off his hand and stepped into the apartment.

"It helps if you hold a handkerchief over your nose and mouth."

I held my folded handkerchief as Kincaid had suggested. It didn't completely mask the odors, but at least it made the stench tolerable.

Years ago the apartment may have been a nice place to live, but that time was long past. The door opened into what was intended to be the living room, dining room combination. The single window directly across from the doorway was covered by a crooked Venetian blind with broken slats. Ryan reached past me and flicked a switch, turning on the ceiling light.

The room was filthy. Obviously Jenny had never bothered picking up trash or cleaning the threadbare carpet. A dilapidated sofa and mutilated coffee table occupied the far end of the room. A cheap dinette set with battered chairs stood in the center of the dining area. The floor and every flat surface was covered with empty food containers, dirty dishes, and unidentifiable trash.

"Your sister was found in the bedroom," Ryan said, leading me down a short hallway.

The first doorway on the left opened into the kitchen. A brief glance showed moldy dishes piled in the sink and an overflowing trash container. The door on the right opened into the bathroom. The toilet had overflowed, depositing sewage onto the floor, filling the small room with the smell of urine and feces.

"Jennifer's body was on the bed," Ryan said, stepping into the bedroom and turning aside so I could squeeze past her.

The room was empty except for a double bed. There were no sheets and a single thin blanket lay crumpled on the bare, stained mattress. The smell was even worse than in the rest of the apartment.

"She was here two days before the body was discovered," Ryan said, as if to explain the putrid odor.

There was no dresser or nightstand where Jenny might have kept clothing or papers. A door to the right opened into a walk-in closet. One dress hung on the clothes rod and a single pair of high heel shoes lay on the floor. There was nothing else in the closet—not even a winter coat.

I stood in the center of the room, feeling tears come to my eyes. My sister had lived and died in this horrible place, and I hadn't given her more than a passing thought for years. Could I have done anything to prevent this tragedy? I was overwhelmed by guilt because I hadn't even tried.

"Have you seen enough?" Kincaid asked.

"Just give me another minute or two," I said.

"Okay," he agreed. "We'll wait in the living room."

The police had been right. There was no clothing or toys or anything else to indicate a little girl had ever lived here. *What did you do with Marie?* I screamed to myself. *Did you sell her to some pervert so you could buy drugs? Jenny, Jenny, what happened to the little sister I knew?*

I forced myself to reach into the bathroom and switch on the light. Nothing happened. Either the bulb was burned out or the switch was broken. From the doorway I could see there was only one cruddy toothbrush on the sink. There didn't seem any point in stepping across the sewage stained floor to check inside the medicine cabinet.

I couldn't believe my sister, who had always been neat and clean, had descended to living in this hellhole. I had an urge to run from the apartment and breathe clean air again, but it was my penance to see everything.

I stepped into the kitchen and switched on the light. Hundreds of cockroaches scurried across the counters and the floor, seeking shelter from the sudden brightness.

The double sink, exuding the odor of rotting garbage, was overflowing with dirty dishes. I stepped to the far end of the kitchen and opened the refrigerator. The light was still working, but there was nothing to see. Except for a crushed milk carton and a sour stench, it was empty. I began opening the wall cabinets. They were all bare except for an empty cereal box. There didn't appear to be food of any kind in the apartment. No wonder Jenny had looked so emaciated. She must have spent all her money on booze and drugs.

There wasn't any point in checking further, but I forced myself to see every horrible nook and cranny. When I squatted down and began examining the lower cabinets I heard a soft scraping noise under the sink. I forced myself to cautiously open the double doors a crack and peek inside, afraid it might be a rat or something equally undesirable.

If I thought I was becoming immune to the horrors of this place, I was wrong. Nothing could have prepared me for the shock of discovering a boy and girl huddled in the tiny space behind the drainpipe.

"Marie?" I asked, so stunned my voice was barely audible.

The girl had one arm protectively around the smaller boy, and seemed to be holding some sort of weapon in her free hand. Her lips were drawn back in a snarl and she looked so wild she frightened me.

"Officer Ryan, would you please come here?" I called, my voice a croaking sound.

Instinctively I reached toward the children. "Don't be afraid," I said, trying to sound soothing. "No one will hurt you."

The girl stabbed at my hand, and when I jerked back, the cut was already dripping blood.

Both officers appeared in the kitchen doorway. "What is it?" Ryan asked before she noticed my wound. "You're bleeding."

I wrapped my handkerchief around the cut to staunch the flow of blood. "I found two kids hiding under the sink. The little girl has a knife."

Ryan crouched beside me and looked into the cabinet. "I don't believe this." She sounded as startled as I had been. "Now I've seen everything."

"I think we've found Marie," I said.

"You kids come out of there," Ryan ordered gently. When the children cringed against the back of the cabinet, she spoke more sternly. "I'm a police officer and unless you want more trouble than you can handle, you'll give me the knife and come out of there right now. Don't make me drag you out."

The girl hesitated like she wasn't certain she should obey.

After a moment she crawled out, tentative and defensive. She held the paring knife in her right hand and looked like she wouldn't hesitate to use it.

"Give me the knife," Ryan insisted. "You don't need a weapon. No one is going to hurt you."

For a moment I thought the girl might attack us, but a light seemed to go out in her eyes and she dropped the knife.

The little boy crawled from the cubbyhole, looking confused and frightened. He immediately ducked behind the girl, using her body like a shield.

"It's all right." Although I was still in shock, I thought my voice sounded nearly normal. "You're safe now. I'm your Uncle Jon and I've come to help."

The two children backed against the far wall, keeping as much distance from the adults as possible. The girl glared at me, her fists raised protectively.

I was horrified. I couldn't see the boy behind her, but the girl was thin and worn, with sad, dark eyes that must have seen too much misery for too long. She was wearing filthy jeans with a gaping tear in the left knee, and a ragged T-shirt that may once have been white. Her hair was stringy and matted from an accumulation of filth. There was a festering scab on her forehead. It was obvious she hadn't washed, or been washed, for a long time. Even from across the kitchen I could smell sour odors emanating from the children.

"Sam, would you please go down to the car and radio for someone from Child Protective Services," Ryan suggested. "Better call for an ambulance too. These kids are going to need medical attention."

"You've got it," Kincaid said, sounding eager to get away from the kids and the apartment.

Except for Kincaid's hurried exit it was a frozen tableau in the kitchen with the kids huddled together against the far wall, me standing with my mouth hanging open, and Officer Ryan standing beside me, our shoulders touching in the narrow space.

Finally Ryan broke the deadlock, stepping forward and

crouching so she was on a level with the frightened kids. "Are you Marie?" she asked.

I could almost see the girl's mind working as she considered whether it was safe to answer. In her world cops were the enemy. After a moment she gave an almost imperceptible nod.

"Who is the boy? Is he your brother?"

She nodded again.

"What's his name?"

This time Marie stared defiantly at the policewoman and didn't answer. She looked so much like a wild animal I wondered whether she was even able to speak.

"Marie, I'm a police officer. Sooner or later you're going to have to answer my questions. What's your brother's name?"

"Are you going to take us to jail?" Marie's voice was aggressive, not soft and frightened as I would have expected.

"No, I'm not going to take you to jail." Ryan's voice was firm, but friendly. "We're going to get you medical attention and food. Now tell me your brother's name?"

"Billy." Marie spit out the name as if giving information was painful.

"There, that's better. Are you hungry?"

"I can take care of me and my brother," Marie said. "We don't need any fuckin' cops."

"How long has it been since you've eaten anything?" When Marie didn't respond, Officer Ryan turned to me. "These kids must have been locked in here for at least three days. You saw for yourself there isn't any food in the place. It wouldn't surprise me if this wasn't the first time they've been left for days at a time without anything to eat."

"Just go away and leave us alone," Marie said emotionlessly. "Mommy will bring us food."

"Marie, you must know your mother isn't coming back. You understand she's dead, don't you?"

"I'm hungry," Billy whispered, peering around his sister.

Marie slapped his arm. "Shut up! I can take care of you. I'll find some food when these fuckin' people go away. We don't need anyone."

"We aren't going away," Officer Ryan said. "Come on now, and don't give me any trouble. We'll all go into the living room and wait for Child Protective Services."

"Can't we take them outside—away from all this?" I asked, waving my hand at the filth in the kitchen.

Ryan shook her head. "Not until Child Protective Services gets here. If we get the kids outside and they run away, we'll play hell finding them again. At least here we can keep them from bolting."

In the front room the children sat together amid the trash on the sofa while Officer Ryan and I took seats at the table. Marie sat upright, but Billy snuggled next to her, his arms tightly wrapped around her waist, his face pressed into her dirty T-shirt.

Now that Billy was no longer hiding behind his sister I could see he was just as filthy as Marie. His unkempt hair was nearly shoulder length and his face was streaked where tears had washed paths in the accumulated dirt. They both looked like street urchins from a Charles Dickens novel.

Marie's eyes were constantly moving, from us to the door and back again. I thought she looked exactly like a trapped animal searching for an escape route.

It was like I'd become immersed in a horrible nightmare. I'd found Jenny's daughter and a son I hadn't realized existed. Now I didn't know what to do or say. For a moment I considered sitting on the sofa and putting a comforting arm around both children, but was afraid Marie would bite me if I touched either of them. So I did nothing.

Kincaid stepped back into the room. "CPS and an ambulance are on the way. It should only be a few minutes." He handed a couple of boxed sandwiches and half-pint milk cartons to the children. "I figured the kids would be hungry so I picked this stuff up at the convenience store on the corner."

Both children ripped off the wrappings and wolfed the food, tossing the papers on the floor to mingle with the other trash.

"What do we do now?" I asked, feeling lost and helpless.

"We wait," Ryan said. "If you're a religious man, you might want to say a prayer or two for the kids. It looks like they're gonna need all the help they can get."

# CHAPTER THREE

**M**aybe I lacked the necessary parental gene, but I'd never been comfortable around children. Even normal, well adjusted kids intimidated me. I never knew whether to treat them like tiny adults or some unique creature. Marie and Billy were definitely not normal, well-adjusted kids. Huddled together on the couch, they looked more like frightened animals than children.

I felt an obligation to say or do something to comfort them, but was afraid they would resist my advances and then I'd look like an idiot. Kincaid and Ryan must have had similar thoughts because we all sat in that horrible apartment staring at each other, without anyone saying a word.

It was a long, uncomfortable fifteen minutes before heavy footsteps came tromping up the stairs and two paramedics hurried into the apartment.

"Hi Liz," the female member of the team said to Officer Ryan. "What've you got? Another body?"

"Not this time," Ryan replied, pointing toward the sofa. "We've got a couple of kids in pretty bad shape. They're going to need a ride to the hospital and some food. It's a good bet they haven't eaten in a couple of days—maybe longer. Someone from Child Protective Services should be here to claim responsibility before you're done checking them out."

The male paramedic went directly to the sofa, opened his bag, and hooked a stethoscope into his ears. He was a big man, looking as if he would have been comfortable with a construction crew. As he crouched and tried to place the stethoscope against Marie's chest, she snarled and attempted to bite him. He jerked away and nearly fell over.

"Damnit, I'm not going to hurt you," he grumbled.

"Here, let me try." The female knelt in front of the sofa and gave the kids a big smile. "Hi sweetheart," she said to Marie. "My name's Suzy and I'm a paramedic. What's your name?"

Marie looked suspicious. Maybe she had dealt with paramedics before when Jenny had passed out from drug usage. "Marie," she finally said.

"I can tell we're gonna be friends, Marie. I need to check you and your brother to make sure you're not sick. What's your brother's name?"

"Billy." Marie sounded reluctant to lower her defenses.

"Okay, Marie, I'm just going to listen to your heart. It won't hurt a bit." Suzy put the stethoscope to Marie's chest. She listened a moment before turning to her partner. "Damn, her heart's going a mile a minute. She's scared to death."

"I'm not scared!" Marie protested.

"Of course not," Suzy agreed. "I can tell you're a very brave little girl. And you're going to need to be brave while I fix the sore on your forehead." She saturated a cotton ball with a liquid and cleaned around the festering scab. "Now, this will sting a little bit."

Marie winced, but didn't make a sound. The paramedic took a spray can of liquid bandage from her satchel. "This won't hurt at all." She shielded Marie's eyes from the aerosol spray as she coated the wound.

"It's all an act," Ryan said to me in a stage whisper.

"What's an act?" I asked

"Not being afraid. I've seen it a million times with kids like Marie and Billy. Abused children learn to put up a façade of fearlessness as a defense mechanism. It's their way of coping with a world full of pain and suffering."

"That's terrible," I said, wondering how anyone could cope with a world where everything and everyone was against them.

Ryan shrugged. "It works for them. It's probably the only

thing that keeps them from curling up and dying." She turned to the male paramedic. "Bill, would you please check Mr. Wilson's hand. The little girl stabbed him with a dirty paring knife."

I unwrapped the handkerchief and extended my hand to the paramedic. The wound had stopped bleeding, but was stinging a bit.

"Doesn't look too bad," Bill said. "It's only a scratch. Are you current with your tetanus shots?"

"I don't know. I think I had one a couple months ago," I replied.

"Then you should be okay." He swabbed the wound with an antiseptic that brought tears to my eyes. "Keep it clean and bandaged," Bill prescribed. "If it's red or sore tomorrow, check with your doctor."

Suzy was still conducting her examination of the children when a tall, hefty woman burst through the doorway like a linebacker attacking an offensive line. She ignored everyone except the police officers.

"Well, what do we have here?" she demanded in a booming voice.

"We've got two children. No known father. Their mother died from an overdose." Ryan nodded in my direction and performed the introductions. "This is Mr. Wilson, the children's uncle. This is Alice Henderson from Child Protective Services."

Mrs. Henderson disregarded me, as if I were irrelevant. Maybe she thought I was somehow responsible for the children's condition, or maybe my sense of guilt made it seem that way.

"Well," she said. "Have you got their things packed?"

"They don't have anything to pack," Kincaid said. "What you see is what you get."

"I suspected as much." Mrs. Henderson acted as if it were normal for kids not to have anything except the clothing on their backs. She walked to the sofa and towered over the children, her hands on her hips. "You, young lady, what's your name?"

Marie glared defiantly at the imposing woman.

"Speak up. I asked your name, and expect an answer."

"Her name is Marie and the boy is Billy," I offered.

"Didn't ask you," Mrs. Henderson snapped without looking in my direction.

"Please tell Mrs. Henderson your names," Ryan said, interceding before I made some comment about the social worker's attitude. "She's here to help you."

Marie thought a moment and must have decided she didn't have any options. "Marie," she said defiantly. "Billy and I don't need any fuckin' help from you or anyone else. We can take care of ourselves."

"Well, we'll see about that," Mrs. Henderson said, ignoring the street language. In her job she had probably heard it all more than once. Then she addressed the paramedics for the first time. "Are they ready to go?"

"As ready as they're gonna be," Suzy said. "There's nothing more we can do for them here."

"Well, then, let's get the show on the road." Mrs. Henderson turned to the children. "Marie, you take Billy's hand and come along with me."

"We have to wait for Mommy," Marie insisted, prepared to defy all of these threatening adults.

Mrs. Henderson turned to Ryan and spoke as if the children weren't there. "Doesn't she know her mother's dead?"

"I'm sure she knows," Ryan said. "Both kids were here for at least two days with the body."

"Your Mother won't be coming back," Mrs. Henderson said. For the first time I heard a touch of compassion in her voice. "She's gone to heaven and won't be able to take care of you any longer. She wants you to come with me so I can give you food and clean clothing."

Marie obviously wasn't convinced she could trust this adult, and for an instant I thought she might resist. Then something in her attitude changed and I wondered if maybe it was a sense of relief because for at least a short while she would no longer be responsible for feeding herself and Billy.

She stood and reached for her brother's hand. "Come on, Billy."

Mrs. Henderson led the way down the stairs and out into the street. I've never appreciated fresh air more in my life. I stood on the cracked sidewalk, drawing in one lungful of air after another, trying to dispel the stench in my nostrils.

"I'll stay with the kids," Suzy told her partner. She opened the ambulance's back door and helped the children up the tall step. "We're going for a ride. You'll really like this."

As Suzy pulled the ambulance doors shut, I saw Billy desperately clinging to his sister. Marie looked like a condemned criminal awaiting execution. I wasn't sure where my duty lay, but I didn't feel right abandoning these frightened kids to the impersonal care of strangers.

Mrs. Henderson turned to the police officers. "Thanks for your help. I'll take over from here."

"Can I hitch a ride with you to the hospital?" I asked Mrs. Henderson.

"I don't think you need to concern yourself any further, Mr. Wilson," she said abruptly. "You go with the officers and see whether there's paperwork you need to process or something."

"I'm their uncle," I insisted, almost losing my temper. It would have given me a great deal of satisfaction to wipe the smug expression from her face. "The children need me with them."

"These kids need professional attention. An uncle who obviously hasn't been interested in them or their welfare isn't going to be helpful now."

I almost snapped back, to deny that I had ignored Marie and Billy, but I knew she was right. One look at the kid's state of neglect was clear evidence no one had shown an interest in them for a long time. Certainly I had never done anything to help. I hadn't even known Jenny had a son, and from appearances Billy was around five-years-old.

Kincaid laid a hand on my shoulder. "Come with us, Mr. Wilson. We'll take you back to your vehicle."

Mrs. Henderson departed without a backward glance, following the ambulance as it pulled away from the curb. I had a funny feeling in the pit of my stomach, as if I were shirking some obligation.

"I don't know whether it's a good idea leaving the kids with that woman," I said, as Kincaid drove toward the police station. "She acted like the evil stepmother."

Ryan turned so she could look over the seat. "I've worked with Mrs. Henderson before. She comes across as being a tough old bird, but kids in these circumstances need an authority figure to take charge. You can bet she'll make certain they're well taken care of."

I had my doubts, but for the moment I had no choice except to tolerate the situation. "I'm Marie and Billy's only living relative. I feel like I should be doing something for them."

"I'd say you've already done something. If you hadn't insisted on checking the apartment, the kids would probably have starved before we found them."

"What's going to happen to them?" I asked, feeling a little better.

"They'll get a complete medical exam, a bath, clean clothes, and something to eat. They'll receive any medical treatment they need, and most likely be given a psychological evaluation. When all that's taken care of they'll be taken to the children's center and Child Protective Services will try to find foster homes for them."

"Will try to find foster homes?" Whatever good feelings I'd just had, suddenly vanished. "Are you saying Marie and Billy might not have any place to go?"

"CPS has facilities where Marie and Billy will stay until they're placed with foster parents," Ryan said. "It isn't the Ritz, but it's a lot better then where they've been living. At least they'll have regular meals and decent clothing."

"How long before the kids are placed with a foster family?"

"That's hard to say. It probably depends on how many foster parents are waiting for children. Billy's young enough that it shouldn't be a problem placing him. Marie may be more difficult. Trust me on this. CPS does a great job with homeless kids. They'll be all right."

"That sounds like you think they'll be separated."

"Hey, I'm a cop, not a social worker. I don't know what's going to happen, but it isn't always possible to place siblings together. Maybe Marie and Billy will be able to stay together, but it's likely they'll end up in different foster homes."

"I want to take them back to Westport with me and give them a home," I said. It was a spur of the moment decision and I had immediate doubts. I was a bachelor and didn't know a damned thing about raising kids. Maybe I had the sudden impulse to be protective because of Mrs. Henderson's attitude. Or maybe I was feeling guilty for not giving Jenny the support she had needed. Either way, Marie and Billy were family, and I had an obligation. "Those kids need to stay together."

"That might not be such a good idea," Ryan suggested.

"It'd be better than splitting them up. All they have is each other. Even a blind man could see that Billy would be totally lost without Marie."

"You'd have to work that out with Child Protective Services," Kincaid said. "In situations like this they have control over what happens to the kids. From the time we called CPS they've technically become the children's guardian."

"So, how do I get Child Protective Services to release them to me?"

"You'll have to contact CPS and see what procedures they recommend," Ryan said. "There's nothing you can do today, and the kids may be in the hospital for a day or two. Your first priority is to make arrangements for your sister's funeral. Then you might consult an attorney to investigate the legal aspects of gaining custody."

"Who should I speak with at Child Protective Services?" I asked.

"I don't know for certain," Ryan said, "but I suspect Mrs. Henderson is the person you'll have to contact. If I were you,

I'd give this some serious consideration before you make a commitment. Unless I miss my guess, those kids are going to need lots of special care."

"Thanks for your concern, but I have to do something to help my sister's children."

"It's your decision," she said as Kincaid pulled into a space behind my car. "Good luck. If there's anything more we can do for you, give us a call.""If you really mean that, you just might be hearing from me again."

I sat in my car a few minutes, digesting everything that had happened. Billy had seemed shy and compliant. At least he did everything his sister told him. That might have been because Marie was stronger and street tough. Being honest with myself, I had to admit the girl frightened me. How would I handle the situation if she physically attacked me or refused to cooperate?

Perhaps I needed to re-evaluate my motives for wanting to take in Jenny's children. Was I acting out of guilt or some higher consideration? Would I quickly begin to resent the burden of raising someone else's kids? More than food and shelter, Marie and Billy needed someone to love them. Would I be able to provide that love? I didn't know. Maybe there weren't any answers. It didn't take an expert to realize both kids had been living in conditions I would never completely understand. Giving them a home wouldn't be easy and I was afraid I might not have the strength to make it work.

Even if I didn't understand exactly what I was getting myself into, my heart told me I had to do whatever was necessary to obtain custody. God help me, I may have failed Jenny, but right or wrong, I wouldn't abandon Marie and Billy.

# CHAPTER FOUR

A s soon as I unlocked the front door, my black Lab, Shadow, burst out, jumping up and down in his usual frantic celebration of my return. I let him out into the fenced backyard and waited while he lifted his leg beside the huge oak at the edge of the yard.

"Well, Shadow, it looks like our bachelor days may just about be over," I said aloud, flopping onto my desk chair as Shadow sprawled beside the desk, head on paws, watching me. "Do you think you'll like having a couple of kids to play with?"

His tail thumped against the desk as he gave me one of those, 'whatever you want is fine with me' looks.

According to my desk clock it was half past three, which was too late to start a new project and too early to phone Linda. I could have contacted her at work, but if the truth be told, I wasn't eager to tell Linda about Jenny's kids and my thoughts about seeking custody. Unless I missed my guess she wasn't going to be thrilled about the idea.

To kill time, I booted the computer and checked my email. There was a message from Henry Jerrold, computer supervisor for Lee's Manufacturing in New York, requesting a quote to design a software program for their shipping department. I had been soliciting Jerrold for several months and had almost given up on winning the account. Normally I would have phoned him immediately to obtain the information needed for an accurate quote, but it was after four in New York and I easily convinced myself Jerrold had probably left for the day. I made a note to contact him in the morning.

That was the first item on the list of tasks I began compiling. I needed to call Child Protective Services and schedule an appointment with Mrs. Henderson. Then I would have to contact Croft Funeral Home about arrangements for Jenny's funeral, and also talk with Father Rose to schedule a funeral Mass at St. Anthony's. I considered adding my attorney, Jim Stanley, to the list, but decided to wait for legal advice until after I'd talked with Child Protective Services.

I hadn't eaten since breakfast, so I fixed myself a ham and cheese sandwich and watched the evening news before calling Linda. She and I had been dating steadily for two years and in March she had accepted my marriage proposal. We hadn't set a date because the nuptials depended on the availability of a suitable reception hall. Personally I didn't want a big wedding with all the trimming, but was willing to go along with whatever Linda wanted.

Finally, at six o'clock I dialed Linda's number, and she answered on the third ring.

"Hi, I'm back from Campbell." I had asked her to accompany me, but she couldn't get the day off on short notice and had been squeamish about visiting the morgue.

"How'd it go?" she asked. "Was it Jenny?"

"Unfortunately, yes. She apparently died from a drug overdose, but we won't know for certain until after the autopsy."

"Oh, Sweetheart, I'm so sorry. It must have been terrible for you."

"It wasn't much fun. The worst part was going to the apartment where she had died. You should have seen it. The place was filthy and smelled like a pigsty."

"No thanks." I could hear the disgust in her voice at the thought of a filthy, smelly apartment. "Why would you even think about going to her apartment? It sounds morbid."

"It was morbid and disgusting, but I had to go. No one in Campbell was aware Jenny had a daughter. One of the cops even suggested Jenny might have sold her daughter for drug money."

"Sold her kid for drug money?" Linda sounded shocked.

"People don't do things like that."

"Unbelievable isn't it? But apparently it happens. Anyway you can understand why I had to go to the apartment to see if there were any clues concerning Marie."

"Don't keep me in suspense. What happened? Did you learn where the girl was?"

"I not only found out where Marie was—I found her. While I was searching the apartment, I discovered not one, but two kids hiding under the kitchen sink. It turns out Jenny had a son I didn't even know existed. Linda, you've never seen anything so pathetic. Those kids looked like they'd been through hell. Would you believe they'd been hiding in the apartment, without food, for at least three days?"

"That's horrible. So what happened to them?"

"Paramedics took them to the hospital and Child Protective Services is looking after them." It didn't seem appropriate to tell Linda about my custody decision over the telephone. She'd already made it very clear she wasn't interested in having a family, and I figured a face-to-face meeting would give me a better chance of winning her over.

"Well, I think it was lucky you found those poor kids before they starved."

"Yeah, they couldn't have lasted much longer," I agreed. "Look, Linda, it's been a long day and I'm totally beat. How about we get together for dinner tomorrow and I can share all the details? By then I'll probably know about Jenny's funeral."

"Sure, I'd like that."

"Would seven be okay?"

"I'll look forward to it."

"Love you."

"Me too."

Since I'd had very little sleep the night before, I crawled into bed early, hoping to get caught up on my rest. I fell asleep almost as soon as my head hit the pillow and immediately began dreaming.

I found myself in a funeral home surrounded by the

sickening odor of flower arrangements. I was drawn toward an open coffin nearly hidden among the flowers. Jenny's body lay in the casket, hands crossed over her bosom, a rosary entwined in the fingers. She was dressed in a flower-print blouse, her hair neatly arranged, and she looked like the teenager I'd known years ago. I was thinking how beautiful and peaceful she looked when suddenly her eyes popped open. She sat up in the coffin, stretched out her arm and pointed a long, bony finger at me. When she spoke, her voice sounded like an echo from Hell.

"Jonathon Wilson, if you don't take care of my children you will never have a moment's peace the rest of your life."

My heart was pounding when I awoke in a cold sweat. Wide-awake, I lay in the dark, staring at the ceiling, a million thoughts racing through my mind. I was torn by one doubt after another, all concerning the wisdom of accepting custody.

There was no question about my ability to feed the children. Along with the insurance settlement from the automobile accident, my parents had left a tidy sum, and I'd inherited the family house free and clear. My software design business was lucrative, bringing in a steady income. I couldn't say I was rich, but I was comfortable and wouldn't have to worry about our next meal.

However, finances were the least of my concerns. I didn't know a damned thing about being a parent. Even normal children required more attention than raising a puppy, and it was pretty obvious Jenny's kids would have special problems. I wouldn't even have a family support mechanism to call on for help. The longer I lay in bed staring at the ceiling, the more I became convinced I had no business seeking the responsibility of an instant family. Even if Marie and Billy got placed in separate foster homes they would almost certainly be better off than if I attempted to be a surrogate father. Maybe I owed something to Jenny and the kids but being an inept parent wasn't going to satisfy my debt.

When I finally dozed again, the same nightmare startled me awake.

My Mother had always believed dreams had mystical meanings, and nearly every morning she consulted a large volume that claimed to interpret dreams. No amount of arguing could convince her that dreams were not a forewarning of the future.

Although I had never subscribed to her theories, I did believe the subconscious mind sorted out problems during sleep and frequently presented a solution. This time when I woke in a sweat, I knew my subconscious had told me I didn't have a choice. I had to make every effort to do the right thing, and that meant obtaining custody of Marie and Billy.

Once I'd made a firm decision, I dropped into a dreamless sleep and was awakened by Shadow letting me know it was time for him to go outside.

As soon as I finished breakfast, I called Child Protective Services. Mrs. Henderson didn't sound enthusiastic about seeing me, but did have some free time that afternoon, and agreed to a two o'clock appointment.

Next on my list was a trip to Croft's Funeral Home to make arrangements for Jenny. Although Westport was a typical small town where everyone knew everyone else, Jenny had been away for so long I wasn't sure whether anyone would remember her. The majority of her school friends probably no longer lived in the area. When kids graduated from high school, they went off to college and many never returned, or they sought more lucrative employment in the larger cities, like Milwaukee, Green Bay, or Madison. Consequently I was determined to have a private funeral with a minimum of stress for everyone involved.

I had dealt with Jeremiah Croft when I'd made arrangements for Mom and Dad, and suspected he would play on my grief and feelings of guilt, in order to sell me the most expensive coffin and funeral available. He didn't disappoint me. In spite of Croft's efforts, I insisted on a simple coffin and a practical vault. There would be a funeral mass and a graveside service, but no open visitation at the funeral home.

I gave Croft all the necessary information and he agreed to

handle arrangements with the Campbell authorities. Since we didn't know when the mandated autopsy would be completed we had to leave the actual date of the funeral open. Croft promised to contact me when he received the body.

I wrote a check to the funeral home, trying to ignore Croft's overdone expressions of sympathy. Then I drove to St. Anthony's where Father Rose had been pastor for well over twenty years.

Agnes Richards, his housekeeper, answered the door and escorted me to the priest's study. Father Rose came around his desk and shook hands. He was a tall, handsome man, still enjoying a full head of thick silver hair. He had always reminded me of Gregory Peck in the movie, "Keys to the Kingdom". If priests ever retired, Father Rose had to be very close to that age.

"Jon, I haven't seen you around Church very often lately," he said, a hint of scolding in his voice. "Have you been attending Mass regularly?"

"Actually I've been pretty busy," I said, feeling like an altar boy sneaking in late for Mass.

"Jon, Jon." He shook is head in disapproval. "How can you be too busy for the Lord? You were here every Sunday when your parents were alive. You must make a commitment to do better in the future."

"Yes, Father. I promise to do better."

"Good," he said, his tone suggesting he didn't have much faith in my promise. "I know you didn't come to discuss your attendance at Mass. What can I do for you this morning?"

Father Rose sat behind his massive desk and peered at me over his bifocals. I settled onto one of the visitor's chairs and told him about Jenny's death and that I had come to make arrangements for a funeral Mass.

We had to leave the date open for the present, but in the meantime Father Rose promised to include Jenny in the prayers for the dead during Masses all week.

When I returned home, I fixed myself a couple of sandwiches for lunch. It occurred to me I wouldn't be able to have such slipshod eating habits when the kids were here. I'd never been a proficient cook, and the thought of preparing nourishing meals on a regular schedule didn't appeal to me. It was just one of the adjustments I'd have to make.

As I drove the twenty miles to Campbell for my appointment with Mrs. Henderson, I attempted to visualize what it would be like to suddenly become a parent. The best-case scenario would be like the warm, fuzzy movie families, where kids thrive on their parent's loving care and develop into model citizens. Somehow I knew it wouldn't be that way. My life was going to be changed forever and I would have more than my share of failures. I just prayed there would be enough successes along the way to make the effort worthwhile.

# CHAPTER FIVE

I found the Campbell Courthouse without difficulty, but became momentarily lost in the annex's maze of corridors before locating Child Protective Service's office. I was five minutes late checking in with the receptionist and then had to fidget, on a very uncomfortable chair, for another twenty minutes before Mrs. Henderson summoned me into her office.

Although I knew seeking custody was the right decision, the closer I came to a firm commitment the more doubts I had. I was halfway hoping Mrs. Henderson would have a convincing argument in favor of leaving Marie and Billy in the child care system.

"Sorry to keep you waiting, but we're extremely busy this afternoon." Her apology didn't sound sincere as she indicated the only visitor's chair in her cramped office. "Please have a seat. What can I do for you, Mr. Wilson?"

"First, how are Marie and Billy?" I asked.

"They're still in the hospital, but I've been told they're doing very well." She glanced at her watch, giving the impression she had better things to do than waste time with me.

Even though her attitude rubbed me the wrong way, I intended to keep the meeting on a professional level. "I've been told Child Protective Services is acting as guardian for Marie and Billy."

"That's correct."

"What are the procedures for me to obtain custody?" I asked.

Mrs. Henderson opened a file, glanced at a couple of pages, and shook her head. "That's a noble gesture, Mr. Wilson, but I doubt whether it's possible. Marie and Billy have suffered severe abuse and trauma. They'll need special care you aren't qualified to provide."

"You can't possibly know what I'm qualified to provide," I snapped. "I can afford to give Marie and Billy any care they require. Wouldn't it be better if a relative provided for the children, rather than have the county footing the bill?"

"This isn't about money," she said, her tone suggesting I'd offended her. "It's about the children's welfare. My job is to give our kids a home and family they can count on."

"I understand that." It was becoming increasingly difficult to remain calm. Maybe the tension was getting to me, but I suspected her negative assumptions were raising my blood pressure. "I'm prepared to provide a good home."

Mrs. Henderson sighed like I was a child who didn't understand. "I assume you mean well, Mr. Wilson, but you obviously don't have any idea of the special problems associated with abused and neglected kids. Children who've been exposed to abuse, drugs, and violence tend to perpetuate that lifestyle in their own families. Our greatest challenge is breaking the cycle of the dysfunctional family."

"Are you suggesting I'd provide a dysfunctional family for Marie and Billy?" I asked, no longer attempting to conceal my anger.

"I'm saying we don't know anything about you except that you've ignored your niece and nephew all their lives. That certainly doesn't imply any great concern on your part." She frowned when she glanced at my left hand and noticed I wasn't wearing a wedding ring. "Are you married, Mr. Wilson?"

I swallowed a sharp retort and tried to regain a calm tone. "No, I'm not married. I don't see where that makes any difference."

"Marie and Billy have just come from a dysfunctional, single parent household. I doubt whether placement in another single parent home will be beneficial. They need a mother and a father to provide positive role models and a firm family foundation."

"It's not going to be a single parent household for long. I'm engaged to a wonderful lady."

Mrs. Henderson looked surprised, as if she couldn't imagine anyone wanting to marry me. "Have you discussed this with your fiancée? Is she prepared to start married life with the responsibility of a readymade family—one with special needs?"

"No, I haven't talked with Linda yet, but I'm certain she'll be loving and supportive." I had no intention of telling Mrs. Henderson that Linda had absolutely no desire to be a mother.

"Perhaps she'll feel differently when she's faced with handling two disturbed children. Marie and Billy need foster parents who can be patient and understanding and provide a decent place to live. Child Protective Services will make certain they have such a home."

"Are you're saying Marie and Billy will have a more stable, loving home with foster parents?'

"I'm saying we can give Marie and Billy what they need, and we don't have any evidence suggesting you can."

I swallowed another angry reply. "Officer Ryan implied Marie and Billy might be placed in separate homes. After the trauma they've experienced don't you think it would be in their best interests to remain together?"

"Naturally it's our policy to place siblings in the same home whenever possible. However, we must focus on what's best for the individual child. Sometimes circumstances necessitate separate placements."

"You mean it depends on whether you can find foster parents who'll accept two kids."

"Mr. Wilson, I don't intend to argue about our policies or procedures. We've had extensive experience working with children like Marie and Billy and we know what's best for them. Our office investigates foster parent candidates thoroughly to determine whether they're qualified and capable of providing a stable, loving environment. As a matter of fact we already have a young couple interested in accepting both of Jennifer's children."

That caught me off guard. Unless this couple was already in the foster parent pool, and had been contacted by Child Protective Services, they shouldn't even know Marie and Billy existed. "Who are these people?" I asked.

"That really isn't any of your business, Mr. Wilson. They're a married couple, and if they meet all our requirements, they'll definitely be better suited than you for taking care of the children."

"So, this couple hasn't been approved yet to be foster parents."

"No, they haven't, but the process has begun and I expect a favorable decision very quickly."

"At this point you don't know any more about this couple than you know about me, and you've already decided they'll be better suited than I am," I said, barely controlling my temper. "I'm a blood relative, and must have legal rights regarding Marie and Billy, which brings us back to my original question. What are the procedures for obtaining custody?"

"If you're determined to waste time and money, you can go through the process of being approved as a foster parent," Mrs. Henderson said. "If you overcome that hurdle, you can petition the court for custody. Children's Court depends on our expertise to determine what's best for the children in our care. I'll tell you right now, you won't have a prayer of gaining custody if we oppose your petition."

"We'll see about that. You're wrong about me and what's best for Marie and Billy. The children need to be with family, and I'll fight to see it happen. If you won't recommend custody, then we'll settle this in court."

"I'm sorry you've taken that attitude, Mr. Wilson. Do whatever you believe you must and we'll do whatever we believe is in the best interests of the children. I don't think we have anything further to discuss."

"Yes we do," I insisted. "I want to fill out the necessary paperwork for approval as a foster parent."

"If you're determined to waste your time, the receptionist

will provide the required forms." Mrs. Henderson had a smug expression. "The approval process is time consuming, and I assure you Marie and Billy will be placed with the first qualified foster parents who will accept them. We will not wait to see whether you're approved."

"Maybe that's something Children's Court will have to decide."

"I can't waste anymore time on this," Mrs. Henderson said. "I believe this appointment is finished."

"Not yet," I said. "I want the children to attend their mother's funeral. I'm sure you'll agree the funeral will provide closure for Marie and Billy."

Mrs. Henderson shook her head. "Attending their mother's funeral may not be in their best interests. I have to talk with the medical doctor and the children's psychologist before I can approve."

"Are you saying you may not let Marie and Billy attend?"

"I don't think it'll come to that, but it's a possibility."

"Let's hope it won't come to that. If I need to have my attorney obtain a court order requiring you to bring the children, I'll do it."

Mrs. Henderson and I did not part on genial terms. I'd lost my cool, but didn't feel guilty. If there is anything that irritates me it's bureaucrats who overrate their importance.

I stopped at the front desk and filled out the paperwork to begin the approval process. If Child Protective Services was going to investigate my qualifications, I realized they could drag out the process forever. I figured my attorney would be able to make certain they moved forward as rapidly as possible.

I pushed the speed limit all the way to Westport, attempting to catch my attorney, James Stanley, before he left his office.

"Hi Madge." I had gone to school with Jim's receptionist, and she'd married the linebacker on my High School football team. "I need to see Mr. Stanley. It's an emergency."

"Hi, Jon. Mr. Stanley just finished his last appointment. I'll see if he's still in the office."

"Tell him it's very important and I have to talk with him today. If he's too busy, I'll find another attorney."

"That won't be necessary," Madge said as she scurried toward Jim's office. After a moment she reappeared. "Mr. Stanley will see you, but he only has a few minutes."

"Thanks." I smiled so Madge would know I wasn't angry at her.

When I entered his office Jim was impatiently putting papers into his briefcase. Madge had probably told him I'd threatened to find another attorney if he couldn't see me, but I didn't care. I'd paid enough fees over the years that he could afford to be a few minutes late to wherever he was going.

"I'm sorry to hear about your sister," he said. "It's a terrible tragedy, coming so soon after your parent's deaths. Does your emergency have anything to do with Jennifer? I'll do whatever I can to help, but I only have a few minutes to spare right now. We'd have more time if you make an appointment for tomorrow morning."

"We need to talk now. This will only take a couple of minutes." I briefly told Jim the details of Jenny's death and that her two children were under the care of Child Protective Services.

"I didn't know Jennifer, but I'm truly sorry she died so young and under those horrible circumstances. What do you want from me?"

"Two things. First, I'm the only living relative, and want custody of the children. Child Protective Services has a typical close-minded bureaucratic attitude toward single parent custody. Because I'm not married and never did anything for the kids while Jenny was alive, they don't believe I'll be suitable. I've already completed the initial paperwork to be approved as a foster parent, but even if I'm qualified, Child Protective Services said I'll have to petition the court for custody."

"I'm not familiar with custody law, but I can look into it for you. It may take a few days."

"We don't have a few days," I snapped. "This needs to be

settled as quickly as possible. I suspect we're going to have to push CPS to complete their investigation."

"I'll see what I can do, but I can't promise fast action. I'll have Madge contact the appropriate people first thing in the morning. I believe blood relatives have certain legal rights in these situations, and it might not even be necessary for you to be approved as a foster parent." Jim glanced at his watch. "You said you had two problems?"

"I don't have the exact date, because I'm waiting for the county to complete an autopsy and release the body, but Jenny's funeral should be in a few days. Child Protective Services isn't sure they'll allow the children to attend. I want you to get a court order or something to ensure that Marie and Billy will be there."

Jim glanced at his wristwatch. "Okay, I'll check into it in the morning. I really have to run to make an appointment."

I reached out and shook his hand. "Thanks Jim. I knew I could count on you to help me. Just remember it's urgent and we have to push matters."

"Don't thank me too soon. This may not be as simple as you imagine. Family should have priority, but the courts give a lot of weight to recommendations from Child Protective Services. We may have a tough fight ahead of us."

"Whatever it takes. I feel very strongly about this. I'm willing to drag the case all the way to the Supreme Court if we have to."

"Court fights can be expensive."

"I understand, but this is something I have to do. No matter how well intentioned they are, I don't believe the state can provide better care for Marie and Billy than I can."

"Okay, I'll see what we can do." Jim glanced at his watch again.

"Good. I'll check back tomorrow afternoon."

I didn't know whether I should have felt excited, anxious, or depressed when I left Jim's office. Maybe I was numb. So much had happened so fast I wasn't certain my mind was keeping up.

There was barely enough time to shower, shave, and dress for my dinner date with Linda. That was another hurdle I wasn't eager to face. I'd tried to sound confident with Mrs. Henderson, but I was pretty certain Linda wouldn't be happy starting married life with the burden of Jenny's kids.

When I arrived home and faced Shadow's frantic greeting it occurred to me it had only been yesterday morning when I'd gone to Campbell to identify Jenny's body. It already seemed like a lifetime ago.

# CHAPTER SIX

Linda came trotting down her porch steps before I had even halted at the curb. She looked more beautiful than usual with the late afternoon sun sparkling in her honey blond hair. With amazing blue eyes and a figure that always turned heads, Linda was by far the most desirable female in Westport. It still amazed me that she had agreed to be my wife.

She had left Westport immediately after high school to attend the University of Wisconsin-Milwaukee. After earning her bachelor's degree in Business Administration, she had accepted a job in Milwaukee and it seemed she would become one of those people who left Westport permanently. Although she'd never married, she had lived with a guy for three years and I suspect she returned to Westport to mend a broken heart after the relationship had fallen apart.

We hugged briefly and Linda gave me a quick kiss on the cheek.

"You look beautiful, this evening," I said, holding her at arm's length.

She looked exasperated, but I knew she loved compliments. "Jon, you always say that."

"Only because it's always true."

I had made reservations at Tony's Country Inn, one of our favorite restaurants. There aren't any elegant eating establishments in Westport, but Tony had good food and the atmosphere was pleasant. Most of the patrons spent the evening in the bar area so the dining room was generally quiet and seldom crowded. It was a good place to relax and have pleasant conversation.

We selected a table near the window where we could watch the sunset over Pigeon Lake. Linda ordered a martini and I had my usual coke while we studied the menu.

Tony's specialty was steak and in my opinion had the best chef in the State. I chose the surf and turf and Linda selected the New York strip. While we ate, I attempted to describe Jenny's apartment and the conditions her children had been enduring. It wasn't ideal dinner conversation, but I avoided graphic details as much as possible. Linda made appropriate responses, but obviously wasn't enjoying the discussion. I saved the bombshell until we were having an after dinner drink. This time I ordered a Manhattan because I was pretty certain I'd need something stronger than coke before the evening was over.

"When I got back from Campbell I talked with Jim Stanley and started the process for obtaining custody of Jenny's kids," I said as casually as possible. "The social worker is adamantly opposed and I'll probably have to fight Child Protective Services in court."

Linda looked at me like I'd just told her I was a serial killer. "You're doing what? Don't you think you should have consulted me before you made a decision concerning both of us?"

"You're right." I hadn't expected her to be enthusiastic, but her reaction startled me. "I should have talked with you first, but there just wasn't time. I was hoping you'd understand."

"Well, I don't understand. I think assuming custody of those kids is a horrible idea. The social worker was right. It would be better for everyone involved if Child Protective Services took care of them. After all, that's why we pay taxes."

"You wouldn't say that if you'd seen Marie and Billy in that horrible apartment. The kids don't have anything or anybody except each other, and chances are Child Protective Services will place them in separate foster homes. I just can't let that happen. They're family and I have an obligation."

"I can't believe you're even considering custody. Your obligation to our future should take precedence over everything else. After all, you hadn't heard from Jenny in years. It isn't like you've been a loving brother and uncle. The last time you saw Marie she was a little baby, and you didn't even know Billy existed."

"That doesn't change my obligation," I insisted. "If I'd been more concerned about Jenny and had tried to help her, maybe none of this would have happened. Maybe she wouldn't have died in that filthy apartment."

"You may think you're doing the right thing, but you couldn't possibly have thought it through. You're feeling guilty and that isn't a very good reason to disrupt our lives. Perhaps you should have done something for Jenny when she was alive, but you didn't. We both know you wouldn't have been able to change anything. Your parents offered to give Jenny and her baby a home, but she turned her back on them. She chose her lifestyle. I really feel sorry for the kids, but they aren't your responsibility. Don't let some misdirected feelings of guilt get you into a situation that's way over your head."

"You're right; I do feel guilty about what's happened. But it's more than that. I have an obligation."

"Don't you think your first responsibility should be to me? After all, you've asked me to be your wife. Isn't there something in the Bible about leaving family and clinging together?"

"Of course I have a responsibility to you—to us. But I can't simply abandon those kids when they need me." I was almost pleading for Linda to understand, but I had a sinking feeling in the pit of my stomach. I suppose in the back of my mind I had always known Linda would reject the idea of custody.

"I'll grant you Jenny's kids need someone, but I don't believe they need you," she insisted. "Child Protective Services has the training and the resources to provide for them. Just think about it for a minute, Jon, what do you know about raising children?"

"Not much," I admitted.

"That's the point. You don't have any experience with children—even normal ones. You've admitted these kids probably have severe emotional problems. They've been neglected and maybe even abused. Their heads are probably all screwed up. Child Protective Services is prepared to deal with children like that. You...we aren't. They know what Marie and Billy need and they can provide whatever help is necessary."

"Don't you think I've argued those points with myself?" I needed Linda's support and she was obviously firmly against having a ready-made family. I had gotten myself into a corner and couldn't see any way out. "I'm not wild about the idea of taking in a couple of kids. I've never seen myself as an instant parent, or some perfect storybook father. But I can give Marie and Billy something social services and all the foster parents in the world can't. I can give them roots and love."

"Oh, come on Jon, be serious. How can you provide love when you don't even know them? You've only seen those kids for a few minutes. Would you be able to love them if they turned out to be little monsters with all sorts of mental and physical problems? Love isn't something you can turn on and off like an electric light, you know. It isn't automatic just because people are family."

"I have to make the effort," I insisted. "Please try to understand."

"What about us?" Linda's cheeks were flushed and her voice had risen above conversational tones. I had never seen her so angry.

"I don't see where this changes anything," I argued.

"It changes everything. We have our lives ahead of us and our plans never included a couple of messed up kids."

"I know that, but we never saw this coming. It's something we have to adjust to and work out together."

"If we're going to work this out together, my vote is for Child Protective Services to handle it. I don't see myself as a mother. We've already talked about having a family and you know I've never been sold on the idea. At least not right now. Maybe in a few years when we've acquired all the things we want. Now you're asking me to take on a couple of kids who aren't ours, who aren't little babies, and who will probably have more problems than we can handle."

"I realize I'm asking a lot. It won't be easy for either of us, but we can do it if we work together." I had finished my Manhattan and considered ordering another one.

"You're not listening to me," she said. "I'm not willing to be the mother of problem children. I won't start our life together with that handicap. Married life isn't a bed of roses, and you want to complicate an already difficult situation. Having those children live with us just won't work. I know I can't handle that sort of commitment and if you were honest with yourself you'd realize you can't either. I hate to make an ultimatum, but you're going to have to decide between me and two children you don't even know."

"Linda, you don't mean that. This has come as a shock and you're upset. I love you and want to spend the rest of my life with you, but I can't abandon Jenny's children."

"Don't you have an obligation to me?" Linda asked. She was so upset I thought she might start crying.

"Of course I do. It hasn't been an easy decision, you know. Please don't make me choose between you and the kids."

"That's exactly what I'm doing. I don't intend to fool myself into thinking I'm cut out to be a mother. And I don't think you're cut out to a father—at least not a father to someone else's problem kids."

"Let's not make a decision now," I suggested in desperation. "Jenny's funeral will be in a few days and Jim Stanley is making arrangements for Marie and Billy to be there. Wait until you've had a chance to meet them. Maybe you'll realize they're a lot nicer than you imagine."

"No, I won't. Don't you see, it isn't Marie and Billy, it's any children. I just can't handle a family at this time in my life. But I can wait until Jenny's funeral for you to make a decision. Hopefully when you've had time to think about it and you see the children again you'll realize this whole custody thing is a horrible idea."

"You're really going to force me to choose between you and

the kids, aren't you?" A difficult situation had suddenly become a no win scenario.

"Jon, I love you and want to marry you, but not under these circumstances. Before we'd been together a year, we'd hate each other. So, yes, as much as I don't want to, I have to insist you make the choice. Either the kids or me. Not both."

"All I'm asking is that you wait until you've met the kids."

"I'll wait until after the funeral," Linda said. "But I already know I won't change my mind. Let's hope you change yours."

We didn't speak on the drive to Linda's house. When I pulled up to the curb she opened her door and began to get out.

"Aren't you going to invite me in?" I asked.

"Not tonight. It'd be better if you went home and did some serious thinking about us and our future—or if we even have a future."

I drove home knowing I wouldn't get much sleep again. Linda and Child Protective Services were both certain I was making a huge mistake. Maybe they were right. Two days ago my life had been blissfully moving along, with a secure and happy future. Suddenly I was faced with the decision whether my prime responsibility lay with two kids I didn't know or with Linda, the woman I'd asked to share my life. I was confused and frightened, and felt trapped.

When I finally fell asleep Jenny came to me in the same dream I'd had the previous night. She sat up in her coffin, pointed at me, and intoned, "If you don't take care of my children, I'll haunt you for the rest of your life." Then suddenly it was Linda sitting in the coffin pointing at me. "If you choose those rotten kids, the rest of your life will be empty and barren."

I awoke in a cold sweat, knowing no matter which decision was made, I was going to be haunted by an unwelcome ghost.

# CHAPTER SEVEN

Generally I'm able to tune out distractions and concentrate on work, but doubts about my ability to be an instant parent and concern over Linda's attitude, made it nearly impossible to focus.

I was attempting to put together Lee Manufacturing's proposal when the phone rang Friday afternoon. An extremely solicitous Mr. Croft informed me Jenny's body had been released and he expected delivery that evening. He assured me everything would be ready for the funeral to be held on Wednesday.

I immediately phoned Father Rose to schedule a funeral Mass for ten Wednesday morning. When I confirmed times and dates with Croft he promised to coordinate the details with the priest.

Then I phoned Mrs. Henderson at Child Protective Services and told her the time for Jenny's funeral Mass at Saint Anthony's. Although she didn't sound friendly, she told me Marie and Billy had been released from the hospital, and were staying with temporary foster parents. Apparently the child psychologist had agreed the funeral would give the children closure because Child Protective Services had decided to allow them to attend. I suggested driving to Campbell Wednesday morning to pick up the children, but Mrs. Henderson immediately vetoed the idea, firmly stating that she would escort the kids. Maybe she was afraid I would kidnap them and take off for parts unknown. After providing directions, we mutually agreed to meet in front of the church at approximately nine-thirty.

Wednesday evening had been the last time I'd seen or spoken with Linda, so my final call was to make a date for the weekend.

"I don't think we should see each other this weekend," she said, sounding formal and cold. "You need time to rethink your decision about Jenny's kids."

"Can't we get together and talk it over?" I asked.

"As long as you're considering custody, we don't have anything to discuss."

Linda left me listening to the dial tone.

Even with the distractions, I managed to finish Lee Manufacturing's proposal and emailed it, hoping I hadn't made any serious or costly mistakes. Their payment would come in handy if I faced large legal bills.

Around five-thirty Jim Stanley returned my call. "I talked with a friend in Milwaukee who is familiar with custody law," he said. "Apparently since you're the children's uncle, you don't need to be approved as a foster parent. It won't hurt anything though, since someone will have to check your background and financial status before the Judge can make a custody decision."

"So, is there anything I need to do?" I asked.

"Not that I can think of. I've still got to do some digging, and we can't do much before Monday. This could get expensive. Are you certain you want to continue?"

"I have no intention of backing out. Just keep me up to date and push this along as quickly as you can."

* * *

Wednesday morning matched my mood—gray and overcast with a promise of occasional light drizzle. There were butterflies in my stomach and I had a vague feeling of dread. It wasn't because of Jenny's funeral. My connections with Jenny were too distant, and it was almost as if I would be attending the funeral of a distant acquaintance.

I dreaded seeing Marie and Billy again, praying they wouldn't behave like the wild children of a Rudyard Kipling story. This would be the last opportunity to influence Linda's decision, and deep in my heart I knew that no matter what happened she and the kids weren't going to hit it off.

After I showered, dressed and breakfasted on toast and coffee, there were still a couple of hours to kill before I had to be at the church. Rather than calling Croft to make certain everything was ready for the funeral, I decided to drive over there. It was better than sitting around the house, twiddling my thumbs.

Croft, obviously proud of his work, insisted I view the body before it was taken to the church. I wasn't eager to see Jenny again, but I had to admit Croft had done a miraculous job in preparing the body.

Jenny looked thinner than I remembered her in life, but not nearly so emaciated as at the morgue. Wearing a beige dress with the traditional rosary in her hands, her hair clean and neatly arranged, and makeup that hadn't been overdone, she resembled a beautiful young woman in peaceful sleep.

Standing beside the casket, I attempted to summon a sense of sadness or grief, but there was only anger. Jenny hadn't intended her life to end the way it had, but I couldn't forgive her for messing up my life along with hers. If I took her kids, I'd probably lose Linda. If I abandoned the kids, the thought of what had happened to them would always haunt me. Either way I'd lose something and I couldn't shake the feeling it was Jenny's fault.

I arrived at St. Anthony's about nine-fifteen and waited on the steps in front of the church. When Mrs. Henderson arrived shortly after nine-thirty and parked in the small lot beside the church, the drizzle had momentarily stopped. Considering how Marie and Billy had looked in Jenny's apartment, I thought they had undergone a remarkable transformation.

Marie had been scrubbed clean and her long auburn hair had been brushed until it shone. The tattered clothing had been replaced by a dress and light spring coat that obviously wasn't new, but was clean and well maintained. I was immediately struck by how pretty she looked; so much like her mother when Jenny had been a youngster. She had her mother's hazel eyes, but where Jenny's had sparkled with joy, Marie's appeared dull and empty.

Even though Billy clung to his sister, I was able to get a really good look at him for the first time. I was surprised at how handsome he was with his dark hair trimmed and combed. He was wearing a white shirt, blue slacks, and a light jacket. His olive complexion made me wonder if his father might have been Hispanic. Perhaps even Jenny hadn't known who the father was.

When I reached for Marie's free hand to escort her into church, she jerked away and thrust the hand deeply into her pocket. I dropped behind a pace while Mrs. Henderson herded the children into the church.

I had always considered St. Anthony's one of the most beautiful churches in the area. The hundred-year-old interior was lined with large stained glass windows that spread a soft, warm glow over the polished wooden pews.

Billy seemed overwhelmed by the people and the soft organ music. Marie didn't show any emotion, but I sensed a hesitation in her step as we walked down the long aisle toward the casket, which had been placed just outside the communion rail.

Although it wasn't standard procedure, I had convinced both Father Rose and Mr. Croft to leave the coffin open until the children had viewed the body. I was afraid if Marie and Billy only saw a closed casket they wouldn't understand that their mother was inside and that she was dead.

It was impossible to tell whether Marie understood the significance of the wax-like figure, or if she even recognized her mother. There was absolutely no reaction. She didn't smile or cry or even frown. Maybe she had never seen Jenny clean and well dressed.

Billy seemed completely mystified and frightened. When Mrs. Henderson lifted him so he could see into the coffin he turned away and buried his face against her shoulder.

"See, your Mother is ready to go to heaven," Mrs. Henderson whispered tenderly, raising a notch in my estimation. "You can touch her, or kiss her, if you want."

Billy buried his face deeper, but Marie reached out and

tentatively touched Jenny. She immediately jerked her hand back.

"Mommy's cold," she said. For an instant I saw a flash of compassion or understanding in Marie's eyes.

Before anyone realized what she was doing, Marie slipped out of her coat and laid it over Jenny's arms. I was stunned, and felt a sudden lump in my throat. I had an urge to reach out and enclose Marie in my arms, but realized she would resist and I didn't want to cause a scene in church. Her completely unselfish act had erased any doubts I'd felt about taking in the children.

"Your mother doesn't need a coat," Mrs. Henderson said. She set Billy down, gently lifted the garment off Jenny, and helped Marie slip it back on. "She's gone to Heaven and won't ever be cold or hungry or sad again."

As quickly as the understanding had come, it was gone and Marie's eyes were again empty, lifeless.

"Come on, children," I said, "let's sit down."

As soon as we turned away, Croft closed and secured the coffin lid.

Mrs. Henderson shepherded the children toward the front pew and slid in first, pulling Billy and Marie after her. I took the aisle seat, with the children safely between us, Marie next to me, and Billy beside Mrs. Henderson.

Linda hadn't arrived by the time Father Rose appeared in the vestibule, lining up the servers for the processional, and I began to wonder whether she would put in an appearance.

When the priest came down the aisle, preceded by an altar boy carrying a tall crucifix and another swinging the thurible, spreading the aroma of incense, Marie whispered something to Billy and he stood so he could see beyond the pew. I watched his eyes widen as he stared in fascination at the priest's colorful vestments and smelled the incense drifting toward us. Father Rose shook the aspergillum in our direction, and Billy flinched from the sprinkle of holy water.

After blessing the coffin, the priest chanted the prayers for the dead, and Marie began crying silently. I put my arm around her and pulled her close as tears began to well up in my own eyes. I had an intense desire to comfort this little girl, to somehow make up for her mother's wasted life and all Marie had suffered. The injustice of her situation made me sad and angry at the same time.

Marie's tears were brief, as if any emotion was an unacceptable chink in her armor. She refused the handkerchief I offered and wiped her eyes on her coat sleeve as she pulled away.

The funeral Mass had already begun when Linda slid into the pew beside me. "Sorry I'm late," she whispered. "I got tied up at work."

I squeezed her hand and smiled to let her know I was glad she had come.

The Mass was beautiful and Father Rose delivered a moving eulogy. I could sense that the children didn't understand what was happening, and wondered whether either one had ever been in a church. Each time Linda and I knelt or stood the children and Mrs. Henderson remained seated. When Linda and I received communion, Mrs. Henderson stayed in the pew with Marie and Billy.

At the end of the Mass, Father Rose led the recessional, followed by the pallbearers Mr. Croft had provided. Mrs. Henderson, the children, Linda and I followed immediately after. I could hear the stirring of the other mourners as they joined the procession.

While the casket was loaded into the hearse a few people stopped to offer their condolences. I introduced Linda to Mrs. Henderson and the children. As usual, Billy buried his face against his sister and Marie glared at Linda, refusing to acknowledge the introduction.

It had begun to drizzle again, so I held my umbrella over the children and Mrs. Henderson. I was afraid the social worker might not allow the kids to go to the cemetery, but she herded Marie and Billy into the back seat of her car and followed Linda and me to Evergreen Hills.

Linda didn't say anything on the short drive, and my

thoughts were on Jenny's unhappy life and her children. Since my heart was now committed to the kids, I was afraid anything I said would further alienate Linda.

A canvas shelter had been erected over the open grave, but wasn't large enough to protect the spectators or the priest. Father Rose stood at the head of the coffin, an altar boy holding an umbrella to shield him from the light rain. No one else had accompanied us to the cemetery.

As a concession to the weather, Father Rose kept the graveside service short, but I was getting soaked anyway. Holding the umbrella over Mrs. Henderson and the kids left me exposed and my overcoat wasn't waterproof.

When we went back to the cars I briefly hugged Billy, but when I reached for Marie, she pulled away. Linda gave me one of those, 'I told you so' looks.

Mrs. Henderson immediately secured the kids in the back seat of her Ford and walked around to the driver's side as if she intended to leave without speaking.

"When can I see the children again?" I asked.

"I don't think it'd be a good idea for you to ever see them again," she snapped. "They're going to have to adjust to their new life and you'd be a needless disruption."

"I am going to see the children again, Mrs. Henderson." Every time I talked with this woman she managed to get my hackles up. "I intend to fight for custody."

"And I'll fight to make certain you don't get custody." She slid behind the wheel, slammed the door, and pulled away; leaving me with the feeling I should have punched her in the nose.

Linda and I drove back to the church in an awkward silence.

"I'm glad that's over. Funerals are always depressing. I'll give you a call this evening." I leaned across the seat to kiss her, but she turned away to open the door.

"Don't bother," she said, sounding angry and bitter. "I heard what you told Mrs. Henderson. Apparently you're still determined to gain custody."

"I don't have any choice," I said. "I'm family and those

children need me."

"Yes, you have a choice and you've obviously decided those children mean more to you than I do."

Linda slid from the car and slammed the door. I sat there for a long time, watching larger raindrops spatter on the windshield, wondering whether I was making all the wrong decisions. Maybe I was getting into something way beyond my ability to handle. I prayed for some easy answers, but knew there weren't any.

# CHAPTER EIGHT

Jim Stanley phoned at nine Thursday morning. "Hi Jon. I've gotta run to court in a few minutes, but thought you'd want to know I've received information on the custody thing—medical and psychological reports. You might want to see them for yourself. They could change your mind about this crazy notion concerning Jenny's kids."

"What time did you have in mind?" I asked. Jim didn't sound like he considered the reports good news.

"I have an hour available at two this afternoon. If this information doesn't change your mind, we'll have to start the paperwork quickly."

"Two o'clock will work for me," I agreed. "Is there any special reason you're suddenly in a hurry about this?"

"We can discuss it this afternoon," Jim said.

When I hung up, my stomach was twisted into a knot. If the reports contained bad news, maybe I didn't even want to read them.

I considered calling Linda at work to share the news, but decided against it. I'd already tried to reach her several times since the funeral and had been forced to leave messages on her answering machine. She hadn't returned my calls and I didn't think her attitude would improve if I bothered her at the office.

Linda's position regarding custody was unequivocal and for a moment I wondered whether she might be right. However, I realized I had to fight for custody, as much for myself as for the children. No matter what anyone believed, or what the consequences might be, if I didn't fight for the kids I'd regret it the rest of my life.

I spent the morning working on the software program I was developing for Lee's Manufacturing. Normally large companies took weeks to make a decision, but Henry Jerrold had jumped at my proposal. His hasty acceptance caused me to check if my bid was too low. After running the figures again, I decided the price was fair and I'd collect a nice fee.

Usually when I got involved writing a program, I became so focused everything else suffered, but this morning it was difficult concentrating. It made me wonder, if I was having a hard time now, what would it be like when I suddenly became a parent?

The pieces of the program weren't falling into place, so I finally gave up the effort at one-thirty. I fed Shadow, gave him fresh water, and headed over to Jim's office.

"Hi, Jon. Mr. Stanley hasn't returned from court yet," Madge said. "It's not that I've been snooping or anything, but I did read the medical and psychological reports." She looked like whatever was in them was not going to make me happy. "I want you to know I think you're doing the right thing."

"Thanks, Madge. It's nice to know everyone doesn't think I'm crazy."

"Well, maybe you're crazy, but in a good sort of way." Madge handed me a sheaf of papers. "Mr. Stanley suggested you read these if you arrived early."

I was surprised that Jim had gotten copies of the reports. I'd figured Child Protective Services would consider them confidential and have fought tooth and nail to keep me from seeing them. It became obvious as I began reading that Mrs. Henderson must have decided the information would discourage me.

I read Marie's medical exam first and immediately wished I hadn't. Even though the doctor hadn't used terminology intended for a layperson, it didn't take a genius to understand the gist of his findings. In my worst nightmare I couldn't have imagined the horrible life my niece had endured.

The report began with the revelation that Marie had been repeatedly raped over an extended period, possibly for years. In the doctor's opinion severe internal damage and subsequent scaring would prevent Marie from ever having children.

*God, that can't be true,* I thought. *She's only nine-years-old. No one could be sick enough to sexually molest a girl that young.* I had to pause and take a deep breath before I could continue.

The sexual abuse was horrible, but it was only the beginning. According to the doctor, there had also been extensive physical torture. It was impossible to read the reports with the doctor's clinical detachment. Every new revelation twisted my gut and I was afraid I might be sick. Childhood should be a carefree, happy time, not a period of pain and torture.

Marie's body bore numerous scars probably caused by cigarette burns. Extensive bruising and long-term welts indicated frequent and severe beatings from belts or similar objects. The doctor didn't believe any of the injuries had been medically treated. Enclosed diagrams were covered with red x's showing the location of each scar or injury. There were even x's on the bottom of her feet.

A serious rash, probably the result of poor hygiene and infrequent bathing, had spread from her knees to her waist, with the worst infection in her crotch. Blood tests and stool samples confirmed intestinal parasites from eating spoiled food. On top of everything else, she suffered from malnutrition and vitamin deficiencies. In a scribbled marginal note, the doctor described Marie as one of the worst cases of abuse and neglect he'd ever seen.

Although I was nauseated and in a state of shock, I forced myself to read Billy's medical report which was only slightly better. There was no evidence of sexual molestation, although the doctor didn't rule out the possibility. Billy had obviously suffered physical brutalization, but there were only a few burn scars and not nearly as much evidence of beatings. The physician speculated that perhaps his age and sex had spared him from the severe and frequent abuse Marie had suffered. I thought there might be a different explanation. After seeing the children together, I suspected Marie had done everything within her power to protect her brother—probably even accepting torture intended for him. However, Billy did suffer from the same rash, parasites, malnutrition, and vitamin deficiencies that affected his sister.

Before finding Marie and Billy in Jenny's horrible apartment I'd considered myself fairly unemotional. Although it had been a terrible tragedy, I hadn't shed tears at my parent's funeral. There hadn't been any deep emotional response to Jenny's death. But what had happened to these two innocent children was more than I could bear.

Tears blurred my vision and I had to wait a moment before attempting to read the psychological evaluations. I wasn't certain I wanted to know how the abuse and torture had affected their minds.

*Jenny,* I thought, *how could you have allowed this to happen?* I still remembered my sister as a sweet little girl who had loved babies and animals. Drugs must have fried her brain until she had descended into an unimaginable hell where she could no longer protect her children. As far as anyone knew Jenny may have participated in the torture.

When I finally gathered enough strength to look at the psychological reports, there was a preamble explaining this was a preliminary examination and further evaluation would be necessary to determine the total extent of psychological damage.

Much of the language was beyond my comprehension, but as I scanned the documents, there was no doubt the children had severe mental problems. Both suffered from symptoms of dissociation, although Marie was more traumatized than Billy. The psychologist described dissociation as a defense mechanism enabling the kids to cope with their environment. I didn't understand exactly what that meant. How could anyone, adult or child, cope with the cruelty they had suffered?

The psychologist suggested if brutally abused children didn't develop the ability to dissociate, they simply curled up and died.

According to the doctor, Marie and Billy both had extremely low self-esteem. Apparently the kids believed they had done something to deserve the abuse, and that they weren't worthy of love.

*God,* I thought, *how could any child believe they deserved such inhuman treatment?* I had to close my eyes and take a deep breath before I had the courage to read further.

As a result of the trauma, Marie exhibited a fear of men, and had little or no respect for women. Understandably, Billy had developed a fear of all adults. He also exhibited an obsessive attachment to his sister, looking to Marie for the support and protection a normal five-year-old would have sought from his parents.

Billy was too young to be expected to read or write, but at nine-years-old, Marie was totally illiterate. The doctor described their intellectual and emotional development as abnormal. Hell, their life had been abnormal, so why shouldn't their emotions have suffered.

In summary, the psychologist recommended extensive counseling, with no guarantee the children would ever completely recover from the trauma they had experienced. She believed they would retain life-long emotional scars, although with proper treatment, love, and a stable environment they could develop into functioning adults.

Mrs. Henderson had been right. The reports scared the hell out me. However they didn't change my mind. If anything, I was more convinced than ever that the children needed me.

"Hi Jon." Jim Stanley's greeting came as a welcome interruption to my reading. "Sorry I'm running a bit late. Come in and we'll talk."

I wiped my eyes and brought my emotions under control as I followed him into the office, dropping onto a chair beside his desk.

"Did you have an opportunity to read the reports?" he asked.

My red eyes and shocked expression should have answered his question.

I nodded and indicated the documents. "Can I keep these?"

"Sure. Those are your copies." When I didn't comment, Jim asked, "So, what do you think?"

"I can't think. Those kids lived in a Hell full of demons and monsters. It's like something from the holocaust. I can't believe children could suffer like that, right here in our county, in this day and age." I shook my head and felt the tears coming again. "It's horrible."

"Yeah, it's the worst I've seen or heard about," Jim acknowledged. "I hope it's made you reconsider your decision to seek custody."

The surprise must have shown on my face. "Of course not. This...this hell the kids have gone through just convinces me they need someone to help them understand there's more to life than torture and abuse."

"Jon, you're letting your emotions speak for you. You have to look at this objectively."

"Objectively!" I snapped. "How the hell can I be objective after reading this stuff? I saw the kids in that apartment. I know how they were forced to live. I wouldn't be human if I even began to be objective."

"Calm down," Jim soothed. "I'm not the villain here. I'm your attorney and I'll do whatever you want, but I really think you should consider this carefully. I've got three kids of my own, who've had a pretty good life. I can tell you from experience, raising children—even normal ones—isn't easy. Marie and Billy have major problems that'll make the job next to impossible. You're opening yourself up for a lot of pain and heartache. I don't think you understand what you're getting into."

I knew Jim was right. I could only vaguely appreciate the problems that lay ahead for the kids and me. Yet there was no doubt that fighting for custody was the only thing I could do. I owed it to Jenny and my parents and the kids—and to myself. No matter how well intentioned foster parents are, they couldn't possibly provide the love and stability Marie and Billy needed. Hell, foster parents could bail out if the going got rough. I couldn't live with myself knowing Marie and Billy were out there somewhere, perhaps shuttling from foster home to foster home, never staying in one place long enough to put down roots.

"Jim, I have to do this," I said. "Maybe I don't understand exactly what I'm getting into, but I don't have any choice. Those kids need me. And maybe I need them."

"Would you like a couple of days to think it over?" Jim asked. "Say until Monday? You might have a different perspective after you've calmed down."

"No! I've already made up my mind. I want you to get on this right now. Today. Do whatever is necessary for me to obtain custody. I'm not going to abandon them to the system."

"Okay, it's your call. You're doing this against my advice, but I'll get the ball rolling immediately."

I felt like I had just stepped into the deep end of the pool with a weight tied to my feet. "So, what's the procedure?"

"I'll file papers with Children's Court. We already know Child Protective Services is going to fight us, but we may get a court date fairly quickly. As long as there's a question of custody, CPS won't be able to place the kids in a permanent foster home, so I suspect they'll ask the court for preference in scheduling."

"You indicated on the phone there was another reason for moving forward quickly," I said.

"Yeah. Frank Johnson, the attorney for Child Protective Services, indicated another couple is nearly approved to be foster parents and they've expressed an interest in Marie and Billy. From their preliminary investigation, CPS favors placing the kids with them. Something about a two parent household being more stable than a single parent environment. It would be in our best interests to schedule a court date before this other couple is approved."

"Do you know anything about these people?" I asked. For no rational reason, I had a nagging concern about this couple's timing. Why would they have requested Marie and Billy at the same time they filed to become foster parents? After reading the psychological and medical reports it was hard for me to believe any young couple would prefer such damaged kids. I realized there were dedicated people who just wanted to do good and this couple might fit in that category, but I couldn't shake the feeling there was something questionable about their application.

"According to Frank, information concerning perspective foster parents is confidential. We'll find out all we need to know when we appear in court."

"Can you at least learn their names?" I asked.

"Possibly. Frank Johnson owes me a favor or two." Jim cocked an eyebrow. "What difference does it make?"

I wasn't sure why I wanted the names, but at the moment it seemed important. "Maybe I'd like to do some investigating on my own. Don't you think it's suspicious that those people are in the right place at the right time?"

"Are you suggesting CPS is trying to blind side us?"

"I don't know what I'm saying. I just have a gut feeling about this couple."

"Don't you have enough on your plate without getting involved investigating something that's a waste of time?"

"You're probably right, but that couple wanting Marie and Billy doesn't seem logical. Don't you think it's strange these people would want to become foster parents and specifically ask for Jenny's kids—kids with major psychological problems?"

Jim shrugged. "Those things happen. It doesn't necessarily imply anything sinister."

"I know, but I'd feel better if I didn't leave this up to Child Protective Services. I'd appreciate it if you'd get the names for me."

"I won't promise anything, but I'll see what I can do. I think you're wasting your time on something that's completely irrelevant."

I stood and reached across the desk to shake Jim's hand. "Thanks. I'd appreciate you doing what you can to speed the process. Please try to see my side of this. I'm going to need your support."

"Just because I think you're making a mistake doesn't mean I won't support you."

When I stepped from Jim's office into the sunlight, fear stirred in the back of my mind. Win or lose, my life would never be the same. I was going to be traveling unexplored jungles and I felt totally alone.

That night I had a new nightmare. I found myself in a dark, cold dungeon, chained against the wall, unable to move. Marie and Billy were across the room, suspended by their wrists from the ceiling, their toes barely touching the floor. They were screaming and pleading for help as devilish figures danced around them, touching lit cigarettes to their naked bodies and beating them with whips. Off to the side Jenny was jumping up and down, clapping her hands in glee, laughing hysterically. With every ounce of my strength I struggled to break free and help the children, but my chains held me securely in place.

When I awoke in a cold sweat, I wondered whether I would need psychological counseling before this was over.

# CHAPTER NINE

When Shadow nudged me at six, my sheets and pajamas were still damp from the night sweats and I shivered as I let the dog out. I considered crawling back into bed, but was afraid I'd have the nightmare again. I showered, shaved, dressed, and tried to keep my mind occupied by working on Lee's software program.

Jim Stanley phoned at eleven-thirty.

"You're not going to believe this," he said, sounding proud of himself. "Children's Court has scheduled a hearing for next Wednesday afternoon, which means Child Protective Services won't be able to place the children in a permanent foster home until after the hearing."

"That's great," I said, feeling relieved because the anxiety wouldn't drag on forever, but dreading the court's decision, whatever it might be. An old cliché flashed through my mind. 'Be careful what you wish for because you might get it.' My problem was that I didn't know what to wish for.

"You don't sound very enthusiastic," Jim said.

"I'm pleased; I just didn't think things would move so quickly."

"Normally they wouldn't, but CPS must be eager to get this settled. You realize if you get custody, it'll only be the beginning. It isn't too late to withdraw your petition."

"Not a chance," I said, trying to sound more confident than I felt. "Do you think there's any possibility of winning against the bureaucracy?"

"I honestly don't know. There's never any way of guessing how a judge will decide, but I figure we've got a fifty-fifty chance or better. The fact that you're a relative should weigh heavily in our favor. Why don't we get together Monday to discuss strategy?"

"Sounds good to me. What time's best for you?"

"Let's hold off making a definite appointment until Monday. We'll have to work around a visitor from Children's Court."

"What visitor?" I asked.

"Children's Court is sending someone to check your living arrangements. It might be a plus if you had everything set up when the inspector arrives. A bedroom for each of the kids would definitely be in our favor. I doubt whether the court would approve of a boy and girl sleeping in the same room, even if they are siblings."

"That's not a problem. I have the bedrooms Jenny and I used as kids."

"Good. Give me a call Monday and we'll go from there."

"One more thing," I said. "Did you learn the names of that couple—the ones who want to foster Marie and Billy?"

"Glad you reminded me. It was like pulling teeth, but Frank Johnson finally told me—with the stipulation that I never tell where I got the information." I could hear papers shuffling in the background. "Here they are. Cynthia and George Blackman."

The names weren't familiar, and Westport is small enough that I'd have known if they were locals. Most likely they were from Campbell, and I didn't have any contacts in the city who could give me information. Then I remembered Officer Ryan's offer to help any way she could. A police officer would certainly know something about a lot of people. I felt uncomfortable phoning her about such nebulous concerns, but I figured the worst that could happen was that I would make a fool of myself.

As soon as Jim and I were finished, I called the Campbell Police Department.

"What can I do for you, Mr. Wilson?" Officer Ryan asked after I'd identified myself.

"This probably isn't a police matter and it may sound paranoid, but I was hoping you could give me some advice." I briefly told her about the medical and psychological reports and explained my unfounded suspicions about Cynthia and George Blackman. The more I talked, the dumber it sounded. I gave Officer Ryan credit for listening patiently.

"That's an interesting theory about the Blackmans," she said when I'd finished. "However, as you said, it isn't a police matter. What did you want from me?"

"I'm not sure. Don't you think the situation sounds a little fishy?"

"Maybe you're looking for problems where there aren't any. Stranger things have happened." She paused a moment. "If it would make you feel better, I could run the names through our database to see if the Blackmans have police records, but that's the first thing CPS would have checked."

"You're right. I just have this gut feeling something isn't kosher."

Officer Ryan must have sensed my disappointment and frustration. "I know you're concerned that Jennifer's kids get a square deal. I was with you when we found them, and I have a soft spot for those children too. But believe me, CPS does a great job. They wouldn't approve foster parents who aren't qualified."

"When I say it out loud, this sounds pretty foolish. I'm sorry to have wasted your time."

"I'm glad you called," she said, sounding gracious. "I know you're not on the greatest of terms with CPS, but you can trust them to do what's best for the kids."

"Thanks for being so patient with my paranoia."

"No problem. You know, maybe I can do something for you after all. The police have some sources not available to CPS. It probably won't do any good, but I can ask the patrol officers to keep an ear open for any street rumors about Jennifer or the kids or this couple."

"Thanks, I'd appreciate that. If you hear anything, please give me a call."

When I hung up I felt like a perfect idiot. Officer Ryan was right in suggesting I was sticking my nose where it didn't belong. I made up my mind to forget the Blackmans until the hearing.

Since I needed moral and spiritual support, I phoned Father Rose. He agreed to see me after seven that evening.

Linda hadn't responded to any of my calls, and I felt compelled to try one last time to salvage our relationship. Since she wasn't answering her home phone, I decided to contact her at the office.

"I don't appreciate you calling me at work," she said angrily when I identified myself.

"You haven't responded to any of my messages, and we need to talk."

"Have you decided to forget this madness about getting custody of Jenny's kids?" she asked.

"That's one of the reasons I called. I have a court date Wednesday to decide custody. Please try to understand that I have to do this. Let's talk about it. We can work something out."

"We don't have anything to discuss as long as those children are an issue."

"Linda, don't say that. I may not get custody, or the kids may turn out to be wonderful children."

"It doesn't make any difference. I'm not cut out to be a mother and I certainly don't want to be stuck with someone else's kids. You've made your choice. Even if you don't get custody, you've already told me those brats are more important than I am. I can't accept that."

"Linda, give it a chance. Don't throw away everything we have together. Your feelings are hurt and you aren't thinking straight."

"No, you're the one who isn't thinking straight. We don't have anything more to discuss. If you keep calling, I'll file harassment charges. Good luck with whatever happens in your life, but you can count me out. It was your choice, not mine."

For the second time in a week, Linda left me listening to the dial tone. Damn, my life had been so organized and comfortable. Now it was falling apart. Was I the only one who believed the kids needed me? Was I deluding myself?

* * *

It was exactly seven o'clock when I rang the rectory doorbell and Agnes Richards led me directly to Father Rose's study.

"Well, Jon, it's good to see you again. I gathered from your phone call you have something serious to discuss. Please have a seat."

"Yes, Father." I said. "I need advice and moral support." I handed him Marie and Billy's medical and psychological evaluations. "Maybe we should begin with these reports."

Father Rose moved behind his desk and began reading. After a few long minutes he looked up, a deep sadness in his eyes. "No matter how often I see it, I never get used to man's inhumanity to man. This is almost beyond human understanding." He leaned back in his chair, steepled his fingers and slowly tapped the index fingers together as he talked. "I imagine it's difficult for you to find forgiveness in your heart for Jennifer's sins. If you're wondering how God can allow such evil to exist, I can't help you. The existence of evil is a mystery we must accept on faith. We have to believe God has a purpose for everything."

"You're right, Father. I don't understand how anyone could torture and abuse helpless children and I don't know whether I'll ever be able to forgive Jennifer, but that's not why I came to see you. I'm trying to obtain custody of Marie and Billy. Everyone tells me I'm crazy—that the kids would be better off with Child Protective Services. I suppose I'd like your opinion and any spiritual advice you can offer."

Father Rose removed his glasses and massaged the bridge of his nose. "Most people think because we wear this collar we have answers for all life's questions. Unfortunately we don't. I can give my opinion, of course. It may be tempered by my years as a priest, but it's still only my opinion."

"I understand," I said, wondering if he was going to tell me I had lost my mind.

"You're not married, are you, Jon?"

"No, Father."

He nodded thoughtfully. "You realize, of course, if you obtain custody of the children you'll have all the responsibilities of a single parent even though you haven't formally adopted them. Parenthood is an awesome responsibility and difficult even when there are two people involved. It's much more formidable for a single parent. Not enough people take parenting as seriously as the calling deserves. It would appear Jennifer's children will need a great deal of special care, both medical and psychological."

I started to speak, but Father Rose held up his hand to stop me. "Sometimes there's no alternative to the State taking care of damaged children. Child Protective Services was created to handle homeless and abused children, and they do an admirable job. There are many dedicated and loving people who work very hard to redeem children such as Marie and Billy. Even so, I'm not convinced it's the best option. One of my favorite charities is the Mission of Our Lady of Mercy in Chicago. They do a fantastic job with throwaway children, but they're still a poor substitute for a loving family. You have the opportunity to offer Marie and Billy the love and stability they can't get from institutions or foster homes. Love and prayer are the two most powerful forces in the world."

"Are you saying you agree with my decision to fight for custody?"

"Personally, yes. However, in the end it depends upon whether God wants these children to be with you. If God wills it, He'll provide the grace necessary to meet the challenge. However I believe God would expect you to take advantage of professional help—doctors and psychologists, teachers and community resources. Most of all you'll have to pray for God to grant you strength and wisdom."

"I've been praying, and I can afford to provide the care Marie and Billy require."

"Then you've got a good start. I believe if God hadn't called you to this task, you wouldn't even be considering custody. We must remember Jesus loved children. He said, 'Suffer the little children to come unto me, and forbid them not; for such is the Kingdom of God'. Three of the gospel writers felt this message was so powerful they all quoted Him."

"I feel in my heart that I have to help these kids, but don't know if I have the strength to handle the responsibility."

"God never gives us a cross we cannot bear," Father Rose said. "I'm convinced Jesus provides special graces to anyone who helps children."

"Then you think I'm doing the right thing?"

"I believe in the long run God will decide whether it's the right thing. I'll pray for you and the children. If you get custody, I'll help in any way I can. St. Anthony's does have a very special resource for cases like yours. For many years before she came to our parish, Sister Joan worked with troubled youngsters in Milwaukee. I'm certain she'll want to assist your children. You may also find comfort praying to Saint Germaine, asking for her intercession."

"Saint Germaine?" I was familiar with a lot of saints, but I'd never heard her name.

"Saint Germaine is the patron saint for victims of child abuse. I believe I have a holy card here somewhere." Father Rose opened a desk drawer and rummaged through it for a moment. "Ah, here we are."

He handed me a card with the picture a young woman sitting on a rock, a sheep at her side gazing intently at her. On the back was a prayer asking for Saint Germaine's intercession.

"She came from a very humble home and was severely abused as a child," Father Rose explained. "Yet she managed to overcome all the obstacles and reach sainthood."

I slipped the card into my shirt pocket. "Thank you, Father. You don't know how comforting it is to have someone on my side."

"God and Saint Germaine are on your side. Pray for the strength you'll need in the days and months to come. It's only normal for you to feel a great deal of bitterness toward Jennifer, but you must rid your heart of all the anger against your sister. Pray for the compassion to forgive her. To give these children the love they'll need, you must love their mother."

After I left Father Rose, I stood beside my car in the gathering twilight, watching the first stars light the sky. I wanted to feel noble and brave, but I was still frightened. I could only hope Father Rose was right about God, St. Germaine, and all the saints being on my side.

# CHAPTER TEN

I'm not a fanatical housekeeper, and with everything that was happening I'd been neglecting my cleaning chores. Any housewife knows it doesn't take long for a house to begin looking shabby. If Children's Court was going to inspect the place, I decided to use the weekend to make certain everything was neat and clean. I grabbed all my cleaning supplies and headed upstairs, planning to begin at the top and work my way down.

It was an uncomfortable sensation entering Jenny's bedroom. After Mom and Dad were gone I had simply left Jenny's door closed and ignored her room. As kids Jenny had always gone ballistic if I invaded her territory, and even now I had the feeling I was intruding. Mom had kept everything exactly as it had been when Jenny moved out so many years earlier, always believing her daughter and granddaughter would return some day.

I sat on the flowered bedspread and looked around at the matching drapes and cream-colored walls. I sensed Jenny's personality still lingering in the room. If there were such things as ghosts, her spirit would certainly be here, where she had spent so many happy hours.

A snow white Teddy Bear, complete with a large red bow, still slumped on top of her dresser. Jenny must have been nine or ten when she won Teddy at the county fair and I remembered how excited she had been. Why had she abandoned her favorite childhood treasure? Had drugs and alcohol already become more important, or had she simply outgrown it?

Faded High School photos of Jenny and her friends were

taped around the edges of the vanity mirror. I felt a lump in my throat as I removed each picture and briefly glanced at it. I spent an extra moment studying the snapshot of Jenny and her date on Prom night. She looked happy in a low cut formal with an orchard corsage on the thin shoulder strap. She must have been a sophomore, attending her last Prom before she ran away from home. The boy looked impossibly young and clean cut in his rented tuxedo. From Mom's description, I was pretty certain this boy was not the one she had left with.

I decided to leave the framed pictures of horses and pastoral scenes hanging on the walls, but felt compelled to erase all other evidence of Jenny. There were too many painful memories. The few items of clothing went into a bag destined for Goodwill. I removed her personal effects from the vanity, dresser, and bedside table, placing them in a box for storage in the garage. Maybe someday Marie would want the mementoes of her mother.

It didn't seem likely the court's inspector would examine the canopied bed for clean sheets, but I put on fresh linen. After dusting and vacuuming, I moved across the hall.

My old bedroom was smaller than Jenny's, without nearly as many ghosts from my childhood. I remembered Mom selecting the Indian motif bedspread and drapes when the Wild West had fascinated me. The posters and pictures scattered around the room reflected my space adventure phase. A plastic model of the shuttle Challenger gathered dust on the dresser. A scuffed baseball glove lay on the closet floor beside my old Louisville Slugger, electrician's tape still wrapped around the cracked handle. Even securely taped, I remembered how my hands had stung every time I hit the ball. I added the bat and glove to the box destined for the garage. Everything else was left in place as I changed the linen, dusted and vacuumed.

It took most of the morning to clean the bathroom. On a day to day basis I had kept the room tidy, but I figured it needed a more thorough cleaning if I wanted the court inspector to approve. Mom had always said that as far as a woman was concerned, the most important rooms in a house were the kitchen and the bathrooms. Consequently I washed the tile walls around the shower area and scrubbed all the porcelain fixtures until they gleamed.

I set to work on the downstairs areas in the afternoon, paying special attention to the kitchen. When I was finished, everything sparkled, looking cleaner than it had since Mom died.

Sunday morning after Mass I tackled the yard. The juniper bushes along the front porch needed trimming, and an accumulation of leaves had to be raked away from the roots. My front yard is small, but the fenced back yard is about a hundred feet deep and fifty feet wide. I hadn't mowed as frequently as I should have, and the lawn looked pretty shabby. I took extra care mowing and trimming the edges.

When I finished, the house and yard might not have impressed a Marine Corps drill instructor, but I was confident they would satisfy a court appointed inspector.

\* \* \*

Eight-thirty Monday morning Kathleen Whitlock phoned, introducing herself as an employee of Children's Court, and we arranged an appointment for early afternoon. Westport isn't a complicated town, but I supplied directions so she wouldn't have any problem locating the house.

I waited until ten to call Jim Stanley.

"It probably won't pay to get together today," he said after I told him about Mrs. Whitlock. "I've got a full schedule tomorrow, and after thinking about it, I don't believe we need to meet before court. The judge might want to see proof of fiscal responsibility, so if you bring copies of your last two tax returns, and your latest bank statement, we should be all set."

"Will do," I agreed, trusting Jim's expertise.

"Great. I'll meet you at the courthouse Wednesday about twelve-thirty. Good luck with Mrs. Whitlock."

After lunch I wandered around the house straightening pictures, doing touch-up dusting and generally killing time. I was bursting with nervous energy and had a major case of butterflies.

It was almost one-thirty when a blue, official looking sedan pulled to the curb. I'm not very good with ages, but guessed Mrs. Whitlock was about thirty to thirty-five. She was wearing a red blouse and tan slacks that were a little tight across the hips. She looked all business carrying a brief case in her right hand and marching up to the porch.

I opened the door before she rang the doorbell, and immediately thought I should have waited for her to push the button so she could hear the chimes. Maybe functioning doorbells were important to Children's Court.

"Mr. Wilson?" She had a nice smile and I liked her right away. "I'm Kathleen Whitlock from Children's Court."

I had forgotten to put Shadow in the back yard and he began jumping around, excited by the prospect of making a new friend. A big, frantic dog intimidates some people, but Mrs. Whitlock bent and rubbed his ears. "Hi, there, big guy, how are you doing?" Shadow was so thrilled he could barely contain himself. "What a beautiful dog. What's his name?"

"Shadow. He gets hyper when he meets new people. He'll settle down in a minute, but it might be better if I put him in the back yard." I took Shadow by the collar and hustled him through the house, grateful Mrs. Whitlock was a dog lover.

When I returned, she had moved into the dining room and was examining the bric-a-brac Mom had kept in the corner china cabinet. "You certainly have a nice old house," she said.

It sounded as if she placed too much emphasis on 'old', but she was smiling. I was probably being paranoid. "Would you like a tour, or do you want to wander around on your own?" I asked.

My nervousness must have been obvious because Mrs. Whitlock laid her briefcase on the dining room table and smiled reassuringly. "Please relax," she said. "I promise this will be completely painless. I'd prefer if you showed me around. Could I see where the children will be sleeping?"

"The bedrooms are upstairs." I led up the staircase and opened the first door we encountered. "This will be Billy's room. I know it's comfortable because it used to be mine."

Mrs. Whitlock wandered around the room, looked out the window, and then opened the closet door. The closet was empty except for a couple of wire hangers and an extra blanket on the shelf. As I had suspected, she didn't check whether the linen was clean. "Very nice," she said, her voice neutral. "It should be a pleasant room for a little boy."

Directly across the hall I opened the door into Jenny's old bedroom. "This is where Marie will be staying. It used to belong to her mother."

She followed the same routine—looking out the window and checking the closet, which was a duplicate of the one in Billy's room. From her expression it was impossible to tell whether she approved or disapproved.

"Very nice," she said. "The vanity is a ladylike touch for a little girl. Is there a bathroom on this floor?"

"It's right here," I said, pushing open the door. "This is a full bath, with tub and shower. I have a half bath downstairs next to my study."

Mrs. Whitlock looked into the tub area and opened the linen closet. Fortunately I had an abundance of towels neatly folded on the shelves.

"The last room is my bedroom. Would you like to see that?"

"I don't believe that'll be necessary," she said. "I'm impressed with the comfortable arrangement you have for two children."

"Thank you. Jenny and I were always happy here," I said. "What's next?"

"May I see the kitchen?"

"Of course."

I was proud of the kitchen, which had been remodeled the year before Mom and Dad's accident. It was a large, well-lit room, with generous cabinets. There was plenty of space to move around the kitchen table and four chairs occupying the center of the room.

Mrs. Whitlock looked into several of the cabinets and opened the refrigerator for a quick glance.

"That's the doorway to the backyard," I said. "The yard is completely fenced and is a great place for kids to play safely."

Mrs. Whitlock peeked out the kitchen window and then walked into the dining room. Most of the furniture in the house had belonged to my parents, and the beautiful old dining table could easily seat six.

"My study is there, off the dining room," I said.

The study door was open and Mrs. Whitlock glanced inside. "I see you have lots of books," she said. "Children who are exposed to books at home generally become the best students. That's quite a computer setup. Do you work from home?"

"Yes. I have my own software design business, so I'm home most of the time. I'll definitely be available for Marie and Billy." We stood for a moment of awkward silence. "Is there anything else you'd like to see?"

"No, thank you. Your home strikes me as a wonderful place for children."

"My sister and I enjoyed growing up here."

"Yes, I can see that."

"I haven't been a very good host," I said, remembering too late that I should be treating Mrs. Whitlock like a guest. "Can I offer you something before you go—coffee, soda, water?"

"No, thanks. I'm on a pretty tight schedule. This is just a routine visit so the Court will have some idea where the children would be living. It's important to their development to have space of their own. I'm pleased to see they'll each have a nice bedroom and plenty of storage space for their clothing." She picked up her briefcase. "Just one last thing. Where are the schools in relation to your house?"

"The elementary school is about four blocks. It's an easy walk through nice neighborhoods." I saw a slight frown and decided she might not approve of the kids walking to school. "Of course

I'll be driving them every day."

"That's great. Easy access to schools is important." Mrs. Whitlock held out her hand and we shook. "Thank you for your courtesy. I have more than enough information for my report."

I escorted her to the car and watched from the sidewalk as she drove away. I had a good feeling about the brief inspection. Her comments had all been positive, and I couldn't see any reason for her to turn in a negative report.

When I went back into the house it occurred to me that when I won custody, I would have to take the kids shopping. I didn't have clothing or toilet articles or anything personal for the kids. A shopping trip with a couple of kids ought to be an adventure in itself.

Getting stuff for Billy would be no problem, but I'd never bought clothing for a little girl, and I was pretty certain Marie wouldn't know what she needed. Considering the rags the kids had been wearing when I saw them, I doubted whether they had ever been shopping. Jenny had probably picked up the bare necessities at Goodwill or some thrift shop, and the kids wore the clothing until it fell apart.

It would have been ideal if Linda had been willing to help, but I knew she had no intention of getting involved. Whatever had existed between us was over. As I thought about her, surprisingly I no longer feel hurt or crushed over the breakup. Maybe I was still numb, or maybe I hadn't been as much in love as I had thought.

However, if Linda wouldn't be available, where could I turn? I didn't know any women well enough to feel comfortable asking them to help me shop for Marie. With the bigger issues on my mind, I'd never considered the day-to-day problems of raising kids—particularly a little girl. Obviously I would need assistance and I had no idea where to turn for help.

I took a deep breath and tried to relax, hoping the details would somehow take care of themselves. My big worry now was the court hearing. If I didn't get custody, I wouldn't have to be concerned about shopping.

# CHAPTER ELEVEN

T he original Campbell Courthouse is a massive, hundred-year-old, granite and marble structure surrounded by manicured lawns. I had been in the modern annex behind the courthouse when I visited Mrs. Henderson, but I'd never been inside the main building. It was impressive, with polished marble floors and a wide staircase leading to the second floor where the courtrooms were located.

Children's Court was in a much smaller room than I expected. The front half contained three rows of pew-like benches with enough space for twenty or thirty spectators. A short aisle ended at a gated divider that reminded me of a communion rail. Immediately past the railing were two tables, with three wooden chairs at each. Against the far wall, an American flag and a State flag flanked the raised dais supporting the Judge's bench.

When I arrived Jim Stanley was at one of the tables talking with a short, pudgy man in a business suit.

"Hi, Jon," Jim said, waving me to the front of the room. "This is Frank Johnson, attorney for Child Protective Services."

I wasn't certain I approved of Jim fraternizing with the enemy, but I shook Johnson's hand and smiled a greeting.

When a court stenographer entered from the doorway behind the Judge's bench, Johnson moved to the table on the right of the aisle and Jim directed me to the left. Everyone stood as Judge Monroe swept in wearing a long, black robe, half-glasses perched on the end of her nose. She was a handsome woman with short gray hair and a motherly expression.

After opening a thick file, and reading for a few moments,

she looked up and smiled. "Good Afternoon."

"Good afternoon, Your Honor," we responded in unison.

"For those who have never appeared in my court, I prefer to maintain an informal atmosphere." She peered at us over the half-glasses. "However I remind you this is a court of law and all parties will conduct themselves accordingly."

She leaned over the desk to address the stenographer. "The issue this afternoon is the custody of Marie and William Wilson, children of Jennifer Wilson, deceased. Let the record show Frank Johnson is representing Child Protective Services, and James Stanley is representing the uncle, Jonathon Wilson. All concerned persons are present."

When the stenographer finished typing, Judge Monroe turned to Johnson. "Please proceed with Child Protective Service's argument."

Johnson stood, but remained behind the table. "Thank you, Your Honor. Have you had an opportunity to review the preliminary medical and psychological evaluations on Marie and William?"

"Briefly."

"As indicated in the reports, these children have suffered severe and emotionally disabling trauma. It's our position the children will require a stable environment with extensive follow-up care. As you know, CPS has considerable experience dealing with damaged children. We believe there is no substitute for a two-parent household and the supervision of our agency to provide the proper environment for this type youth.

"Although Mr. Wilson is their uncle, he has not had any recent contact with the children. We could not find evidence he ever made attempts to alleviate the horrible conditions under which Marie and William lived. This apparent lack of concern is a clear indication Mr. Wilson never had an ongoing interest in the children's welfare."

Johnson's allegations stung and I would have stood to refute his charges, but Jim placed a restraining hand on my arm.

"Further, Mr. Wilson is a bachelor with no experience as a care provider," Johnson continued. "We question his qualifications to properly supervise Marie and William. Their removal to Westport, where Mr. Wilson resides, would make it difficult for the children to receive adequate professional care.

"As mentioned in my brief, CPS has located a young couple who have expressed a desire to accept Marie and Billy in foster care."

Judge Monroe held up a hand to interrupt. "Your brief indicated this couple has not yet been approved as foster parents. Is that still correct?"

"That's correct, Your Honor. However our preliminary research suggests Mr. and Mrs. Blackman will be ideal foster parents. At this time, I make a motion that the hearing be continued until CPS has completed their investigation and approved the Blackmans."

"How long do you estimate before the Blackmans are approved?" the Judge asked.

"Not long, Your Honor. A matter of only two, maybe three weeks."

"You've indicated the children are currently in a temporary foster home."

"Yes, Your Honor. Actually, as a temporary measure, Marie and William have been placed in separate homes."

Judge Monroe made a notation in the folder. "I will consider your motion and make a ruling shortly. Do you have anything further to add?"

"We believe it would be in Marie and William's best interests if they remain in foster care under the jurisdiction of Child Protective Services where we can provide qualified foster parents and adequate supervision."

Johnson sat and Judge Monroe turned to us. Her expression remained neutral.

"Mr. Stanley, do you have anything to say in favor of your client's petition for custody?"

"Yes, Your Honor." Jim stood, but also remained behind the

table. "Mr. Wilson has the highest regard for the professionals in Child Protective Services and greatly admires the work they've done with the children of our community. He also has great respect for the foster care program which we consider the best in the state."

"Mr. Stanley," Judge Monroe interrupted, "the court acknowledges Mr. Wilson's admiration for our child welfare system. There's no need to polish the apple. Please state your case without the platitudes."

"Sorry, Your Honor." Jim didn't sound contrite. "I would like to enter copies of Mr. Wilson's last two Income Tax Returns and his most recent bank statement." Jim walked to the bench and handed the papers to Judge Monroe. "I believe these clearly show Mr. Wilson has the financial resources to provide Marie and William with whatever care they may need. He lives approximately twenty miles from Campbell and there is easy access to any services not available in Westport. I'm sure Mrs. Whitlock's report indicated Mr. Wilson owns his home, with separate bedrooms for the children. He lives in a quiet, upper class neighborhood with schools and medical care convenient to his residence."

Judge Monroe nodded.

"Mr. Wilson has not had recent contact with the children through no fault of his own," Jim said. "His sister had not communicated with the family for several years. Although Mr. Wilson repeatedly attempted to contact his sister, he received no response, and consequently lost track of where she and the children lived. His first indication the children were in Campbell was when the police notified him of his sister's death. If Mr. Wilson had not insisted on searching for the children, it's entirely possible they would have starved in that apartment. Had he been aware of the conditions under which Marie and William existed, he would have taken steps to rectify the situation. We believe his desire for custody at this time indicates his deep concern for Marie and William's welfare."

Jim took a sip of water from the glass on the table. "We

maintain his marital status has no bearing. We could cite numerous cases where courts have awarded custody, and even finalized adoptions, to single parent households. There's no evidence such placements have been detrimental to the children involved. If necessary, Mr. Wilson has the financial resources to hire domestic help, and will provide the children with whatever medical or psychological care they require.

"It is our opinion, whenever possible, preference should be given to blood relatives. To the best of our knowledge, Mr. Wilson is Marie and William's only living relative.

"Children who have suffered severe trauma need the stability and love only family can provide. There is no guarantee Mr. and Mrs. Blackman will be approved as foster parents, or that the process will be completed in a reasonable time frame. While waiting for a permanent disposition, CPS has found it necessary to separate Marie and William. More than normal, these children are dependent on each other, and we believe separation is detrimental to their recovery. Therefore we request that you deny Mr. Johnson's motion for continuance and award custody to Mr. Wilson."

Jim sat down and Judge Monroe scanned the tax returns. "Mr. Wilson, I have a few questions for you."

"Yes, Your Honor." I stood.

"You may remain seated. As I said, this is an informal proceeding. First, are these returns representative of your income?"

"Yes, Your Honor. I'm self-employed and the income does vary. However, I have a large, steady client base. With current projects, I should maintain an annual income of approximately sixty thousand dollars."

"What exactly do you do to earn this income?"

"I'm a software designer, developing specialized programs for businesses. With changes in technology there's always a demand for updated software to meet expanding needs. Consequently I not only have income from new accounts, but a steady residual income from my current customers."

"I see you operate your business from home. Will your work interfere with your ability to properly supervise the children? Or putting it another way, will supervising the children interfere with your ability to maintain your income level?"

"I realize I'll have to make adjustments to my schedule in order to accommodate the added responsibilities, but I don't believe the children will interfere to any appreciable degree. Marie and Billy will always be my number one priority."

Judge Monroe wrote something on a notepad. "One last question. Why do you want the responsibility of raising these children? You must realize they'll have special problems and needs that would tax the patience of the most experienced parents."

"Yes, Your Honor." I paused a moment to gather my thoughts. "I've seen the conditions Marie and Billy endured and I'd be living in a dream world if I didn't realize they have unique problems. I honestly don't know how well I'll do as a parent, but I'm prepared to seek any professional assistance and advice required. Marie and Billy are my sister's children and I believe I can give them security and love. They need roots and a link to their heritage only family can provide."

"Thank you, Mr. Wilson." She made a long notation before addressing the entire court, "Gentlemen, does anyone have further comments?"

"No, Your Honor," Jim and Mr. Johnson answered.

"Good. Then I'm going to retire to my chambers and weigh the evidence before rendering a decision. Court will recess for one hour."

Jim turned to me when Judge Monroe left the room. "Well, we've got an hour. Do you want to grab a cup of coffee?"

"Okay with me."

"Frank, would you like to join us?" Jim asked the CPS attorney.

"No thanks," Johnson said. "I've got to catch up on paperwork. I'll see you in an hour."

In the small café across from the courthouse, we each

ordered coffee and a Danish.

"Well, what do you think?" I asked.

"Your guess is as good as mine," Jim answered. "In jury trials you can read clues from the jurors—how they look at the defendant or other body language. But with a judge you just never know. In the end it comes down to a choice between family or the system. I got the impression Judge Monroe wasn't happy with Marie and Billy being placed in separate temporary care, but I don't have any idea how she feels about kids in the system. We'll have to wait for her decision."

"Just for the sake of argument, if she rules against us, what are my options?"

"I don't know. I told you up front I'm not familiar with custody law. Most likely it would depend upon the basis for the ruling. If she decides on a continuance, we'd have another shot then. I'm sure there's an appeal process, but I'd have to look into it. Let's not worry about that right now."

"What is this continuance Johnson requested?"

"Basically it means Judge Monroe wouldn't make a decision today. If she grants Johnson's motion, everything will stay as it is now, with the kids under CPS's wing until foster parents are found, or the Blackman's are approved. Then we'd be back in court and CPS would have a much stronger argument."

"That doesn't sound like something we want to happen. The kids would be in limbo for weeks."

"That's right."

"Well, do you think she'll grant the continuance?"

"All we can do is hope she doesn't, although a continuance would be better than a ruling against you." Jim glanced at his watch. "We'll know in a few more minutes."

We returned to the courtroom fifteen minutes early and Johnson came in five minutes later. We all sat in silence until the stenographer entered, followed immediately by Judge Monroe.

She sat behind the bench, scanning her notes, drawing out the dramatic tension.

"Gentlemen, I realize this is not a landmark case, but I would like to present a brief explanation of my decision." She slipped off her half-glasses and stared intently across the bench.

"The problem of abused, neglected, and abandoned children has grown more severe during the last several years. Or perhaps we've just become more aware of an existing condition. Unfortunately, the State has been forced to assume many of the duties traditionally belonging to parents. The orphanages of the last century have given way to organizations such as Child Protective Services and the foster care system. Our State has an excellent program for dealing with children such as Marie and William, and our foster parents are second to none. Many foster parents come to love their foster children as if they were their own. CPS provides an essential service when family cannot, or will not, do the job society demands. Statistics suggest the majority of children placed in foster care mature to become useful and productive citizens.

"Those same statistics indicate a percentage of children raised by their biological parents become delinquents and social outcasts.

"I believe these statistics mean there is no guarantee children raised by their natural families will fare substantially better than youngsters placed in foster care. However, whenever possible, I believe children have the best chance for success with family, and it's generally desirable for siblings to provide physical and emotional support to each other.

"Therefore I am going to deny Mr. Johnson's motion for continuance and award temporary custody of Marie and William to Mr. Wilson—with these stipulations. First, this custody proceeding will remain open and subject to review in ninety days. At that time a decision will be made regarding permanent placement. During the period of temporary custody, Mr. Wilson will be required to provide Marie and William whatever medical and psychological care Child Protective Services recommends. If these medical expenses become a financial burden, Mr. Wilson may apply for Aid to Families with Dependent Children. Finally, Mr. Wilson will make monthly reports regarding the children's progress and will agree to periodic inspections by an authorized representative from Child Protective Services or this Court.

"Are there any questions about, or objections to, this decision?"

No one spoke.

"Good. Court adjourned."

Jim turned to me and held out his hand. "I don't know whether to offer congratulations or condolences."

I shook his hand. "I don't know which I need. If I heard the Judge correctly, I'll only have custody for three months and then we have to go through this again."

"That's it in a nutshell."

"So in effect, custody is still up in the air. It seems to me Child Protective Services came out ahead on the deal."

"Not really. Monroe could have granted the continuance and left things as they are. The ninety days will give CPS time to approve the Backmans, but you'll have Marie and Billy with you rather than in separate foster homes. With the kids in your physical custody you'll have a decided advantage as long as Marie and Billy make measurable progress. I'd say today is a small victory for the good guys."

"Okay, I'll take what I can get. When will I be able to pick up the kids?"

Jim turned to Mr. Johnson, who was putting papers in his briefcase. "Frank, when can we claim the children?"

"Give me an hour to get it set up and they'll be waiting at the CPS office."

I didn't know how to feel—whether to shout with joy or break down and cry. In an hour I would be taking on the responsibility of a son and daughter and my life would never be the same. Now that custody was suddenly a reality, I felt as if an immense burden had been placed on my shoulders. I could only pray the burden wouldn't be more than I could handle.

# CHAPTER TWELVE

W hile waiting for Marie and Billy, I went across the street for another cup of coffee in the little café. There weren't any other customers, so I was able to sit in a booth and stare out the window at the traffic moving past the courthouse.

I wished there was something to occupy my mind other than the demons of doubt that began to raise their ugly heads. Would I be a good parent? Was three months long enough to establish a relationship? Maybe temporary custody was to my advantage. If I absolutely couldn't make it as a parent, the ninety days would allow me a graceful exit. But I had no intention of giving in to negative thinking. I had to believe the three months would prove to everyone, including myself, that I was capable of providing a good home for Jenny's children.

The café's strong brew was beginning to make me jittery, so I decided to try walking off my nervous energy. I strolled as far as Campbell's main street and back again, twice. It didn't help. Time was dragging and the hands on my watch seemed to be standing still.

After forty minutes I couldn't wait any longer, so I wended my way through the maze of corridors to the CPS offices, hoping Marie and Billy would be available early. Then I cooled my heels in the waiting area for another half hour before being ushered into Mrs. Henderson's small office.

"Well, Mr. Wilson, you're going to get your opportunity to have a family." She didn't appear happy to see me. "I disagree with Judge Monroe's decision, but for the next three months we'll have to work together for the children's benefit."

"You'll see that Judge Monroe was right," I said, determined not to let her irritate me.

She looked at me with the disdain a professional might have for an amateur. "Well, you have three months to prove your point. Before we can release Marie and William you'll need to complete some paperwork." She handed me a clipboard. "Please fill in the top form where I've made x's. The bottom one is a release. Read it carefully before signing. You'll be agreeing to accept responsibility for the children and promising to follow the Court's guidelines."

I completed the top sheet, supplying my personal information: name, address, and phone number. After scanning the release form, I scrawled my signature at the bottom and filled in the date. I don't know whether I felt relieved or trapped. For better or worse, I was now Marie and Billy's guardian for at least ninety days.

"I've put together a file to provide basic information." Mrs. Henderson handed me a manila envelope. "There are copies of the children's birth certificates, all the medical and psychological examinations completed to date, and a list of pediatricians and child psychologists we recommend. Of course you're free to choose your own professionals, but these people are highly qualified and you'd be wise to select from the list. Do you have any questions?"

"Judge Monroe ordered monthly reports and periodic inspections," I said. "Do we set up a schedule today?"

"There are standard report forms and a schedule of filing dates in the envelope. Need I remind you the reports must be submitted on a timely basis or it will be grounds for revoking custody?"

She wasn't making it easy for me to control my temper. "The reports will be on time," I snapped. "What about the inspections?"

"Our policy is to conduct unannounced inspections of our foster parents. It's important to observe conditions as they exist on a daily basis, not during a staged visit."

"Suits me," I acknowledged. "I'm sure I can phone if there are any other questions."

"Certainly. The packet contains a list of phone numbers and emergency contacts." Mrs. Henderson stood. "Now I'll take you to the children."

She led me along the sterile corridor, unlocked a door to a room obviously intended for children, with books and toys on child-sized tables and chairs. For a moment I didn't see the kids on the far side of the room huddled behind a table. Billy was clinging to Marie, her arms wrapped protectively around her brother. I had a momentary flashback to the kids hiding under the sink in that horrible apartment. Marie's eyes had the same trapped look of a wild animal. It made me wonder if either child had made any progress during the time with Child Protective Services, or whether the week's forced separation had aggravated the situation.

"Children, this is your Uncle Jon," Mrs. Henderson said in a soothing voice. "He'll be taking you to your new home where you'll be living with him."

"You're really going to like our house," I said, trying to put a tone of excitement in my voice, even though I felt just as awkward as the last time I'd seen them. "It has a big yard to play in, and you'll each have a bedroom of your own."

I hadn't expected the kids to be bubbling over with enthusiasm, but I had hoped for some sort of positive reaction. There was nothing.

With Mrs. Henderson hovering over us, I felt I had to take the initiative, so I reached for Marie's arm to help her up. She jerked away, but did untangle herself from Billy, looking defiant as she helped her brother to his feet. Billy was obviously frightened, but Marie seemed resigned to whatever fate awaited her. Although she didn't resist when I took her hand, it felt limp and cold. My custody wasn't starting out as a very warm, fuzzy relationship.

"Okay, kids, let's go shopping," I said, trying to sound upbeat. As I led them from the room, I turned to Mrs. Henderson.

"Thanks for your help."

"The children have already had lunch," she said. "Don't let them overeat or have a lot of rich food. They still aren't adjusted to regular meals, and they'd probably get sick." As we walked down the hallway she called after us. "Good luck."

My Buick had front bucket seats, and since the kids obviously didn't want to be separated, I buckled them both in back. I made an effort at conversation as we drove to the Wal-Mart located off Highway 37, but could have been alone in the car for all the reaction I got. I didn't know whether they were shy or frightened or just didn't understand what was happening.

Although I maintained a firm grip on Marie's hand and Billy was clinging to his sister, I felt a moment of panic when we entered the store. This Super Wal-Mart was always crowded and I was afraid we might get separated. Wouldn't it be the perfect beginning if I had to explain to a cop that I'd lost my kids during the first hour of custody? I considered stopping at the pet department for a couple of collars and leashes, but decided that would probably get me arrested for child abuse. My best bet was to keep a tight grip on Marie because I was pretty certain Billy wouldn't voluntarily let go of his sister.

My second panic attack came as we approached the girl's department. It was a huge area, with a jungle of racks and shelves. Where should I begin? How would I figure out the correct sizes? Obviously I couldn't go into the fitting room with Marie. A middle-aged Wal-Mart employee was stocking racks, and I considered asking for help, but there was no simple way to explain why a nine-year-old girl needed assistance in the fitting room.

I saw racks of what appeared to be girl's underwear and stockings, so I pulled the kids in that direction. Fortunately the underwear had age ranges on the packages and I figured I'd take the manufacturers word for the sizes being correct.

"How about these?" I asked, showing Marie a nine pack of print briefs. "Aren't they pretty?"

Marie shrugged, like she didn't care what I chose.

"Okay," I said, trying to sound enthusiastic. "Looks like you're going to let me pick for you today. But I'll bet it won't be long before you have definite opinions on what you want."

I tossed the underwear pack and two six packs of white crew socks into the shopping cart. Since sleepwear was right next to the underwear section, I selected a nightgown by holding it up to Marie, checking size and color.

"How do you like this?" I asked.

Marie shrugged, still without expression.

"Look, you're going to have to help me. I don't know what you like."

"I hate it," Marie snapped.

It wasn't the reaction I wanted, but it was better than nothing. "Okay, you pick one." Obviously a man had no business choosing clothing for a young girl.

She pointed to a blue, flowered gown. It looked close enough to the right size, so I added it to the cart.

I was beginning to wonder if I had the patience to be a parent. We were only a few minutes into the shopping trip and I already had an urge to simply grab clothing from the racks and run to the checkouts.

"I think jeans and T-shirts will do for today," I said, selecting a pair of jeans and holding them in front of Marie. "These look pretty good."

Again Marie had no response. I put two pairs of jeans in the cart, figuring we could buy a more varied selection when I turned this chore over to a qualified shopper. Then I added several T-shirts to the growing pile.

"I think you should have something a little nicer for special occasions or when we go to church," I suggested. "Would you like to help me pick out a nice dress?"

I led Marie to a rack of dresses, and after looking at several, selected a blue plaid, pleated skirt and long sleeve white blouse. "Don't you think this would be a great outfit?"

This time Marie nodded, which I considered a major improvement in our relationship.

With enough clothing to get Marie through the next several days, we went to the boy's department and selected jeans and T-shirts for Billy. I could have accompanied him in the fitting room, but that would have left Marie unattended, which I didn't think was such a great idea. Since I couldn't chain her to a post, I figured it would be best to keep her in sight. Consequently I chose Billy's sizes the same way I'd picked for Marie—by holding up clothing and guessing.

We added underwear, socks, and a blue plaid dress shirt with button down collar. By the time we got to the pajamas, Billy realized he had a choice in the process. He looked at every pair of pajamas on the rack and chose the gaudiest ones—red bottoms with a blue Superman top. I hoped the colors weren't so loud they would keep him awake.

After selecting dress and casual shoes for both kids, we headed over to the personal hygiene area where I grabbed combs, hairbrushes, toothbrushes, toothpaste and children's vitamins. We were passing the accessories counter when it occurred to me Marie needed something to control her long hair. I selected a couple of barrettes and a pretty band for holding a ponytail in place.

I figured our final stop had to be the toy department. When I suggested that Marie could have her choice, she didn't respond. Considering that there had been no toys in Jenny's apartment, I wondered if Marie had ever been allowed to select a toy, or whether she had ever owned any playthings. Remembering how much Jenny had loved her white Teddy, I selected a big, stuffed Teddy Bear for Marie. When I handed it to her she hugged it and buried her face in the soft fur.

"Is this really mine?' she asked, like she didn't believe. "Can I keep it?"

"Absolutely. It's yours forever."

Billy was getting into the swing of shopping. "Can I have anything I want?" he asked.

"You sure can," I agreed, pleased that at least one of the kids was cooperating.

The choices overwhelmed Billy. He wanted everything that grabbed his attention, and would have easily filled several shopping carts with his selections. When I limited him to one choice, he finally decided on a set of die-cast cars.

We went through the checkout and I paid for everything with my credit card. When I took the Teddy from Marie so it could be scanned, she looked at me with an expression that said, 'I knew you weren't going to let me keep it'. She was surprised when the clerk returned the stuffed animal, and hugged it so tightly I don't believe I could have gotten it away from her again.

This brief shopping trip had convinced me there was a long, hard adjustment ahead, and I wasn't going to be able to handle it alone. One of my first priorities had to be finding someone to help with the kids. If there wasn't a woman available who knew what children needed or wanted, I was going to be in desperate trouble.

# CHAPTER THIRTEEN

It was past my normal suppertime when we left Wal-Mart. I didn't have the energy or desire to cook a meal, but testing Marie and Billy's social skills in a public restaurant wasn't an option I wanted to exercise. That left a choice between take-out or frozen dinners. I assumed Mrs. Henderson's warning against rich food, meant cake or ice cream and didn't include pizza. I called over my shoulder. "Are you guys hungry? Would you like a pizza?"

"I'm hungry," Billy said in a soft voice. Marie didn't respond. In the rear view mirror I could see her staring vacantly out the window.

My heart went out to her. What was it that had wounded her the most? Was it that the basics—food, clothing, shelter—had been so hard to come by? Was it her mother's addictions and lack of motherly love? Or was it that her dreams had failed her? I didn't know the answers and probably never would.

I used my cell phone to order a large pizza from Kendall's Pizzeria, so it would be ready when we reached Westport.

Since all attempts at conversation were met with silence, I gave up the effort. When Jenny and I had been kids we never could have ridden so passively. At the very least we would have been horsing around or arguing. Maybe Marie and Billy had never really been children. When other youngsters were swapping baseball cards or giggling over a valentine, these kids had been scrounging for food or dealing with a drugged out mother.

We picked up the pizza at Kendall's drive-up window and the aroma of spices and melted cheese quickly filled the car.

"Well, here we are," I said, pulling into my driveway. "This is your new home."

I hadn't expected the kids to jump up and down with excitement, but something more than complete silence would have been appreciated. It just wasn't natural for children to completely suppress their emotions.

While helping Marie and Billy with their seat belts I could hear Shadow's nails clicking on the floor as he ran back and forth from the front door to the front window. I hadn't thought to put him in the back yard before leaving for Campbell, and now I was afraid his enthusiasm would overwhelm the kids. Marie and Billy may never have been exposed to a big dog's frantic greeting. Ninety pounds of canine energy could be scary.

"I forgot to tell you I have a dog," I explained. "He's very friendly and loves children, but he gets excited when he meets new people. Don't be afraid. He doesn't bite and he won't hurt you."

Carrying the pizza in one hand, I led the kids onto the front porch and opened the door. Shadow burst out, prancing up and down, happy to see me and overjoyed at meeting new friends. Billy gave a brief shriek and hid behind Marie. She stood defiantly, one hand clutching her Teddy Bear, the other balled in a fist ready to defend herself and her brother. I grabbed Shadow's collar and nearly dropped the pizza.

"Don't be afraid, he won't hurt you," I repeated, trying to calm the dog and simultaneously nudge Marie through the doorway. "Go ahead into the house. I've got a good hold on Shadow. He'll calm down in a minute."

Marie edged into the house, keeping herself between Shadow and Billy. Although she was obviously frightened, she apparently had every intention of protecting her brother. If this huge black animal was going to attack, he would have to get past her before he could hurt Billy.

I kept a firm grip on Shadow's collar as we all went into the kitchen. "I'll feed the dog first, and then we can have our pizza."

"Does he eat people?" Billy asked, peeking from behind his

sister.

"No way. He only eats dog food." I filled Shadow's dish and set the bowl in the usual place beside the refrigerator, but he was too excited to eat, so I put him into the back yard. Shadow would love having two new friends. I just hoped the kids would adjust to the dog.

I put some paper towels on the table as plates, and opened the pizza box. "Okay, kids, let's eat. But be careful, it's probably hot."

Billy grabbed a piece and tried to stuff it all into his mouth.

"Take you time," I said. "There's plenty for all of us. If we run out, we'll just get another one."

I left the kids to help themselves while I carried in our bundles of purchases. It required a couple of trips to haul everything from the car to the upstairs bedrooms, but I was only out of the kitchen for about ten minutes.

When I rejoined the kids, the pizza had disappeared except for a single square in the middle of the carton. Both kids had tomato sauce smeared around their mouths and Billy had several spots on his T-shirt. They must have swallowed the pieces whole in order to have demolished a large pizza so quickly.

"It's been a long day, kids," I said, wiping their hands and faces with paper towels. "Why don't we put away your new clothes, take a warm bath, and get ready for bed?"

I led them upstairs and showed them their rooms and the bathroom. Marie and Billy stood silently as I sorted the clothing, cut off tags, and put everything away in the dressers and closets. After gathering the empty bags and other trash, I ran warm water into the tub until it was about half full. I was pretty certain they hadn't bathed on a regular basis and wondered if they even understood the fundamentals of washing. Hopefully they had learned something while they were with Child Protective Services. At that moment I would have given my left arm for an experienced woman to supervise their baths.

"I'll help Billy with his bath, and then you can take one by yourself," I suggested.

"I can take care of Billy," Marie snapped, a spark of defiance in her eyes. "We don't need your goddamned help."

As exhausted at I felt, I was tempted to let her take care of the baths, but realized if this custody period was going to work, the kids had to understand who was in charge. If I let Marie boss me around, I would never be able to exercise control.

"I know you've been taking care of Billy, and you've done a great job," I said, as patiently as possible. "But now it's my responsibility to take care of you both, so we'll do things my way."

For a moment I thought she might argue, but she simply glared at me.

Normally I would have told Marie to wait in her room while Billy was washing, but since she had probably assumed most of a mother's responsibilities, I decided it wouldn't hurt for her to remain in the bathroom.

"You can watch to make sure I do a good job," I said.
I helped Billy undress, and happily didn't see any sign of the rash mentioned in the medical report. There hadn't been any medication in the packet Mrs. Henderson had given me, so I assumed the rash had been treated and cured while the kids were in the hospital.

I lifted Billy into the tub, soaped up a washcloth, and scrubbed him all over. I had expected a five-year-old to struggle, at least when his face was washed, but he remained completely passive. The idea of an unresponsive little boy in a bathtub was alien. When I'd been Billy's age I'd spent hours splashing and playing with toy boats.

Satisfied Billy was clean, I pulled the plug, lifted him onto the bath mat, and wrapped him in a big towel. While the tub was filling with clean water, I got fresh underwear and the nightgown for Marie.

"I'll get Billy ready for bed while you're bathing. Just give a holler when you're finished. You can dry off with this towel," I said, indicating a large, red towel sitting on the vanity.

With no indication of female modesty, Marie began to strip off her clothes. Although I felt like a voyeur, I needed to examine her rash, so I remained in the room until she was naked except for panties. Although there was a small area of redness on the inside of her thighs, it appeared her rash had healed. That was one less thing for me to worry about.

Marie was slipping off her underwear when I closed the bathroom door and took Billy into his room. I finished toweling him off, combed his hair, and dressed him in his Superman pajamas. He preened in front of the mirror, fascinated by his image in the gaudy outfit.

I didn't think Marie had been in the tub long enough to clean herself, when she appeared in the doorway wearing her nightgown. Her hair was still dripping, so I picked up her towel, wiped away a spot of tomato sauce from her cheek, and vigorously rubbed her dry. Then I used one of the new brushes to straighten her hair. It wasn't a very professional job, but at least I managed to untangle most of the snarls.

"How about if we all say our prayers together?" I suggested.

"I won't say any fuckin' prayers," Marie said, her fists balled at her sides, obviously prepared to defy me. "Prayers are stupid."

"Prayers aren't stupid," I insisted. "It's important to thank God for all He's done for us, and to ask Him to bless our loved ones."

"God never did anything for us," she hissed. "He never listens to our prayers."

Her outburst shook me. I suppose I'd taken it for granted that all kids believed God loved them and listened to their prayers. Had Marie's life been so terrible she had given up on God? Somewhere along the line her helplessness in the face of abuse must have destroyed her faith in everything—in herself, her mom, and God.

It would only make matters worse if I insisted, even though I made a mental note that one of my responsibilities would be teaching her to trust God again. "Okay, Marie, if you don't want to pray, you don't have to. Billy and I are going to say our prayers and you can listen."

"Billy's just a baby and doesn't know any better." Marie

sounded too cynical for a child.

I knelt beside his bed and motioned for Billy to join me. He had no idea what was expected of him, but cooperated when I showed him how to make the sign of the cross and hold his hands in prayer. Then I helped him repeat the Lord's Prayer, and we finished with a string of God blesses, "God Bless Mommy and Marie and Uncle Jon."

I gave Billy a hug, helped him into bed, pulled the sheet and blanket up to his chin, and kissed him on the forehead. He looked tiny and frightened. "Sleep well. If you need anything, just call and I'll be here for you."

When Marie and I left the room I switched off the light, but left the door ajar so the room wouldn't be totally dark.

"The same goes for you," I told Marie. "If you need anything, just call and I'll be here for you."

I attempted to hug her and she went stiff and tense. "Marie, what's wrong?" I asked.

"Are you going to fuck me now?" she asked, her voice pathetically passive.

For an instant the words didn't register. Then it was like someone had punched me in the gut. No one had ever shocked me so deeply. I couldn't understand a world where an innocent child was resigned to being molested. My first impulse was to gather her in my arms and reassure her that she was safe and never had to be afraid again. Then I realized touching her would be a mistake. In her world all men must have been potential abusers.

"I won't ever hurt you," I stammered. "Why would you even think something like that?"

"My other uncles fucked me." Marie hugged her Teddy Bear, looking frightened and defenseless.

I was so repulsed that for a moment I thought I'd be sick. No wonder Marie had been so withdrawn all afternoon. She must have been dreading bedtime. I should have realized Jenny had probably introduced her temporary boyfriends as Uncle Bill or Uncle Bob or Uncle Something. It was a helpless sensation, knowing there was no way to convince Marie I wasn't that kind of uncle. How could any words reassure a little girl who'd been repeatedly abused by her mother's drug partners?

"That's never going to happen again," I promised, tears beginning to fill my eyes. "No one is ever going to hurt you as long as you live here."

Marie looked dubious as she crawled into bed and pulled the covers tightly to her chin. She had no way of knowing I could be trusted, that her new life was going to be different from everything else she'd experienced. When I leaned over to kiss her forehead, she cringed back against the pillow. Would she ever be able to gamble on reaching out to anyone?

"Good night," I said, feeling inadequate. "I'll be here if you need me. I promise you no one will ever hurt you again."

I switched off the light, left her door ajar, and went downstairs. For a long time I sat in my darkened study trying to understand how Jenny could have allowed her children to suffer such profound hurts.

I had completely forgotten Shadow in the backyard until I heard him whining at the door. When I let him in, he made a quick tour of the kitchen, and began sniffing and scratching at the cabinet doors under the sink.

"What's wrong, boy?" I asked. "Do you hear a mouse?" I opened the door a crack and cautiously peeked in. Marie and Billy hadn't eaten the entire pizza after all. They'd hidden several pieces in the far corner of the cabinet. It was heartbreaking to realize they felt the need to prepare a cache against the day there wouldn't be anything to eat.

The pizza hoard was too much for me and I let the tears roll down my cheeks. In an abstract way, I had known the kids had suffered terribly, but nothing had prepared me for Marie's question or their need to hide food. I prayed I would have the strength and wisdom to help them forget the past and move forward. Maybe I couldn't do it alone, but I vowed to do everything in my power to make both kids feel safe and loved.

When I went upstairs at eleven, I looked into Billy's room and experienced a moment of panic. His covers had been tossed aside and his bed was empty. Had the kids somehow managed to sneak out of the house and run away? I quickly stepped across the hall to check Marie's room and breathed a sigh of relief. Both kids were snuggled together, sound asleep.

Shadow looked up from his guard post beside Marie's bed. His tail thumped on the carpet and he grinned at me like he was saying, "You aren't alone in protecting these kids. I'll make sure they're always safe."

As I went to my own room, I realized my reservoir of tears wasn't empty.

# CHAPTER FOURTEEN

If I'd believed having the kids with me would allow a good night's sleep, I was sadly mistaken. My jumbled thoughts refused to settle as I tossed and turned for hours. I had thought the medical and psychological reports gave me an understanding of what Marie and Billy had suffered, but I was wrong. The cold, clinical descriptions of their physical and mental scars had only given a brief glimpse of the pain and fear they lived with. Did I have the mental toughness to handle further revelations?

When sleep finally came, I was tormented by the nightmare of the kids being tortured in the dark dungeon, and woke in a cold sweat. At least Linda, and all the others who had warned against custody, hadn't appeared in the dream saying, 'I told you so'.

Shadow's cold nose jolted me awake at quarter past six and I rolled out of bed feeling exhausted. On the way downstairs I peeked into Marie's bedroom where the kids were still huddled together, sleeping peacefully. Marie looked like an angel hugging her Teddy Bear and Billy was a cherub snuggled against her. Were they tormented by nightmares of their own? God, how I wished it was possible to erase their past and allow them to move forward with a clean slate.

I let Shadow out, cleaned up the mess from last night's pizza, and checked to see if there was anything to prepare for breakfast. I hadn't thought far enough ahead to go grocery shopping and my pantry was nearly bare. A half loaf of bread and one egg remaining in the carton wouldn't go very far, but there was a nearly full box of raisin bran and almost a gallon of milk. Marie and Billy would have to do with cold cereal until we got to the store.

When Shadow returned from his morning duties, I kept him downstairs so he wouldn't wake the kids. I had a good start on a grocery list when the youngsters began stirring and Shadow bounded off to greet his new friends. I followed him up the stairs and found Billy and Marie sitting in the center of the bed cringing away from Shadow's advances. Knowing he wasn't allowed on the furniture, Shadow could only stretch his nose across the bed in an effort to reach the children. As I watched, Billy timidly reached out and patted Shadow's head.

"I'll bet you're hungry," I said, calling Shadow away from the bed. "You get dressed and we'll have breakfast."

I laid out a pair of jeans, a T-shirt, socks and the new athletic shoes for Marie. Then I took Billy into his room and helped him dress.

Surprisingly both kid's new clothing fit decently—not perfect, but acceptable. Billy's jeans were half a size too large, but I figured if they didn't shrink in the wash, the boy would grow into them soon enough.

"You look great," I said. They were both so visibly pleased with their outfits I suspected they might never have owned new clothing before. Or maybe just having clothing that wasn't old and torn was a special treat. "You guys wash, comb your hair, and I'll meet you downstairs when I'm done here."

Marie and Billy weren't in the bathroom long enough to have cleaned properly before I heard them clomping down the stairs. After straightening the beds I checked the bathroom, finding the toilet waster bright yellow. They must have been afraid to flush in case the bowl would overflow like it had done in Jenny's apartment. Their toothbrushes hadn't been used and there was no evidence they had touched the soap. I considered calling them upstairs to discuss morning hygiene and flushing toilets, but changed my mind. If I scolded them every time they failed to meet my expectations, I'd constantly be nagging. The last thing they needed was criticism.

I grabbed toothbrushes, a hairbrush, and comb and headed for the downstairs bathroom. After supervising their tooth brushing, I combed Billy's hair and brushed out Marie's snarls. I considered arranging Marie's long hair in a ponytail, but wasn't sure how to do it. Just another thing someone would have to teach me.

In the kitchen I filled three bowls with cereal. Before I could add milk and sugar, both kids were using their hands to stuff raisin bran into their mouths.

"Wait a minute," I said, laughing to show I wasn't angry. "That isn't the way we eat cereal. It tastes better with milk and sugar. Then we use spoons—not our fingers."

They looked at me like I was speaking a foreign language. "You have used spoons before, haven't you?" I asked.

"Of course," Marie said, sounding angry. "We're not goddamned babies, you know."

"We're not goddamned babies," Billy repeated.

"I never thought you were, but we have different rules here than you're used to. From now on, you'll eat with forks or spoons."

"We didn't use a spoon last night," Billy protested.

"You're right," I agreed, wondering if children always took everything so literally. "It's okay to eat some foods, like pizza, with your fingers. Which reminds me, I found the pizza you guys hid under the sink. As long as you live here, you never have to hide food. If there are leftovers we put them in the refrigerator so they won't spoil. We'll always have enough to eat."

Marie didn't say anything, but I could tell she was skeptical.

After I added milk and sugar to their bowls, they reluctantly picked up their spoons. Neither one did very well with the utensils. After a few tries they had milk running down their chins and cereal spilled on the table. However they dug in with an appetite and soon asked for refills.

They finished every crumb of the raisin bran and probably would have eaten more. I suppose if I'd spent most of my life hungry I'd also have stuffed myself whenever food was available.

I wiped the milk off Billy's chin with a damp washcloth, and handed it to Marie so she could clean herself.

I didn't know if it was safe to let the kids fend for themselves, but realized I couldn't hover over them forever. I might as well start right away giving them a little slack.

"While I make a shopping list you kids can explore the house, or play in the back yard."

Shadow tagged along as they went outside, the screen door slamming behind them. Unless they climbed the fence they couldn't go anywhere and maybe they would begin to play with Shadow. Bonding with a pet would be good for them and I didn't think Shadow would let them get into trouble.

After finishing the grocery list, I stood at the kitchen door watching them play. Billy had apparently discovered if he threw a stick, the dog would chase and retrieve it. This time when Shadow returned the stick, Marie reached out and slapped him.

"Don't hit the dog," I yelled, stepping onto the back porch. "That's no way to treat a pet."

"He's a stupid fuckin' dog," Marie explained. "I told him to give me the stick and he gave it to Billy."

"You have to remember dogs aren't as smart as people." I attempted to sound calm and reasonable. Maybe all of Marie's lessons had been enforced with some form of physical punishment. "He doesn't understand what you want, and won't learn anything if you hit him." Marie looked skeptical. "Shadow is your friend. Did you know he slept next to your bed last night to protect you? It's okay to scold, but don't ever hit him again. Do you understand?"

Marie nodded, but obviously thought I was crazy. In her world, hitting and being hit was the way of life.

"Anyway, it's time to come in. We're going to the grocery store to see if we can find some good stuff to eat."

When we got to the supermarket, I let Marie push the shopping cart, and with Billy never more than a step or two from his sister, I didn't have to worry about them wandering off and getting into something they shouldn't. Although I had an extensive list, as we walked the aisles I kept adding items I hadn't thought of. Maybe men lacked the necessary shopping gene, because I'd never been able to master the skill. Mom had always been able to buy a week's worth of groceries in one trip, but I had to run to the store at least every other day.

We were rounding the potato chip aisle when I nearly collided with Linda. Her lipstick and hairdo were perfect and she looked as beautiful as I ever remembered.

"Hi, Linda," I said, my heart doing a little flip. I hadn't seen her since the funeral. "What a pleasant surprise. How are you?"

"I'm fine," she said, obviously not pleased with meeting us. "I see you have Jenny's brats with you."

My temper flared. "They aren't brats," I snapped. "They're my children and they're good kids."

I must have stunned her with my angry reply because her cheeks colored. "Whatever," she said in an icy tone. "I don't have time for chitchat. I have to get back to work." She turned abruptly and walked away.

"She's a bitch," Marie said.

"A bitch," Billy echoed.

I started to say something about their language, but couldn't fault their assessment. She had acted like a first-class bitch. "You may be right," I agreed, finally realizing my relationship with Linda was over. I didn't feel nearly as heartbroken as I had expected. "Come on, kids. Let's finish our shopping."

By the time we'd walked the last aisle the cart was nearly overflowing. Since it was still early in the day we only had to wait behind one elderly lady at the checkout. A young girl, already bored with her duties, ran the groceries past the scanner, and generally ignored my attempts at conversation. I paid with my debit card and blinked at the total. Feeding kids was going to be more expensive than I'd anticipated.

We loaded the groceries in the trunk, and when the kids were crawling into the backseat I noticed something sticking out of Marie's jean pocket. "What's this?" I demanded, pulling out a candy bar. "We didn't pay for the candy, did we?  Do you have anything else?"

"No," Marie said, sounding angry or defiant, but definitely not contrite.

"We'll see about that."  Maybe I should have accepted her word as a sign of confidence, but it was time she learned trust must be earned.  I patted her down, and found two packs of chewing gum and a roll of lifesavers in her pockets.  "Stealing is bad enough, but lying is even worse.  I won't be able to trust you if you aren't honest."

"It's only some fuckin' candy," Marie pouted.

There was so much to teach the kids and I didn't have a clue where to begin.  At some point I'd have to address the street language, but right then, my concern was with shoplifting.

"Do you have anything?" I asked Billy.  If he'd seen his sister take candy, most likely he'd have followed her example.

Billy contritely handed over two candy bars he'd hidden under his T-shirt.  "Is that all?"  He nodded, but I checked his pockets without finding any other loot.

"Taking candy without paying for it is theft, and stealing is a crime," I said.  It was hard to scold them, knowing how they had been raised. Maybe the only way they'd survived was by stealing something to eat.  I'd read somewhere about tough love, and knew this was where I had to apply it.  It would definitely be a poor beginning if I let them get away with swiping anything.  "Maybe you had to steal before you came to my house, but now we have enough money to buy whatever we need."

"It's okay to take candy from a store," Marie protested.  "People who have stores must be rich.  They won't miss a few pieces of fuckin' candy."

"Whether they're rich or not doesn't make any difference.  Stealing is never okay and I won't allow you to take merchandise without paying."

"No one saw us," Billy said timidly.

"That doesn't make it right," I scolded.  "We're going back into the store to pay for this."

"They'll put us in jail," Billy wailed, beginning to cry.

"I won't let anyone put you in jail, but you have to learn not to take things that don't belong to you."

"I'm not going back in that fuckin' store," Marie said.

"Watch your language, young lady. You are going back, even if I have to carry you."

Defiance flashed in Marie's eyes, but was gone immediately. "I hate you," she hissed.

As I hauled them back into the supermarket, a vision of my first monthly report to Child Protective Services flashed through my mind. Everything is going fine, except the kids were busted for shoplifting on the first day.

One of the checkout lanes was empty so I approached the cashier from the wrong end. "I just checked out a moment ago and didn't realize I'd forgotten to pay for this candy. Would you please ring it up for me?"

I paid cash and gave the candy back to the kids. No one talked as we returned to the car and I helped them buckle in. We were pulling out of the parking lot when Marie spoke.

"Are you going to send us away now?"

"No, of course not." Was that the way it had always been with them? They did something an adult didn't like and they were either beaten or pushed out onto the streets. "I know things are different living with me, and we all have a lot to learn, but you're my kids now and we'll work things out. You never have to worry about being sent away just because you make a mistake or did something I think is wrong."

In the rearview mirror I could see Marie had the emotionless expression that told me she had tuned out. How long would it take before that look went away forever? Would she ever feel safe and secure?

My attempts at fatherhood were going to be an uphill struggle. It was still early on our first full day and I had the problem of morning hygiene, eating with utensils, hitting Shadow, unacceptable language, and stealing. Obviously I required help with Marie and Billy, and I needed it as soon as possible.

# CHAPTER FIFTEEN

Twenty-four hours with Marie and Billy had convinced me there would be dozens of problems beyond my ability to handle. Maybe if I'd begun this parenthood thing with infants, I wouldn't have felt so inadequate. Starting with damaged kids, who had experienced a life beyond my comprehension, was obviously going to be a real challenge. However, I had no intention of allowing Child Protective Services to win. If I didn't have the necessary experience or skills, I would take advantage of people who did.

When we finished putting away the groceries, I sent the kids into the backyard to play with Shadow and began making phone calls.

All the medical doctors on Mrs. Henderson's list were located in Campbell, which was too far to take the kids in an emergency. The Westport clinic was about a mile from the house, and since they had a pediatrician on staff, I arranged an appointment with Dr. Ruth Greco. There was a three-week waiting period for new patients, so I grabbed the first available opening and asked to be called if there were any cancellations.

The Westport clinic also had a psychologist on staff, but I figured it would make more sense to continue with a doctor who was already familiar with Marie and Billy. When I phoned Dr. Deana Scott, the child psychologist who had done the children's initial examination, the receptionist recognized their names and scheduled an appointment for Wednesday.

I don't consider myself a very religious person, but I did realize we all needed to believe in something bigger than ourselves. While the kids were learning to trust me, establishing faith in God would help us all. My final call was to the number Father Rose had given me for Sister Joan. She must have been anticipating my call because she agreed to meet us in the church hall at six that evening.

Supper consisted of meatloaf, mashed potatoes and green beans. I'm not a great cook, but Mom had believed men should know their way around a kitchen, so I was at least capable of making basic meals.

The kids pitched in like they really enjoyed my efforts, which was flattering. However I realized anything I prepared was better than what they had been eating.

There was a fair-sized stack of dishes in the sink and this was as good a time as any to introduce the kids to household chores. Mom had also insisted that Jenny and I do our share of kitchen cleanup. If it hadn't left me with emotional scars, I didn't figure it would hurt Marie and Billy.

As expected, the kids weren't enthusiastic, but they didn't have a choice. I washed, Marie dried, and Billy stacked the finished product on the table.

I had anticipated the possibility of one or more broken dishes, but hadn't anticipated the kid's reaction. I didn't see what happened, but apparently Billy let a glass slip out of his hand and it shattered on the floor. By the time I turned around Billy had run to the far side of the table and was holding both arms over his head as if protecting himself from expected blows.

"I'm sorry," he wailed, crying as if he were terrified. "It was an accident. I didn't mean to break it."

Marie moved so she was between me and Billy. "It wasn't Billy's fault," she said defensively. "I dropped it."
Obviously both kids expected me to react violently and Marie was prepared to accept whatever punishment would be directed at Billy.

"Hey, it's okay," I said. "It's only a glass. We have plenty of glasses. You didn't cut yourself, did you?"

Both kids remained in defensive positions and neither replied, but I didn't see any blood so I figured they were unharmed. "Let me clean up the broken glass before someone gets hurt." I swept up the pieces, put them in the trash can, and resumed washing the dishes as if nothing unusual had happened.

It wasn't more than a minute later when Marie dropped a plate. I was pretty certain she had broken it on purpose, testing my patience. Apparently if adults didn't react the way they expected, the kids needed to test whether a non-violent response was an anomaly.

"Maybe we'll have to get some plastic dishes until you guys get more practice at handling dishes," I joked as I swept up those pieces. "Just try to be careful. I don't want you to hurt yourselves."

We managed to finish without any more broken dishes, but I was pretty certain the kids weren't done testing me.

The last plate was safely placed in the kitchen cabinets around five-thirty, so I quickly helped the kids wash their faces and hands before we drove to Saint Anthony's for our appointment.

Sister Joan was a petite lady, dressed in a skirt and sweater. A medallion around her neck was the only sign of her vocation. Women's ages were always a mystery to me, but I guessed she was in her mid-forties, although I could have been off ten years in either direction.

Marie assumed her usual detached attitude and Billy hid behind his sister when Sister greeted us with a smile.

"You children can play in here while I talk with your Uncle." She ushered Marie and Billy into an empty classroom where there were toys, paper, crayons, and books to keep them occupied.

When we stepped across the hallway to another classroom, Sister Joan exuded an air of competence that made me believe she would be great with children. "Now, Mr. Wilson, how can I help you?" she asked.

"First, you might want to scan these reports." I handed her copies of the medical and psychological histories and continued talking while she read. "I have temporary custody of Marie and Billy—for at least the next three months. As you can see from the reports, both kids have had a rough life. I'm beginning to believe I may have gotten in way over my head. You've heard stories about children in India who were raised by wolves. That's Marie and Billy. It's as if they've been living in a cave all their lives."

"Maybe they would have been better off being raised by wolves rather than by the beasts they lived with," Sister Joan said when she finished scanning the documents. "Father Rose briefly explained about the children, but I had no idea they'd suffered so greatly. They certainly haven't had many good experiences in their lives.

"For several years I worked with abused and neglected children in the Milwaukee area. My chosen vocation demands that I practice forgiveness, but the injustice of mistreated youngsters always makes me feel angry and helpless. It's hard to understand how a merciful God can allow such cruelty to exist. But we must have faith and believe everything has a purpose. Of course I'll help your children in any way I can."

"Heaven knows I need help," I said, feeling as if a weight had been lifted from my shoulders. "I don't think Billy has had any religious education, and Marie has had very little. She's only nine-years-old and has already lost faith in God." I told Sister Joan about Marie refusing to say her nighttime prayers. "I want them to believe there is a caring and loving God, because they need to know there can be good in the world."

"All children need a spiritual foundation," Sister Joan agreed, "but particularly children who've been abused. Over the years I've learned that youngsters who claim to have given up on God are actually rebelling against the injustices they've experienced. They really want to believe there is a Higher Power Who loves them and listens to their prayers. Unfortunately, when Hell is the only reality they've experienced, it takes a great deal of love and understanding to reestablish their faith."

"So, where do we begin?" I asked.

"Let me talk with the children for few minutes so I'll have a better idea of where they are and what they need."

When we entered the children's classroom, Billy was pushing a toy truck around the floor. Marie was seated at one of the tables using crayons to draw on a large sheet of paper. From the doorway I couldn't see her picture very clearly, but it appeared to be a hodgepodge of swirls and scrolls, all done in dark colors.

"You can wait across the hall, Mr. Wilson," Sister Joan said. "I want to talk with the children alone."

It was a long, anxious half an hour before Sister Joan returned.

"How did it go?" I asked, having visions of Marie shocking the nun with her denials and street language.

"Billy was fine, but Marie didn't want to cooperate," Sister said. "After what she's experienced from adults some resistance is to be expected. Generally it requires a few sessions to establish any degree of trust. Your assessment concerning their religious education was correct. At some point, Marie may have been exposed to minimal religious training, but as you've already noticed, she has a strong sense that God abandoned her. Billy doesn't have any concept of God. In a way that's better because we don't have to deal with prejudice and abandonment. However, they're both well behind their age groups. Until Marie has at least minimal reading skills she would be lost in a class of children her age. Unfortunately we don't have an appropriate catechism class for either of them."

I felt crushed. "What can we do if you don't have a class for them?"

"Just because they aren't ready to join a regular class, doesn't mean I can't work privately with them. It'll be a slow process and I'll need your cooperation if we're going to achieve anything."

"Of course I'll do anything I can."

"I'm not a trained psychologist," Sister Joan said. "but I can make some suggestions based on my previous experiences. Our biggest obstacle is their low self-esteem and our need to convince them they're worthwhile human beings that God truly loves. It's important for you to spend time reading religious stories to them. Children love stories, and religious tales can go a long way toward awakening their desire to learn. I can loan you suitable books, but there are many others you can buy or pick up at the library. Marie seems to enjoy drawing and should be encouraged along those lines. I suggest you provide paper, pencils, and crayons for both of them. Every child should have an opportunity to be good at something and all children are natural artists. It's important to praise their efforts, even if their work seems bizarre. Don't expect perfection. Support their small triumphs and be patient."

"I'll do my best," I promised. Just knowing Sister Joan was going to be working with the children made me feel more confident than I had in several days.

"I'm sure you will. Our regular catechism classes are out for summer vacation, but Marie and Billy should begin lessons immediately. I'll be available for an hour every Tuesday and Thursday evening beginning at six-thirty. It's important for you to reinforce their lessons by taking them to Mass every Sunday. The children will come to appreciate the importance of religion if they see it's a strong force in your life."

"The kids only came to live with me yesterday, but I fully intend to take them to Mass regularly," I said. "Billy and I have already begun evening prayers, but as I told you, Marie refused to join us."

"Give her time. When she begins to realize she's safe and loved and that God has answered her prayers, one day she'll simply kneel beside you and Billy. Be patient." Sister Joan stood, signaling an end to the interview. "Is there anything else?"

"Just one more thing," I said, hoping she might have an answer to one of my bigger problem. "I'm a bachelor and don't have any experience with little girls. At Marie's age, and considering her previous experiences with men, I don't think it's appropriate for me to help her with feminine hygiene. I don't believe she's aware of most of the things a nine-year-old girl should know. I was hoping you might have a suggestion."

Sister Joan considered my request for a moment. "There's an older lady in the parish who's raised several youngsters of her own, and might be the ideal person to work with you. Her children are scattered around the country and she lives alone. Let me ask if she's interested in taking on the job as your housekeeper, with the added responsibility of helping with Marie and Billy. Although some people consider her abrupt, she's a good Christian woman with a strong personality. I believe she's financially comfortable, and would probably work for an affordable salary if she agrees to accept the position."

"That would be wonderful," I said.

"Good. Give me your phone number and I'll call when I've spoken with her."

After the kids took their baths and got into their pajamas, we sat on the living room sofa and I read one of the books Sister Joan had given me. It was a simple story about a little Shepherd boy with a sick lamb. Billy sat close enough to see the lavish illustrations, but Marie scooted to the far end of the couch and I wasn't even certain she was listening.

"Read it again," Billy begged.

"Okay," I agreed, wondering if anyone had ever read a story to the kids.

After the third time through the book, I decided that was enough for one evening. I had to promise to read another story the next evening before Billy agreed to go upstairs.

I put them in their separate beds although I figured Billy would join his sister sometime during the night. When I hugged Marie she didn't stiffen, and didn't cringe when I kissed her on the forehead. If she was beginning to trust me, even a little, maybe we were making progress.

# CHAPTER SIXTEEN

Saturday morning was dark and depressing, with a steady drizzle dripping off the eaves and sheeting the windows. I retreated to my study, but couldn't summon the ambition to work on Lee's software program. The study door was open and I leaned back in my chair to watch Marie and Billy quietly working at the dining room table.

Their new art supplies were scattered across the surface and a few pieces of drawing paper had fallen to the floor. Marie labored studiously on a large sheet, taking her time to complete a picture. Her back was toward me, but I knew that even as she concentrated on her drawing there would be a haunted, sad look in her eyes. Billy was facing toward me, the tip of his tongue working at the corner of his mouth, as he scrawled hurriedly through the pages of a coloring book. If I hadn't known better, I would have thought he was a perfectly normal five-year old.

I couldn't avoid thinking how different Marie and Billy were from Jenny and me at the same ages. It would have been impossible to spend a rainy day in the same room with my sister without a major squabble. Mostly it would have started with Jenny pestering me until I yelled at her and she began crying. Then Mom would have settled the conflict by separating us, allowing Jenny to stay at the table and sending me to my room. At the very least there would have been noise of some sort— laughter, running, loud games, arguing.

It just wasn't natural for Marie and Billy to always be so quiet. During the short time they had been with me, I'd never heard them argue or shout or run through the house. When I thought about it, I realized I'd never even heard them laugh. Was it possible they had never learned how to laugh?  Had they been punished if they drew attention to themselves?  Did they avoid conflicts with each other because they had to be united against the adult world?

*Damn it,* I thought.  *There were so many questions and not a single answer.*

At ten o'clock my attempts at doing something productive were interrupted when Sister Joan phoned to tell me Emily Hall was open to the possibility of working as our housekeeper.  I immediately dialed the number Sister provided.

Mrs. Hall answered after the second ring and I introduced myself.  "I believe Sister Joan talked with you about me and my children."

"Yes, she did."  Her voice sounded strong and confident, like a woman accustomed to being in charge.  "Sister told me you have a bachelor household and recently obtained custody of your dead sister's children.  According to Sister Joan, the children are little more than savages and you need help civilizing them."

Her attitude raised my hackles.  "Marie and Billy aren't savages," I snapped.

"Don't get your dander up," Mrs. Hall snapped back.  "Children who don't know their catechism certainly aren't civilized.  Do you need help with them or don't you?"

"Actually I need help with the girl," I conceded.  "Marie's nine-years-old and needs a woman's influence."

"Nonsense.  Both children need a woman's influence.  A bachelor has no business trying to raise kids."  I attempted to reply, but Mrs. Hall ignored me and kept talking.  "As I told Sister Joan, I'm not a nanny or a babysitter.  However, I'm willing to hire out as a housekeeper, and I suspect you need one."

After only a few sentences I was convinced that no matter how desperate I might be, Mrs. Hall wasn't the housekeeper we needed.  "I appreciate your offer," I said, "but I'm really looking for someone to help with the children."

"I understand that," Mrs. Hall snapped.  "Do you think I'm dense?  I'd consider it my duty to work with the children, but I don't intend to baby-sit while you go gallivanting all over the countryside." I tried to speak again, but Mrs. Hall wouldn't be interrupted. "Before I agree to anything, I'll have to see your house and meet the children. If I decide to work for you, I'd be available Monday through Friday, from two in the afternoon until nine at night."

"Those hours would be great," I said, beginning to feel overwhelmed. "But I don't know if I'm ready to hire anyone right now."

"Don't talk such foolishness. From what Sister told me you need help immediately. You aren't going to find anyone else in this town that'll put up with wild children. Sister gave me your address. I'll stop by this afternoon at two, and if everything is agreeable, I'll start immediately."

It didn't seem like she was going to let me say no. "What salary would you require?" I asked, hoping she would want more than I could afford.

"How would I know before seeing what I'll be getting into?" Mrs. Hall snapped. "We'll talk about wages if I decide to work for you." There was a loud click and I was left listening to a dial tone.

I was tempted to call back and tell Mrs. Hall not to bother coming over, but I desperately needed someone, and at the moment there weren't any other choices. She had referred to Marie and Billy as wild, which they weren't, unless she meant wild in the sense they were untrained, which certainly was true. Maybe a take-charge person was exactly what we needed. I wasn't about to let a female tyrant take over my household, but it made sense to withhold judgment until I'd interviewed her in person. I took a deep breath and prayed she would turn out to be the sweet, grandmotherly type.

The prospect of gaining a housekeeper forced me to consider a major problem. If Mrs. Hall was suitable for the job, she probably wouldn't appreciate Marie and Billy's street language. It was time to address that problem. There had to be an alternative to spending the rest of my life scolding them every time they used a cuss word. I believed there was a solution, and now was a good time to find out if my idea would work.

When I joined the kids at the dining room table, Marie was working on a picture that looked like a domestic scene with a green house, red stick figures, and blue furniture.

"That's very pretty," I said.

She flipped the paper over so I couldn't see the drawing. "It's dumb," she said, but I suspected she was pleased with my compliment.

"Mine's pretty too," Billy said, shoving the coloring book in front of my nose. He had scribbled various colors on the page with no effort to stay within the lines.

"Yes it is," I agreed. "But I'd like you both to put down your crayons for a minute. We're going to have a family discussion."

Billy looked curious, but Marie had a suspicious frown. Evidently family talks were a foreign concept.

"Before you came to live here, you both learned a lot of bad words," I explained. "I understand that's the way people talked where you were, but it isn't nice."

"What's a bad word?" Billy asked. Marie looked like it didn't make any difference to her.

"That's a good question," I agreed. "They are words bad people use. Good people only use nice words."

"But what's a bad word?" Billy insisted. "I'm not bad. I'm good."

"Yes, you're a good boy and Marie's a good girl." Apparently I was going to have to be more specific. "There are lots of bad words and I can't think of them all right now, but goddamned, fuck, and shit are examples. When people hear you say those words, they'll think you're bad kids, even though we know better. From now on, we're all going to use only good words."

"If you don't tell us all the bad words, how will we know when we use one?" Marie asked. She was wearing her emotionless expression, but joining the conversation suggested she was at least partially interested.

"That's another good question. At first you won't always

know the bad words, and sometimes you'll forget. Whenever you say a bad word, I'll tell you, and suggest a good word to use instead."

"Are you going to send us away if we use bad words?" Marie asked.

"Of course not." I replied calmly, although I wanted to scream that this was her home and she didn't have to always feel concerned about being sent away. "You'd never learn if I sent you away for making a mistake. Tell you what; let's make this a family project. Sometimes I might use a bad word, so if any of us use a word we shouldn't, we'll just say, 'that's a bad word', and we'll use a good word instead."

"If we say you used a bad word, you'll hit us," Marie said.

"Absolutely not." Had punishment always been the result of criticizing an adult? "I won't ever hit you. What's fair for you is fair for me. Do we have a deal?"

Marie nodded, but I could tell she didn't believe me. Billy was more enthusiastic, like it was a new game. "I want to know all the good words," he said. "No bad words for me. I'm a good boy."

Only time would tell if our first family discussion bore fruit.

# CHAPTER SEVENTEEN

I t had stopped raining and the sun had appeared when the doorbell chimed at precisely two o'clock. I was soon to learn that punctuality was one of Emily Hall's many positive characteristics.

The house had been dusted and vacuumed, faces and hands were scrubbed and shinny, and we were all wearing freshly laundered clothing. I had explained we were going to meet a lady who might be our housekeeper and warned Marie and Billy to be on their best behavior.

Mrs. Hall was as overwhelming in person as she had been over the phone. The image of a take-charge woman definitely suited her personality. Even standing still she gave an impression of motion. She wasn't fat, but did look like she had enough heft to put in a good day's fieldwork.

"Good afternoon, Mr. Wilson," she said, exuding energy. "You may address me as Emily when the children aren't present. Otherwise I'm Mrs. Hall." She turned to the kids who were standing beside me, their mouths open, awe struck. "You may call me Mrs. Hall. I don't abide children who address adults by their first names." She enveloped Marie in a hug, and then held her at arm's length. "You must be Marie. You certainly are a pretty young lady."

Marie looked subdued, like she'd just encountered an elemental force. I knew exactly how she felt.

"I'm handsome," Billy proclaimed.

"Yes you are." Emily swept Billy into her arms and smothered him in a hug.

"You're going to choke that poor dog, holding him like that,"

Emily scolded. I had a firm grip on Shadow's collar to prevent his normal enthusiastic greeting. "Let him go. He won't hurt anything. What's his name?"

"Shadow." I released my grip and the dog bolted toward Emily, jumping up and down, his tail nearly shaking off his hind legs. He was the only who didn't appear intimidated. Maybe he sensed something we didn't.

Emily pushed him down and vigorously rubbed his ears. "Not a very imaginative name, but at least Shadow is better than Blackie. Kids need to have a dog of one kind or another. Teaches them responsibility. Always had one or more around when my kids were growing." Emily straightened up. "Well, no sense in just standing here staring at each other. Let's take a look at the house."

Marie, Billy, Shadow, and I followed in procession as Emily swept through the downstairs. She opened all the doors, made a quick tour of each room, checked all the kitchen cupboards, and shook her head as she looked in the refrigerator. She opened the back door and surveyed the yard, but didn't go outside.

I should have been guiding the tour and making comments, but somewhere along the way I had completely lost control.

Emily slowed as she began climbing the stairs, using the banister for support. "Got a touch of arthritis," she proclaimed. "Doesn't bother me much, except when I climb steps. Don't have any stairs at my place." The way she said it made me feel guilty for not having an escalator.

She was like a whirlwind sweeping through the bedrooms, opening cabinets and doors, even checking the linens and looking under each bed. She didn't say a word and it was impossible to determine whether she was satisfied or disappointed.

"You kids go outside and play with Shadow," she ordered as soon as we had returned to the living room. "I have to talk with your Uncle Jon." When Marie and Billy hesitated, she made a sweeping motion with her hands to shoo them out. "Go on now, scoot. Nice day like this, kids should be outdoors."

Marie and Billy ran outside, the screen door banging behind them, and Emily plopped down on the sofa. "You aren't much of a housekeeper, are you?"

My house might not have won any awards, but I was proud of my general housekeeping. "I do all right," I said, letting my irritation show.

"Nonsense. Never did know a man who could properly keep a house. You need a woman to get things in order."

Sister Joan had been conservative when she'd said Mrs. Hall was abrupt. I thought she was irritating and downright bossy. However, I did have to admit she had gotten the kid's attention, and seemed to know what she was doing. If she was willing to take the job, I figured we could try it for a week or so. "Would you like to read the children's medical and psychological reports before you decide about the position?"

"Don't need to read reports. Never had much truck with all that professional mumbo jumbo. Besides, I've already made my decision. I'll take the job. But we'll have to make a few changes around here."

I figured now was a good time to exercise some authority. "We can talk about changes in a minute. Right now I insist you read these. If you're going to work here, you have to be aware of what the kids have gone through. They have special problems." I handed Emily the reports.

"All children have problems of some kind," Emily complained as she reluctantly scanned the documents. After a couple of paragraphs she slowed down and began to read more carefully. Tears formed in her eyes. "Allergies," she said, taking a handkerchief from her purse to blow her nose. "They don't usually bother me. It must be the weather."

When she finished the reports, she dabbed at moisture in the corner of her eyes. "This is horrible. Sister Joan told me the children had been abused, but I had no idea how much they'd suffered. It doesn't seem possible anyone could do things like that to such sweet children"

"Yes, they are sweet kids," I agreed, "but they do have special problems. Billy is already beginning to adapt to his new home, but Marie hasn't been able to accept the fact she's safe and secure. Both kids need love and understanding more than they need discipline."

"Of course they need love." Emily had regained control of her emotions and was back to her forceful manner. "Love to children is like water to flowers. It's essential for proper growth. If you give any child love and a little recognition, the rest will take care of itself. But kids also need discipline, which is just a different kind of love. They need someone to take charge and set boundaries so they learn acceptable limits. Doesn't mean you have to beat or torture them. The worst thing you can do is treat Marie and Billy differently than normal children."

"I agree, but it's going to take time and patience." I took a deep breath. Maybe Mrs. Hall wouldn't be a tyrant after all. "Are you still interested in the job?"

"Of course." Emily sounded as if I had hurt her feelings. "You didn't think I'd abandon those children just because they have a few problems, did you? You mean well, but they need to have a woman around. From what I just read, they've only had bad experiences with men."

"I think I can pay a fair wage, but we may have to cut back on the hours you suggested."

"Isn't that just like a man, putting money ahead of the children's welfare. I don't intend to work by the hour and punch a time clock. Can you afford two hundred dollars a week?"

"I'm not putting money ahead of the kids, and I can afford two hundred right now, but I don't know what expenses I'm going to have. The kids have doctor's appointments coming up and my insurance won't cover them while I have temporary custody."

"Jon, you have to learn to set your priorities, and right now the kids should be at the top of your list. I'll start for two hundred a week. If you find the bills are piling up, we'll sit down and work something out."

"You're hired," I quickly agreed. "When can you start?"

"I've already started. To begin with I'll work from two until nine, Monday through Friday. We can adjust the hours later if need be. That way I can fix a nutritious supper for the children. You've probably been feeding them pizza and TV dinners. Kids need vegetables and solid food."

"I've cooked a decent meal for the kids every night," I protested.

Emily ignored my objection. "We have some immediate concerns. Neither one of the children have enough clothes. I didn't even see jackets in their closets. What did you plan to do if we have a cold snap? I'll make an inventory of their wardrobes, and Monday I'll take the children shopping. What about cleaning supplies? There isn't enough here for even one good cleaning. Your pantry is a disaster. You don't have any of the food children need. I suppose when you lived alone, you didn't eat anything except sandwiches. Never did know a man who could take proper care of himself. I didn't even see any cookies in your cupboards. Do you think growing children can get by on just three meals a day? They need a couple of snacks along the way. Nothing's better than milk and cookies. You'll have to make do this weekend, but Monday we'll stock up. You have enough money for food and clothing, don't you?"

Emily wasn't even out of breath after reciting the long litany of my sins.

"Of course I have enough money," I snapped. "It's not like I'm on welfare. I don't have a problem taking you shopping."

"Absolutely not. You'd just be in our way. Give me some money and I'll take the children." Emily stood up. "Now you show me where I can hang my coat and purse and I'll get busy. I'll be all afternoon just making a list of the things we'll need."

"I thought you weren't going to work Saturdays."

"I don't intend to make a habit of it, but if I don't make a list today there won't be time to shop on Monday. Those children can't do without proper food and clothing one day longer than necessary."

"Okay," I said, resigned to Emily taking temporary charge.

"Where do we start?"

"Sister Joan told me you work from home. You just go into your study and get busy. Nothing I hate more than someone hovering over me while I'm working. I can find my way around, just fine."

I retreated to my study; feeling like Mom had sent me to my room. I was wondering whether I had made a wise decision. I needed a housekeeper, not a warden. I didn't know it then, but Mrs. Hall was going to be a positive influence and our savior. If she wasn't an angel, she was the closest to one I'd ever see in this lifetime.

# CHAPTER EIGHTEEN

We had an early Sunday breakfast before I dressed the kids in the outfits we'd picked up at Wal-Mart. I combed Billy's unruly hair as best I could, and then brushed Marie's hair. As a final touch I clipped on the barrettes to hold it in place. She looked so sweet I couldn't avoid giving her a hug. She didn't return the hug, but at least she didn't resist.

"You sure are pretty when you're all dressed up. Come see for yourself." I led her into my bedroom where there was a full-length mirror on the closet door.

Billy followed along. "What about me? Don't I look pretty?"

I laughed, giving him a hug. "Of course not. Boys don't look pretty, but you certainly are a handsome young man."

When she stepped in front of the mirror, Marie was obviously startled and pleased by her image. She probably had never seen herself clean and wearing a lovely outfit. Turning her head slightly so she could see the barrettes, she reached up to gingerly touch them. For a fleeting instant I thought I saw the ghost of a smile.

Billy pushed in beside her. "Look at me. I'm handsome."

"I'll bet you're the best looking kids in town," I agreed. "But that's enough admiring ourselves in the mirror. If we don't get going, we'll be late for Mass."

Ten-thirty Mass was the most popular service and the church was already crowded. Since the pews always filled from the back, forward, we had to sit near the front. When I genuflected and stood aside to let the kids enter first, Billy imitated me, but Marie sidled into the pew without attempting to genuflect.

I knelt to say the preparatory prayers and Billy knelt beside me, but couldn't see over the back of the pew, so he stood on the kneeler.

"Where's God," he whispered. A few worshippers turned and smiled at us.

"God is everywhere," I whispered back. "But in God's House, He's mostly at the altar."

"I don't see Him," Billy complained.

"He's invisible," I explained. "You can't see God, but He's here with us."

Momentarily satisfied, he looked around at the candles and colorful statues and stained glass windows. "He sure has a nice house," Billy whispered.

When the organ music began everyone except Marie stood for the processional. Billy followed my example, standing, kneeling, and sitting when I did. Although she followed the proceedings with interest, Marie remained sitting throughout the Mass. It was going to take time before she trusted God enough to participate.

On the way out of church we met Sister Joan on the front steps. She smiled at all of us, but focused on Marie. "My goodness, Marie, you look very, very pretty this morning." I thought I saw a smile beginning on Marie's lips, but it never developed.

"I'm handsome," Billy announced.

"Yes, you are a very handsome young man. I'm so happy to see both of you at Mass this morning."

An elderly woman approached Sister Joan. "Good morning, Sister. Do you have a moment?"

"I'll see you kids at class Tuesday evening," Sister said as she moved away.

"I've got a special treat for us this morning," I announced after we were all securely in the car. "We're going to have dinner in a restaurant."

Billy gleefully clapped his hands, always excited by a new adventure. It was likely the kids had never been in a restaurant.

Marie accepted my announcement in her usual stoic manner, as if nothing—good or bad—was going to penetrate her shell.

Calhoun's Kitchen is a locally owned restaurant offering the best fried chicken in the State. On Sundays they have an 'all you can eat' option served family style. Normally I ordered from the menu because I can't eat enough to make the option worthwhile, but I was curious to see how much the kids would consume if they weren't limited.

When the waitress began bringing dishes of food, the kids immediately attacked the chicken platter. Billy grabbed a drumstick, but Marie, being more practical, selected a breast, the largest piece on the plate. Both kids would have ignored the dressing, mashed potatoes, and whole kernel corn if I hadn't put a portion on each of their plates and insisted they at least try some.

"It's okay to eat chicken with your fingers," I told them, "but you have to use a fork for the other stuff. Take as much as you want. Just put the bones on your plates and help yourselves."

They both quickly picked the bones clean and reached for more. I showed them how to use napkins to wipe grease off their faces and hands. Marie did well, but Billy quickly forgot, wiping his hands on his pants and his mouth on his shirtsleeve. I was afraid they might eat until they got sick, but after each finished three big pieces, along with a helping of side dishes, they seemed satisfied. Maybe they realized no one was going to take the food away, or maybe the kids were becoming accustomed to regular meals.

"As a special treat, how about having ice cream for dessert?"

Billy probably didn't know what dessert meant, but he knew about sweets. "I love ice cream," he said, clapping his hands.

"Do you like strawberry? That's my favorite kind."

Extra desserts weren't part of the 'all you can eat' option, but when both kids asked for a second helping, I gladly paid the additional price.

All things considered, I was proud of the way they had behaved in the restaurant and in church. It was comforting to know they could act civilized although I didn't fool myself into believing the problems were over.

At home we settled down for a quiet Sunday afternoon. I began watching a TV movie while the kids occupied themselves with paper and crayons. If anyone had observed us, they would have considered the kids part of a normal family.

Although Billy still tended to seek protection behind Marie, he was beginning to come out of his shell. In many ways he already acted like a normal five-year-old.

It was Marie who worried me. I had yet to see a full smile, and she never showed emotion. Not anger or fear or joy or anything. It just wasn't normal for a nine-year-old to keep everything locked inside.

The movie wasn't very good, and by three o'clock I was beginning to doze when Detective Kincaid called.

"What can I do for you?" I asked when he identified himself. He was the last person I'd have expected to be calling on a Sunday afternoon.

"Congratulations," he said. "I hear you've gotten custody of Jennifer's kids."

"Actually it's only temporary. We have to go back to court in three months."

"I have two kids of my own, so I know you've got your hands full right now. I hate to add to your problems, but I've got information you should be aware of."

The last of my drowsiness vanished as I sat upright. "What are you talking about?"

"Do you remember Liz Ryan offering to check if there were any street rumors about Jennifer or the kids?"

"Of course. She told me she'd ask around when I talked with her about the Blackmans."

"You were right about the Blackmans, by the way, but I'll get to that in a minute. Have you ever heard the names Henry Washington or Pusher?"

"No, I don't think so. Am I supposed to know them?"

"Actually, Pusher is Henry Washington's street name, and

there isn't any reason for you to have heard of him. He runs a stable of prostitutes and is one of the major drug suppliers in Campbell."

"Are you saying he was Jenny's pimp and drug connection?" I checked to see if the kids were paying attention because they didn't need to hear my end of the conversation. They were both occupied drawing pictures and didn't have the slightest interest in my phone call.

"Jennifer worked freelance for the most part, and as far as I know she never had a regular pimp," Kincaid said. "But Pusher was one of her drug connections. The word on the streets is that her overdose might not have been accidental—at least not in the way we suspected."

"You're telling me Jenny was murdered?" I'd adjusted to the idea that my sister had accidentally killed herself, but the thought she might have been murdered was shocking.

"It's not that simple," Kincaid said. "You have to remember my information is based on rumors, although more often than not, what you hear on the streets is just as accurate as the evening news. There's no evidence Jennifer was murdered, and if she was, there's no way we could prove it. Personally I still believe she came into possession of more drugs than she'd ever seen and accidentally overdosed."

"I'm sorry, but you've lost me somewhere along the line. I don't have any idea what you're talking about."

"Sorry if I've confused you. Let's see if I can clarify. Remember this is just street rumor." He paused a moment like he was gathering his thoughts. "According to our sources, Jennifer got involved in a major drug deal that went bad. I don't know whether she was part of the operation or if she just stumbled onto the opportunity of a lifetime. However it happened, the word is that she ended up holding a few kilos of pure China White and several hundred thousand dollars."

"China White?"

"That's the street name for Asian heroin."

"So you think Jenny was murdered because of the money and

drugs?"

"Let me tell this my way so I don't get you more confused. When the money and drugs went missing Pusher began looking for Jennifer, but I don't think he killed her. Street drugs are always stepped on several times, and getting hold of pure heroin was too much for her. Like I said, I still believe she overdosed."

"Hold on a minute. You're losing me again. What does 'stepped on' mean?"

"At every stage of distribution, suppliers step on or cut the product by adding a filler, like sugar, starch, quinine or something similar, to dilute the pure China White and make it go further. By the time it reaches the user, it's probably not more than fifteen, twenty percent pure."

"So you think taking the pure drug is what killed Jenny?"

"Seems logical. At any rate, the word is that when Pusher found Jennifer she was already dead or at least in a coma. Other than one partial bag, there weren't any drugs or money in the apartment. Losing all that merchandise, along with a bundle of cash is the sort of thing that can put a supplier out of business permanently, if you get my meaning. Chances are the drugs or the money didn't belong to Pusher and he has to answer to someone higher up the supply chain. Word is he's under a lot of pressure to make good on the loss, and doesn't have the resources to replace either the junk or the money."

"Do I have this right? You're saying that somehow Jenny ended up with all those drugs and a couple hundred thousand dollars?"

"I don't know for certain, but that's the word on the street," Kincaid agreed.

"So, what happened to all that stuff? It must have been a pretty big bundle."

"At least a couple of large suitcases, and no one knows where it is. That's what Pusher is desperate to find out. If he'd reached Jennifer soon enough, he'd have made her beg to tell him what she did with the stuff. He missed his opportunity with Jennifer, but he did manage to locate her most recent boyfriend. We found his body in the freight yards. Whoever worked on the poor guy made him suffer a long time before he finally died. Again, word is the boyfriend didn't know where the drugs and money are, and Pusher is still looking."

"If he murdered Jennifer's boyfriend, why don't you arrest him?"

"It isn't that easy. We can't bust someone because of street gossip and there's no hard evidence linking Pusher to any of this. Believe me, we'd love to slam the door and throw away the key if we could."

"It sounds like a mess, but I still don't see where any of this concerns me."

"I'm getting to that. Apparently Pusher didn't realize Jennifer had any kids. Marie and Billy must have been hiding when Pusher was in the apartment. The suitcases were too large to conceal in the kitchen cabinets, so he apparently never looked under the sink. Because the kids are his last chance to recover the product he has to get hold of them to find out whether they know where Jennifer stashed the loot. He isn't a very patient man, and he isn't going to ask the kids to 'pretty please' answer his questions."

"Are you suggesting Pusher might be coming after Marie and Billy?" I'm sure Kincaid could hear the fear in my voice.

"Yeah, he doesn't have any other option. Marie and Billy are in serious danger unless we find the stash before Pusher locates the kids."

"Marie and Billy couldn't possibly know anything about this. If you didn't find anything in the apartment, it isn't likely the kids have a clue where she hid the stuff."

"Maybe, maybe not. But Pusher won't be satisfied until he finds out for himself. He has to hope one of the kids heard or saw something. Actually I'd like to talk with Marie and Billy myself, but I've already gotten a turn down from CPS and Children's Court. They won't allow us to question the kids until we get an okay from their psychologist, and that could take weeks. Unfortunately Pusher doesn't have legal restraints, and he can't afford to wait."

"What do you mean?" This was beginning to sound like a 'B' grade movie, and they didn't always have happy endings.

"As I said earlier, your suspicions about Cynthia and George Blackman's motivation and their interest in the kids, were right on target. Word is Pusher brought them in from out of town as a way to get at Marie and Billy. He went to a lot of trouble to set up the Blackman's histories with stolen identities and paid references. We don't even know their real names, but they both vanished immediately after you got temporary custody. Obviously Pusher couldn't afford to wait three months for another shot, so he abandoned the foster parent scam."

"So, that should be the end of it," I said hopefully.

"Don't we wish? I doubt whether Pusher is going to give up so easily," Kincaid warned. "I wanted to give you all this background so you could be on the alert."

"Are you saying Pusher might still be after the kids?"

"I don't think there's any doubt about it. He can't afford to lose either the drugs or the money, and if he's got pressure from up the line, it's more than likely a life or death situation for him. He needs to get at those kids. We're keeping an eye on him, but we can't watch 24/7. He probably wouldn't come after the kids personally anyway. He's got plenty of muscle on his payroll to do the dirty work."

"Don't just tell me my kids are in danger." I felt like shouting into the phone. "Tell me what I can do to protect them."

"Do you have a fax machine?"

"Yes"

"Good. I'll fax you mug shots of Pusher and the main people he's liable to send after the kids. They're all black and should stand out like a sore thumb in a lily-white town like Westport. But I wouldn't rule out him sending white muscle. Keep an eye open for any suspicious people in your neighborhood, and stay close to the kids. I doubt whether Pusher would attempt to grab them in a public place, but that would depend on how desperate he is. It's more likely he'll try something at your house. I've already notified the Westport police and they've promised to increase patrols in your neighborhood. Don't tell anyone I suggested this, but if I were you, I'd get myself a gun and keep it close. If these guys show up in Westport, shoot to kill. I guarantee you they aren't very nice people."

I gave Kincaid my fax number. "Thanks for the advice, but it'd make things a lot simpler if you could arrest Pusher."

"If we're lucky we'll bust him and his gang for something else before they have a chance to look for you and the kids, but I wouldn't count on it."

When I hung up, I was shaking.

Dad's old hunting rifle and shotgun were still in my closet. I hadn't used them in years, and didn't even know if there was ammunition in the house. My first priority was to make damned sure both weapons were loaded and ready to go.

The fax machine was churning out the mug shots when I took the kids upstairs. I tried to pretend everything was normal as they bathed and got ready for bed, but I was scared like I'd never been in my life. After everything Marie and Billy had suffered, it didn't seem fair to have this threat hanging over them.

When they were tucked in for the night, I went into my study and examined the stack of mug shots. It was a mean looking group of hoodlums. The evil in their eyes scared the hell out of me.

I leaned back in my chair and closed my eyes. I had to do something to protect my family, and couldn't walk around town carrying a rifle. When I picked up ammunition, I'd also buy a pistol small enough to carry in a pocket. If the kids needed me, I would be prepared.

With everything else, Mrs. Hall would be starting work on Monday. Whether she liked it or not, I intended to go with her and the kids on the shopping trip. I still had to decide how much, if anything, to tell her about this new development.

I already knew I'd get very little sleep until Pusher's threat was resolved.

# CHAPTER NINETEEN

I t was nearly nine Monday morning when the kids finished
breakfast of scrambled eggs, sausage links, and toast. With
no ammunition for either the rifle or shotgun, I was a
nervous wreck, and felt vulnerable. My anxiety wasn't going to
get any better until I had a useable weapon.

I left the breakfast dishes in the sink, herded Marie and
Billy into the car, and headed for Hensley's Sporting Goods
Emporium.

During the summer a lot of hunters, fishermen, and campers
passed through Westport heading for the forests and lakes north
of town. Consequently, Hensley's was a larger operation than a
town the size of Westport could normally have supported. They
not only carried an extensive line of fishing and camping gear,
they also maintained a large inventory of guns and ammunition.
For me, the biggest advantage was that Ralph Hensley was one of
my best friends, and I was hoping I could impose on that
friendship.

The last year Westport's football team had won the
conference championship, Ralph and I had teamed in the
backfield. A lot of people considered us the best halfback,
fullback combination in school history. I still held the single
season rushing record and Ralph had scored more career
touchdowns than anyone in the conference. A knee injury
during my senior year had ended my football career, but Ralph
had gotten a scholarship to State and had been on his way to
bigger and better things.

Many people, including myself, thought he would have been
a high draft choice with the Pros if he'd played his final year of

eligibility. Midway through Ralph's Junior season, his father had suffered a massive heart attack, and Ralph had dropped out of school to run the family business.

Although he was married and had a couple of kids, we still got together occasionally for a night on the town or a weekend fishing trip at his Dad's cabin. I was hoping our friendship would convince him to bend a few rules.

All the way across town I kept glancing into the rearview mirror to see if we were being followed. I'm not sure what I was looking for—maybe a big black limousine full of gangsters carrying Tommy guns, like in the movies about the prohibition era. I realized I was being paranoid, but I'd never been the target of an angry drug gang, and I was scared.

When we reached Hensley's I parked in front of the entrance and hustled the kids inside. Keeping a firm grip on Marie's hand, I went directly to the back of the store where the firearms were displayed. There were only two customers. I recognized both of them, so I was pretty certain we wouldn't be ambushed between the aisles.

"May I help you find something?" The pimply-faced clerk didn't look like an assassin—more like a high school kid with a summer job.

"Is Ralph in this morning?" I asked.

"Yes, sir, he's in the stock room," the young man replied. "I'll get him for you."

The clerk disappeared through a swinging door. I nervously scanned the store, having the feeling someone might be sneaking up on us.

"Hey, Jon, it's good to see you," Ralph said as he came from the stock room wiping his hands on a shop towel. "Been a long time."

"Ralph, I'd like you to meet my kids." He was well aware I wasn't married, but in a small place like Westport, the story about Jenny and the custody hearing would already be all over town. "Marie and Billy, this is Mr. Hensley. He's one of my best friends."

"Hi kids." I was grateful when Ralph didn't attempt to reach over the counter and shake hands. I was never sure how Marie would react and it wouldn't help my cause if she bit him. "So what can I do for you this morning, Jon?"

"I'd like a box of twenty gauge number 8 buckshot, a box of 30-30 hollow point, and a pistol."

"It's a little early for hunting, isn't it?" he asked, reaching under the counter for the ammunition. "Can I sell you a hunting license?"

"I'm just stocking up. Maybe I'll do a little target practice."

"Here's the ammo." He put the boxes on the counter. "What kind of pistol did you have in mind? A handgun will require some paperwork and possibly as much as a three day wait."

"I need to talk with you about that," I said. "Can we step to the end of the counter?"

Ralph looked curious. "Sure."

"You kids wait right here where I can see you," I said. "Don't go wandering off."

"What's up?" he asked. "Are you planning to rob a bank?"

"Ralph, I need a big favor. I have to have the pistol right away, this morning."

"That's a possibility, but I don't have any control over the approval. After you complete the Firearms Transaction Record, I'll call it in to NICS and they'll run the information through their database. If the system isn't jammed with requests, we can get immediate approval, but sometimes we have to wait as long as three days."

"What's the NICS?" I asked.

"The National Instant Criminal Background Check System. Like the name implies, they'll check you out to make certain you aren't a criminal or some sort of subversive."

"I can't take a chance on waiting." I briefly explained about Jenny and Pusher and the warning I'd gotten from the Campbell police.

When I finished, Ralph looked at me like he was waiting for the punch line. "You're pulling my leg, right?"

"This isn't a joke. These guys are for real, and they're dangerous. One way or another, I'm going to do whatever is necessary to protect my kids."

Ralph's expression changed to a look of concern. "You're serious, aren't you?"

"Damned right. That's why I need the pistol this morning."

"If my kids were in that kind of danger, I'd do anything I could to protect them." He put his hand on my shoulder. "I understand why you want the pistol, but shouldn't you let the cops handle this?"

"If there hasn't been a crime, all the cops will do is keep an eye open for strangers and schedule more frequent patrols through my neighborhood. That isn't enough and you know it. After everything my kids have suffered, I'll die before I let Pusher get hold of them."

"Damnit Jon, I know how you feel—how I'd feel if it were my kids, but if I don't follow the rules, I could lose my license and that would shut me down."

I couldn't blame Ralph for not wanting to risk his business. He had his own family to consider. "I understand," I said. "If you can't help me, maybe you know people who could get me a pistol without waiting. I can't walk around town carrying a shotgun."

"I didn't say I wouldn't help. If my kids were threatened, I'd be carrying a pistol myself. Let's fill in the Transaction Record and I'll call it in to NICS. If we don't get immediate approval, I'll bend the rules a little."

"Thanks, Ralph." A sense of relief washed over me. "I won't forget this."

"Don't worry. I'll remind you if I ever need something." He unlocked the display case and picked out a .32 caliber Berretta automatic. "This would be perfect. It's small enough to carry concealed, but it packs a solid punch." We walked back toward where Marie and Billy were waiting patiently, and he handed me a yellow sheet. "Fill this out and we'll see what happens."

It was a fairly simple form, which I quickly completed. Ralph took it into the office and I waited impatiently for about fifteen minutes.

"Looks like we were worried for nothing. NICS didn't discover your secret criminal history. You've been approved."

"Thanks, Ralph. I really appreciate this."

He put the Beretta and a box of .32 shells on the counter. "Let's hope the cops handle the problem before it gets to Westport and you won't need to use the pistol."

As soon as I secured the kids in the back seat, I loaded the Beretta's magazine, jacked a round into the chamber, made certain the safety was engaged, and placed the pistol on the seat beside me. For the first time since Kincaid had phoned, I felt reasonably secure.

# CHAPTER TWENTY

E mily Hall arrived precisely at two, armed with her shopping lists. I had purposely left Marie and Billy in the backyard playing with Shadow.

"I need to talk with you before the shopping trip," I said. "Things have changed since Saturday afternoon."

She sat on the sofa while I told her about Detective Kincaid's phone call. The story must have shocked her because she didn't once try to interrupt. Her expression changed from shock to anger and her eyes filled with tears.

"I don't need to tell you I'm scared, and worried about the kids," I concluded. "But it isn't your problem. You didn't sign on to risk your life."

"Are you going to run away from the trouble?" she asked. "Do you intend to return the children to Child Protective Services?"

"Of course not. They need me more than ever. For better or worse, they're mine and we'll face this together."

"So what's this foolishness about things changing? As long as those children are living here, they need a woman around. I don't intend to leave them in a bachelor household where they'll be eating nothing but sandwiches and pizza. If they're going to grow up as proper adults, they'll need more help than a man can give them."

I felt like giving her a big hug. "You realize you'll be in danger if you stay with us."

"Hogwash. Isn't it just like a man to think all females are helpless? With traffic the way it is, I'm taking my life into my hands every time I cross the street. God isn't going to let anything happen to those kids. That's why He sent us to protect them. Maybe He wants me to watch your back."

"Emily, you don't know how much I appreciate this."

"Stop blubbering before you embarrass me," she said. "Do the children know about Pusher and the danger?"

"No. I didn't think it would help anything to scare them. They've had enough problems."

"That's the first intelligent thing you've said all day." She stood up. "Now, let's get the kids ready so I can take them shopping."

"That's another thing," I said. "I'll have to go shopping with you."

Emily sighed like having me on the shopping trip was more of a problem than Pusher's threat. "We'll be perfectly safe without you hovering over us. Never did know a man who was anything but a nuisance in a store."

"It isn't open for debate," I said. "I'll stay in the background and keep my mouth shut. You won't even know I'm there, but I'm not letting Marie and Billy out of my sight until this thing is resolved."

Emily didn't look pleased with my decision, but knew better than to argue. It made me feel like maybe I'd won a minor victory.

She called the kids in and began getting them ready. Although it was a warm day, I slipped on a light jacket. I needed the larger pockets to conceal the pistol and still have it available quickly.

I wasn't happy about driving to the Wal-Mart in Campbell, but Pusher wasn't likely to have people staked out in all the discount stores, and Westport didn't have any shops where we could purchase everything on Emily's list. Also, the Campbell Wal-Mart had a fully stocked grocery department, and we wouldn't have to expose ourselves at several locations.

We shopped for clothing first. Marie and Billy pushed the cart while I hung back, scanning the other shoppers. Every time anyone got too close to the kids, my hand tightened around the pistol. If I didn't get over my paranoia, I'd be a basket case before we were done.

Emily acted as if everything were completely normal, although I noticed she also kept an eye on the other customers. She was one of those shoppers who had to examine every piece of merchandise before making a decision. I wanted to hurry her along, but figured she'd do her own thing no matter what I said.

By the time we finished in the grocery department there were two overflowing shopping carts. I paid with a credit card because I wasn't sure there was enough in my checking account to cover the total.

My nerves were strung tight as we moved through the parking lot and stowed the purchases in the trunk. Fortunately there weren't any sinister looking strangers near the car and no one attempted to grab the kids. However, I wasn't able to begin relaxing until we were on the highway.

\* \* \*

Dinner ran later than usual, but was worth the wait. Emily proved to be a great cook. She whipped up a fantastic chicken, broccoli and cheese casserole. I hadn't enjoyed a meal as much since Mom had died.

By the time we finished eating and washing the dishes, it was time to get the kids ready for bed. I helped Billy bathe before Emily went into the bathroom with Marie. There was quite a bit more splashing than when Marie bathed alone, and I figured Emily was getting her properly cleaned. When they came out, Marie almost sparkled.

"We're going to have to get your hair trimmed," Emily commented as she began brushing Marie's hair. "Not real short, but long hair isn't stylish, and there are too many snarls."

Marie had retreated into her shell, but I could tell she wasn't completely unhappy to have Mrs. Hall fussing over her.

Although Emily complained about her arthritis, she knelt with Billy and me for our nighttime prayers. When Marie remained aloof, I was afraid Emily might insist on her participation, but she surprised me by not saying anything.

After the kids were safely tucked in bed, Emily gathered her coat and purse. "You make certain all the doors and windows are bolted," she ordered. "And be sure to give those kids a nutritious breakfast. They need something warm in their tummies to start the day."

When I heard her car pull away, I collapsed onto the sofa, feeling emotionally drained. I wasn't sure how long I'd be able to take the pressure. If I were able to sleep at all, the pistol would be under my pillow and the shotgun within easy reach. I hoped that between us, Shadow and I would be able to keep the kids safe

# CHAPTER TWENTY-ONE

I t shouldn't have made any difference, but I couldn't get comfortable with the pistol under my pillow. When I moved it to the bedside table, I fell asleep almost immediately, and slept better than I had for several days. Tuesday morning I didn't feel completely refreshed, but my batteries had been partially charged.

For breakfast I selected the easiest meal available; frozen pancakes, heated in the microwave. They might not have met with Emily's approval, but at least it was a warm, filling breakfast.

As I watched Marie and Billy getting syrup all over their hands, faces, and clothing, I decided pancakes hadn't been the wisest choice.

"So, how did you like Mrs. Hall?" I asked.

"I hate her," Marie said angrily. "I hope she dies!"

Her burst of emotion startled me. I could have sworn Marie had been warming to Emily during the few hours they'd been together. Was this some sort of defense mechanism? Did Marie believe that by refusing to allow anyone to get close, she couldn't be disappointed or hurt?

"You don't want Mrs. Hall to die," I said. "It might take a little while to get used to her, but I think she's a very nice lady and she'll be a big help around here."

"She's a worthless bitch!" Marie shouted. "I hate her!"

"Marie! That's a bad word and I don't want you using it again." Marie glared at me. Without experience dealing with an angry child, I wished there was a definitive manual on child rearing, so I could check the index and find an answer for every situation.

"If you give Mrs. Hall a chance, I know you'll like her," I said. "She's already helped with the shopping, and you have to admit she's a better cook than I am."

"I won't ever like her!" Marie had begun to sob, like a bubble of repressed emotion had burst. "I hate her! She's a worthless bitch, just like my mother."

"You don't mean that," I said. The depth of Marie's pain and bitterness made me feel totally inadequate. "Your mother wasn't worthless."

"Yes she was!" Marie was sobbing so violently she could barely talk. "She never stopped people from hurting us, and Mrs. Hall won't keep the bad people away either!" She pushed back from the table, knocking over her chair, and ran from the room.

For a moment I couldn't do anything except stand with my mouth open. Jenny had obviously been a sorry example of motherhood, but I hadn't realized the magnitude of Marie's hostility. Had she been exposed to other women who had reinforced her negative view? Did she consider herself worthless? All I knew for certain was that Marie's outburst was beyond anything I was prepared to handle.

Billy had remained at the table, tears running down his cheeks, his body racked by sobs. Although I wanted to go after Marie and reassure her, Billy also needed to be comforted. I wrapped my arms around him so he could cry against my chest.

"There, there," I soothed. "Don't cry. It's going to be all right."

He pushed away and stood with his tiny fists held aggressively toward me. Although Marie's outburst frightened him, he was determined to protect his sister. "I won't let you hurt her," he sobbed.

I reached out to hug him again, but he backed away.

"I'm not going to hurt Marie," I promised. "She's upset, and we need to tell her everything will be all right." Obviously Billy wasn't convinced. The only response to anger he'd ever experienced had been more anger. "You can come with me and bring Shadow. You know he won't let me hurt Marie."

When we reached the living room, Shadow went directly to the hall closet, whining and scratching at the door. Marie was huddled in the far corner, partially hidden behind the coats.

"You can come out," I said, trying to sound comforting. "I know you're upset, but it's okay. No one is going to hurt you."

Marie cringed against the back wall, her arms raised to protect her face and head. All of her life adults had been instruments of control and pain. She had no reason to believe I wouldn't beat her.

"Don't be afraid. I'm not going to punish you." I instinctively realized it would be a mistake to try to touch her. My only option was let her stay in the closet until she was ready to come out. "If you feel safer in the closet, you can stay there as long as you want," I said. "Billy and I will clean up the breakfast dishes and leave you alone until you feel better."

"No," Billy shouted, crawling into the closet and snuggling against his sister. Shadow joined them, curling at their feet.

"Okay," I said, feeling like I had become the enemy. "I'm going to wash the dishes. You can both come out when you feel like it. Nothing bad is going to happen."

Leaving the closet door ajar, I went into the kitchen, and began clearing the table. Billy's spilled syrup had dripped onto the floor, creating a gooey puddle. I used the sponge mop to clean the spill and ended up mopping the entire floor. The last thing I needed was Emily scolding me for leaving a sticky mess.

The kids hadn't stirred from the closet by the time I finished cleaning up, and I wasn't sure what to do. I tried to remember how Mom had handled situations like this. When I had been a kid and something had upset me, I had generally run to my room to pout. After a few minutes I had always been willing to relent, but hadn't known how to gracefully ease off. Mom had always given me time to stew before she came up with an excuse to entice me out of my room. If it had worked for me, maybe Marie and Billy were waiting for the same opportunity Mom had given me.

"You know, it's a nice warm day," I said loud enough for them to hear. "Wouldn't you like some ice cream? If you guys are ready by the time I change my shoes, we can drive to the Dairy Queen and get a treat."

I made a production of going upstairs, waited a few minutes, and came back down. Both kids were perched on the living room sofa, a relieved Shadow sitting in front of them, grinning and wagging his tail. I hoped it meant Marie was giving me a chance to prove I wouldn't hurt her.

"Okay, let's clean the syrup off your hands and then go get a treat," I said, acting like the incident had never happened.

\* \* \*

When Mrs. Hall arrived at two o'clock, I decided not to tell her about the breakfast episode. We had enough to worry about. Right now Pusher was a more immediate concern than Marie's outburst.

"The kids have a catechism class at six-thirty," I said.

"I was wondering if you'd have sense enough to think of religious training," Emily said. "But catechism classes are Mondays and Wednesdays and they're in recess for the summer. I should know after having taught third grade catechism for more years than I care to remember."

"Sister Joan is giving them private lessons until they get caught up to the other kids," I explained.

Emily nodded, as if that made perfect sense. "I'll be sure to have dinner early enough. Now you go into your study and do whatever it is you do. I'll take care of Marie and Billy for the rest of the afternoon."

I retreated into the study as Emily opened the back door and called. "Marie! Billy! Come in the house. It's time you learned how to take care of yourselves."

"I can take care of me and Billy," Marie said. "We don't need you."

"Don't give me any sass, young lady. The first thing you have to learn is to listen to me and keep quiet. Is that clear?"

I didn't hear any response from the kids, and could picture them standing rigid with their mouths open, completely awed.

"Don't dawdle. We're going upstairs and putting away all that clothing we bought yesterday."

As they climbed the stairs, I booted up my computer and tried to concentrate on Lee Manufacturing's software program. I hadn't accomplished anything for several days and couldn't afford to lose the contract. With the pistol on the printer stand and the shotgun standing next to the bookcase, I felt fairly secure, and was able to actually be productive.

"Uncle Jon," Emily called, sounding upset. "Would you please come here for a moment?"

I saved my computer file and trudged upstairs, wonder what was wrong. There hadn't been enough time for them to put away all the clothing.

Emily was standing in Marie's room, facing me with hands on her hips. The kids had moved to the far side of the room, like they wanted to distance themselves from whatever was going to happen.

"I understand you've been making the children's beds every morning." The way she said it made me feel like she was a cop accusing me of a criminal act.

"Sometimes I help them straighten things," I admitted. After Marie and Billy had moved in, I had shown them how to make their beds. When they did a sloppy job, or neglected to make their beds at all, I took them back to their rooms and supervised the chore. It hadn't been more than a couple of days before I had decided it was easier to just make the beds myself.

"Isn't that just like a man, taking the easy way out," Emily scolded. "No one ever said being a parent was going to be fun and games. You aren't doing the kids a favor if you don't teach them to do things for themselves."

I was embarrassed, but didn't intend to give up without a struggle. "No one has ever taken care of them and maybe they could do with a little pampering. They certainly don't need me harping at them every day."

"Hogwash! Just because they used to live in a pig sty isn't any reason to keep them in one."

"Our house isn't exactly a pig sty," I protested.

"Well, it'll get that way if you don't teach them to take care of themselves and accept responsibility? It gives children a sense of pride and belonging if they're productive members of the family."

She turned to Marie and Billy. "Your rooms are a mess and your beds haven't been properly made."

"I did good," Billy complained, looking as if he might begin crying.

Marie glared at Mrs. Hall, but didn't say anything. They might sometimes complain and groan when I gave orders, but they never questioned instructions from Emily.

Billy's protest made no impression. "Hogwash," she said. "First you're going to pick up all those dirty clothes and put them in the hamper where they belong."

Both kids gathered up the socks, underwear and jeans that lay scattered around each room. Emily made them check under the beds for anything that might have ended up there. When they had it all, Emily marched them to the clothes hamper and had them put in their bundles. "That's where dirty clothing belongs, not on the floor. From now on, you'll pick up after yourselves or I'll know the reason why."

Then she pointed at the toys and books still on the floor. "Everything must have a place. When you're done with something you will put it where it belongs. Responsible people don't leave things lying around where innocent folks can fall over them and break a leg?"

She waited impatiently while they picked up and put away every item. "That's better. Now at least we can walk without tripping over something," she said. "Now I'll show you how to properly make a bed."

"I made mine good," Billy suggested hopefully.

"Balderdash. You can't look at that bed and say it's properly made. Pay attention while I show you how to do it, because if I find you haven't done a proper job, you'll do it over until you get it right."

Emily pulled all Marie's bedding back and began with the sheet, pulling it snug to the top of the bed and smoothing it from side to side. She did the same with the blanket, and folded the top of the sheet over the top of the blanket. Finally she smoothed the bedspread over the bed, fluffed the pillows and covered them with the spread.

"That wasn't so hard, was it?" Emily deliberately pulled back the covers and sheet, balled up the pillows, and turned to Marie. "You make the bed again, like I just showed you."

For a moment I though Marie would rebel, but she must have realized she wouldn't be able to resist Mrs. Hall.

It took a few minutes, with reminders from Mrs. Hall, but when Marie was finished, Emily gave her a big hug. "See, doesn't that look nice. You did very well for the first time. That's the way I expect you to make your bed every morning."

Marie didn't say anything, but I could see she was pleased at the praise. Maybe Emily was right. The kids would develop a sense of pride by helping themselves.

Emily went through the same procedure in Billy's room. "Doesn't that look much better?" she said when he finished his bed. "It's so much nicer climbing into a well-made bed at night."

Both kids were beaming from Emily's praise.

When they were finished upstairs Emily and the kids moved into the kitchen. Although I couldn't understand the words, I heard Emily delivering a non-stop monologue while she rattled pots and pans. Pretty soon the delicious aroma wafting from the kitchen reminded me I was hungry.

After dinner Emily washed faces and hands, while I slipped on a light jacket and put the pistol in my pocket. It felt sacrilegious taking a gun to church, but I had no intention of leaving the kids unprotected.

# CHAPTER TWENTY-TWO

ister Joan took immediate charge when we arrived for our first catechism lesson, making it clear I wasn't welcome in the classroom. "You can wait here, or you can come back," she said, closing the door in my face. "We'll be done at seven-thirty sharp."

I didn't see any point in telling Sister about Pusher's threat. It was problematical whether drug people would attempt kidnapping the kids from a church building, but I wasn't about to take a chance. I sat in an empty classroom across the hall, and waited impatiently, never taking my hand off the Beretta.

At seven thirty-five the classroom door opened and Sister Joan came out.

"So, how'd it go?" I asked.

"Very well for the first time," Sister said, sounding upbeat. "Billy was cooperative, but I don't think Marie was quite in the spirit of things." She put her arm around Marie's shoulders. "It was only the first lesson, and you'll feel better about class the next time, won't you?" When Marie didn't respond, Sister handed me a small booklet. "This is the basic text we'll be using. It would be helpful if you went over the material with the children before our next session."

As we were driving home I asked how they'd liked the class. As usual, Marie didn't respond, but Billy seemed excited. "It was fun. Sister Joan told us stories about Jesus when he was a little boy, and how God loves all little boys and girls."

"Anything else?" I asked.

"She taught us why God made us," Billy said.

"And why did God make you?" I pulled into the driveway and

turned so I could see over the seat.

Billy squeezed his eyes shut and searched his memory for the correct answer. "God made us to know and love Him in this world and to be with Him in the next," he said proudly.

"It's a goddamned lie!" Marie hissed.

I bit my tongue to keep from criticizing her language. "You don't really believe that." I said.

"Yes I do. God doesn't give a shit about us. It's all a lie."

"Why do you believe God is a lie?" I asked. Marie had the ability to shock me every time she revealed the extent of her pain.

"When I was little Mommy took me to church." I could see Marie was struggling not to cry. "She told me God loved me and if I prayed to Him He would protect me. When my uncles hurt me I prayed for God to make them stop and He didn't. And I prayed for Mommy to make them stop and she didn't. God doesn't care about me because I'm no fucking good."

Suddenly tears were streaming down Marie's cheeks and she was sobbing. My heart ached for every belief that had failed her. How could I convince her God was real and that He loved her? How could I reassure Marie that in her warped way, Jenny had loved her daughter?

"Marie, that isn't true," I said. "You're a dear, sweet girl. I love you and God loves you and I'm sure your mother loved you very much."

"No she didn't. She hated me. Mommy said if I hadn't been born things would have been different. I ruined her life because I'm no fucking good."

If there had been a way for me to take away Marie's pain and put it in my own heart, I would gladly have done so. How could Jenny have said such a horrible thing to her daughter? How could I explain that alcohol and drugs had destroyed her mother's mind until she had said and done things she didn't really mean? I reached out and pulled her to me, hugging her against my chest. For once, Marie didn't resist.

"Your mother didn't mean what she said. You have to believe

God really loves you, and I love you. You're a very precious, wonderful little girl. You're important to me and Billy and Mrs. Hall. I don't know why God didn't answer your prayers before, but He's answered them now. He brought you to live here and He gave me the job of protecting you. I promise no one is going to hurt you ever again."

I held Marie until she stopped sobbing. Before we went into the house I wiped her face with my handkerchief, but her eyes were red rimmed and she was still sniffling. Emily looked at me with a question in her eyes, but didn't comment. It was only after we had tucked the kids in bed that she confronted me.

"What did you do to make that child cry?" she demanded.

After I told her about Marie's tirade against God, Emily had tears of her own.

"That little girl has so much pain," she said. "Jon, we have to do something to help her believe again."

"I know. I'm trying, but it's going to take time. We have an appointment with the psychologist tomorrow. Maybe Dr. Scott can give me some ideas about how we can help both of them."

"I don't have much faith in head doctors and all their mumbo jumbo, but if she can do anything for our children, I'm all for it."

I hadn't missed Emily referring to Marie and Billy as our children. It made me feel good to know she had taken a personal interest.

"I don't know when we'll be back from the appointment," I said. "You can come in late tomorrow, or take the whole day off."

"Of course I'm not going to do either," she snapped, resuming her usual abrupt manner. "Without everyone tramping through the house I'll be able to scrub the kitchen floor and properly clean the bathrooms."

When Emily left I trudged upstairs, wanting nothing more than the oblivion of sleep. It had been a hard day and I was emotionally drained. Twice Marie had broken out of her shell and I'd seen the raw pain in her heart. I was angry with Jenny and all the people who had injured Marie, but I was also overwhelmed with my own guilt. For nine years I hadn't done a damned thing to help her.

# CHAPTER TWENTY-THREE

Psychological Associates of Campbell was located in a sprawling, single story building on Clifton Court, a cul-de-sac of medical and dental practices. The generous waiting room had a pleasant atmosphere, with colorful landscapes hanging on the pastel walls and an abundance of live plants on the end tables between comfortable chairs.

While Marie and Billy sat passively in the waiting room chairs, I registered with the receptionist, filled in the required paperwork, and asked if I could talk with Dr. Scott before she saw the children.

I had barely settled into a chair when the receptionist called my name. I didn't feel comfortable leaving the kids unprotected in the waiting area, but it wasn't likely Pusher's thugs would bust into the office, guns blazing. If they even suspected we were in Campbell, it would be more reasonable for them to ambush us in the parking lot.

If I had been expecting a psychologist to look like the stereotypical librarian, Dr. Scott was a pleasant surprise. She was tall, slender, very attractive, and appeared younger than I had anticipated.

"Good afternoon, Mr. Wilson," she said, flashing a brilliant smile. "Please have a seat."

There was no desk, and the furniture was grouped to resemble a living room. The setting was obviously designed to encourage relaxation, but it didn't work for me. I sat nervously on the edge of an easy chair.

"I realize this appointment is for Marie and Billy," I explained. "But as you know, I have temporary custody—which hopefully will become permanent in ninety days—and I've got a million questions."

Dr. Scott selected a chair across from me. "I understand. Actually I wanted to talk with you. Helping Marie and Billy will require an extended series of visits, and your cooperation will be essential."

"I intend to do everything possible for the kids, but first I have to tell you about something critical that came up over the weekend." I gave a brief summary of Detective Kincaid's warning. "I haven't mentioned this to the kids because Billy wouldn't understand, and Marie would be more frightened than she already is."

"I agree." Dr. Scott's expression remained unconcerned, like she didn't consider the danger serious. "We have more than enough issues to address without worrying the children about something that may never happen."

"Were you aware the police contacted CPS and Children's Court for permission to interview Marie and Billy? The cops want to find out if the kids know where Jenny hid the drugs and money. According to Detective Kincaid, the court refused permission until you agree the kids are ready."

Dr. Scott looked startled, as if she were more disturbed about police interrogation then the threat to the kid's lives.

"I hadn't been aware of any of this," she said. "However, I agree with the court. At this point an interrogation would definitely be stressful and counterproductive."

"I suspect you'll eventually hear from the police because they'll be pushing for permission. Detective Kincaid believes the only way to positively protect the kids from Pusher is to take the drugs and money out of circulation."

"I doubt whether that's true, but I won't be giving permission for anything that would be detrimental to Marie and Billy." She changed the subject, like she'd already dismissed the danger. "You did say there were questions, didn't you?"

Her blasé attitude made me wonder if she was the psychologist we needed. She should have taken the threat seriously since she had to be aware of the type of scumbags who had been around Jenny and the kids. If Marie and Billy hadn't needed immediate psychological help, I might have walked out. However, I decided to withhold judgment until this session was over.

"In the handful of days I've had the kids, I can see an improvement in Billy. I think he's beginning to adjust to his new environment, but Marie is another story." I briefly told Dr. Scott about Marie remaining in some sort of impenetrable shell most of the time, her fear of sexual abuse the first night, her foul language, her anger and antagonism toward Mrs. Hall, and her tirade against God. Dr. Scott listened intently, not giving any indication of her feelings.

"I read your initial evaluation and it helps me understand some of their behavior," I said, "but I was hoping you could provide additional insights."

"I'll certainly do my best," Dr. Scott said. "I'm not surprised Marie is resisting her new environment. After so many years of fear and abuse, it's difficult for her to believe she's safe and protected. There have been so many broken promises; it's likely she fully expects this new situation to deteriorate into violence. However, I've only seen Marie and Billy once. Until I've had an opportunity to evaluate them in depth, my insights have to be very general."

"Anything would be helpful. Sometimes I feel totally inadequate, as if I'm way over my head."

"That's understandable. Abused children have special problems and their personalities are more complicated than most people realize. You appear to be quite concerned about Marie's behavior, but only briefly mentioned Billy."

"I'm not ignoring Billy," I explained, "but he really hasn't been a problem. Other than an unhealthy dependence on his sister, he doesn't seem much different from a normal five-year-old. Of course there are problems with his social skills, but he's been open and eager to learn."

"I would have expected that," Dr. Scott agreed. "Billy suffered torture and abuse, but I believe Marie shielded him from much of the ill treatment. Although he'll always have psychological scars, they aren't nearly as deep as they would have been without his sister's support and protection. Even in the short time I talked with him, I saw every indication his adjustment to being normal should be fairly rapid."

"But not Marie?" I asked.

"I didn't say that. Marie will require a number of sessions before I can make a prognosis. I'd prefer not to comment without a stronger basis to judge."

"How long will that take?"

"Honestly, I don't know. If things go well, I can probably give you an estimate after a few consultations. However, in the meantime I can provide some general insights concerning the problems you mentioned."

"I'd appreciate that," I said.

"As to their street language, I'm sure you're aware we all develop our vocabularies from our environment. Children don't want to be different, so they make every effort to fit into the world around them. Normal children, who have been exposed to proper influences, use foul language for the shock value. I suspect Marie and Billy have heard gutter language all their lives and simply don't realize it isn't appropriate. If you're patient, don't get angry, and provide them with an acceptable vocabulary, I believe the inappropriate language will simply disappear."

"Actually, we've made progress along those lines." I told Dr. Scott about my bad word, good word strategy.

"I'm impressed," Dr. Scott said. "That was an excellent idea. It'll help them correct their vocabulary without constant censure. You obviously understand Marie and Billy need love and support more than criticism."

"I'm trying."

"I know you are," she agreed. "On that first night, Marie feared sexual exploitation because that's the only experiences she's had with men. She's never perceived adults in a protective role, and it'll take time for her to feel secure. It's encouraging that Billy hasn't shown any fear toward you. All the males they've known have been abusive and used their superior strength to dominate the children."

"One reason I hired Mrs. Hall is to provide a strong female role model. She exudes a sense of security and strength," I said. "What shocked me was Marie's vehement reaction to her."

"Marie's reaction to Mrs. Hall was predicable. From what you've told me, Mrs. Hall appears to be a commanding personality. I suspect Marie is fearful Mrs. Hall will assume the dominant female position, and upset her relationship with Billy. I don't know when Jennifer abdicated her parental duties, but from an early age Marie was forced to do all the things expected of a parent. Perhaps from the time Billy was born—when Marie was only four-years-old—she may have changed diapers and assumed the responsibility for feeding Billy when food was available. Billy may be overly dependent on his sister, but the mother role is even more important to Marie."

"A nine-year-old assuming the role of a mother couldn't be healthy," I protested.

"No, it isn't, but Marie believes her motherly role is the only thing giving her value. When other successes give her a sense of worth, she'll voluntarily relinquish her need to be Billy's mother."

"That makes sense," I agreed. "What sort of successes did you have in mind?"

"Nothing spectacular, I assure you. Giving Marie chores and providing a sense of being needed is a great start. Praise for all accomplishments, no matter how small, will do wonders for her self-esteem."

"If I praise Marie and give her household responsibilities, she'll learn to accept Mrs. Hall?"

"It'll help, but like all things with children, the problem is more complex. Marie not only fears men because of repeated sexual abuse, but experience has taught her women are weak and helpless. She saw men dominate her mother, who either couldn't, or wouldn't, protect the children. Children need to see that adults are in charge, that they're fair, and will protect them. It'll take time for Marie to picture any woman, or any adult, in a strong protective role."

"Does any of this have to do with Marie's defensive shell?"

"It has everything to do with it. Since children are powerless to defend themselves against abusive adults they dissociate in order to survive the pain and degradation. Basically it's an effort to bear the intolerable by stripping away the emotional content. I know it's difficult to understand, but children close their minds and retreat into a state of denial where they can believe the awful things are happening to someone else. For many children, if they didn't dissociate they wouldn't be able to retain their sanity. However, while the emotions aroused by abuse and rejection are locked away in this protective denial, they don't just sit there. They earn emotional interest. It's like pressure building in a boiler without a safety valve. In some ways her relationship with Billy has been her safety valve, her fragile connection to a sense of value."

"Are you saying Marie's problems stem from a feeling of being worthless?"

"Not really. All her psychological problems are related, but the issue of self-worth is complicated, and I'm afraid I'm oversimplifying it. All children want to be accepted and believe they're worthwhile human beings. Children who are repeatedly abused physically and verbally are plagued by humiliation and shame. They believe there is a reason for being badly treated; that if they were worthwhile or loveable, adults wouldn't abuse them. Consequently they begin to believe they're responsible in some way for the cruelty. They tell themselves this is happening because 'I'm bad' or 'Or no one cares about me, so I must be worthless'."

"I can't believe any of the mistreatment was Marie's fault." I said. The more Dr. Scott attempted to explain, the more my heart ached for both children.

"I'm speaking more of generalities than specifically of Marie's case. Certainly the abuse wasn't her fault, but she isn't ready to believe she didn't trigger it in some way. Remember, the dissociation is the result of nine years of brutalization, and won't be resolved in a few days. It's going to take time, patience, and love to penetrate her shell. Give her respect and take her seriously as a participant in managing her life. The anger concerning Mrs. Hall and God is a positive indication she's begun to respond. Any emotion—joy, sorrow, anger—is a crack in the shell. I must warn you, though, when children begin to come out of their shells, they frequently behave worse than before. They're testing whether their behavior will trigger abuse, or whether they actually are safe and loved."

"Believe me, I've seen the anguish and the lack of trust."

"Bringing them for counseling is a step in the right direction. We need to encourage them to talk, to bring their pain out in the open where we can deal with it. That's my job, and to a certain extent, your job. Show them patience and love. Don't expect too much too soon. Positive male and female role models will be a major contributing influence. Make a point of praising every constructive thing they do. Your principal job will be to elevate their self-esteem."

"That's a big responsibility, considering what you've told me."

"Yes it is. But I have every confidence you can handle it. I can see you really care, and that's the first step in reaching them." Dr. Scott glanced at her wristwatch. "We're almost out of time and I'd really like to visit with the children for a few minutes. I realize the trip from Westport is an inconvenience, but at least for the next month or so, the children need to see me three times a week. Perhaps you can set up a series of appointments with my receptionist while I talk with them."

Dr. Scott came to the waiting room with me and collected Marie and Billy while I walked up to the reception desk. After our discussion, I felt better about her as the children's psychologist, but her lack of concern about their physical safety still bothered me. I decided we would continue with her for the time being, but I would do whatever necessary to keep the kids alive long enough to learn there were things in the world like love and security and happiness. If that meant changing doctors, I would do it.

There was no reason to suspect that Pusher knew the children were seeing a psychologist, but maybe he had sources in CPS. If we established a predictable routine, and he learned about our visits to Dr. Scott, it would be easier for him to get at the kids. Even as I thought about it, I realized I was paranoid, but I wasn't going to take any chances.

The receptionist must have thought I was eccentric when I set appointments for the next month, alternating days and staggering times.

When we left the building, I stood in the entrance for a moment scanning the parking lot. Although I didn't see anyone lurking in ambush, I kept my hand on the pistol as we walked to the car.

It was nearly four when we arrived home. Emily was bustling around the kitchen and Shadow was frantically happy to see us. The house was filled with the strong smell of detergent and floor wax, overlaid with the aroma of something delicious in the oven. I wondered if the kids experienced the same sense of security and warmth I felt at being in our own home.

# CHAPTER TWENTY-FOUR

Thursday morning rain was being driven against the west side of the house by a thunderstorm wind. It was not a fit day to be outdoors, but it was cozy and dry inside. I was feeling lazy and was forcing myself to be productive when Mrs. Henderson phoned.

"Ann Riley will be conducting the court ordered inspection this morning," she announced. "She'll be leaving here in a few minutes and should be at your house in less than an hour."

Thunder rumbled in the background and sent a wave of static through the phone line. "We'll be here," I promised.

Mrs. Henderson must have been aware of Pusher's threat, since Detective Kincaid had asked CPS for permission to interview the kids. When she didn't mention it, I didn't bring it up. She couldn't know Kincaid had warned me, so it did make me wonder why she didn't feel it necessary to alert me. Maybe she was hoping something would happen to cause the court to terminate my custody. It must have been a bitter pill for her to learn the Blackmans had been a scam.

I considered calling Emily and asking her to come early enough to be available during the inspection, but decided against it. There was nothing she could do. The house was already spotless, the breakfast dishes had been washed, and the beds were straightened. Shadow had left a few muddy tracks in the kitchen when he returned from his morning duties, but I'd already wiped them up.

Marie and Billy were drawing pictures at the dining room table, papers and materials scattered over the surface. Neither of the kids had welts or bruises and even a casual observer could see they weren't being starved. It looked like the ideal domestic scene of a happy family on a dreary day.

I didn't believe Mrs. Henderson would be setting us up for Pusher, but there was always the possibility someone would follow Mrs. Riley. Even though I realized it was paranoid, I wore my shirttail out to conceal the pistol I shoved into the back of my waistband.

When a gray sedan pulled up to the curb I watched until the woman driver popped open her umbrella and hurried up the walk toward the house. No other cars had entered our rainy street, so I was pretty certain Mrs. Riley hadn't been followed. As usual, Shadow beat me to the door and was jumping up and down with excitement. I took a firm grip on his collar when I answered the bell.

The woman standing on the porch was middle-aged and a bit overweight, but had a pleasant face and friendly smile. When she didn't whip a gun out of her purse, I figured it was safe to invite her inside.

"Good morning, Mr. Wilson." She collapsed her umbrella and stepped into the hallway. "I'm Ann Riley. I believe Mrs. Henderson called earlier to let you know about my inspection." She didn't appear intimidated when Shadow nearly pulled my arm out of the socket attempting his normal, frantic greeting. "What a beautiful dog." She held her hand so Shadow could sniff it, and then briefly scratched his head.

"He does get excited when he meets new people," I said. "Let me take care of him and we can talk." I couldn't put Shadow outside in the rain, so I closed him in my study.

"I should have done that before you arrived," I apologized when I returned. "Can I take your coat?" Even after the short walk from car to porch, her raincoat was soaked, the water dripping small puddles on the floor.

"Thank you." Mrs. Riley slipped out of her coat, which I hung in the hall closet when I stood her umbrella beside the door.

"This is all new to me," I said nervously. "What do we do during an inspection?"

"Inspect is probably too harsh a description of my visit," she said, flashing a warm smile. "Really, all I want to do is visit with you and the children for a few minutes."

Considering Mrs. Henderson's attitude toward my custody, I couldn't help but believe the inspection would be a bit more critical than a simple visit. Mrs. Riley probably had orders to discover evidence of abuse and neglect.

"Please don't be nervous," she said. "I simply have to verify Marie and Billy are being properly cared for and supervised."

"Marie and Billy are in the dining room," I said leading the way. "Kids, I'd like you to meet Mrs. Riley. She's from Child Protective Services and has come to see how you're doing."

Marie glared briefly at Mrs. Riley, and then concentrated on her drawing as if the social worker wasn't there. Billy held up a page of garish circles and scrawls. "I made a pretty picture," he said proudly.

"You certainly did," Mrs. Riley agreed, examining the picture. "Is that the sun shining on your new house?"

All I could see were scrawls of color, but Billy looked seriously at his picture and must have decided Mrs. Riley was right. He pointed at a blob of color in the lower corner of the drawing. "This is our car."

"It's a lovely car." Mrs. Riley obviously had a better imagination that I did, because nothing on the paper even remotely resembled an automobile. Perhaps deciphering childish scrawls was a skill I would acquire.

She walked around the table and looked over Marie's shoulder. "That's really very good," she said. "You're an excellent artist."

Normally Marie glowed when her artwork was praised, but since Mrs. Riley had arrived she had retreated into her shell and simply ignored the social worker. Some of Marie's drawings were bizarre and I leaned over to check this one. She was doing a beautiful job of copying a magazine picture of a barn and a field of flowers.

"Both the children are talented artists," I said. "We've got more pictures in the kitchen if you'd like to see them?"

"Yes I would." We stepped into the kitchen and Mrs. Riley examined the dozen pictures held to the refrigerator by little magnets. She oohed and aahed appropriately, loud enough for the kids to hear.

"Did you want to talk with the children now, or would you like to see their rooms?" I asked.

"Why don't we look at the living areas first," Mrs. Riley suggested.

She didn't make any comments as she walked through the bedrooms checking the closets and dresser drawers. No one could complain the kids didn't have enough clothing because Emily had made certain the closets and dressers were stuffed full. When Mrs. Riley examined the bathroom, I wondered if she was counting to see if there were enough toothbrushes. I breathed a prayer of gratitude for Emily, confident the kids had an excess of everything CPS would consider important.

We had finished the upstairs inspection when I heard a sharp noise that sounded like a slap, and Billy began to cry. "Excuse me," I said, rushing toward the dining room.

I scooped Billy into my arms. "What happened?"

"Marie hit me," Billy wailed.

"Why did you hit your little brother?" I asked, attempting to keep my voice calm. From personal experience I knew siblings had conflicts, but Marie and Billy had never even had an argument. This was not a good time for their first squabble.

"He broke the goddamned crayon," Marie said, her voice emotionless, matter of fact.

"Goddamned is a bad word," I said. "You've got plenty of crayons."

"He broke the one I was going to use."

"That's no reason to hit him. We've talked about this before. You don't hit people just because they do something you don't like."

"He's a stupid ass. He did it on purpose." Marie picked up her drawing and began tearing it into pieces. "That sonofabitch ruined my picture."

"Marie! Sonofabitch is another bad word. You know we don't use those words in this house. And we don't hit people. Tell Billy you're sorry, and then go to your room to think it over." I could sense Mrs. Riley standing behind me and visualized her putting big black marks on her report.

"I hate you!" Marie shouted. She threw the torn picture on the table and ran from the room.

I suspected she was testing me, just as Dr. Scott had predicted, but it was a lousy time for her to act up. Or maybe, in Marie's opinion it was the perfect time.

Billy had stopped crying so I put him down. "Marie didn't mean to hurt you," I said. "She was just upset. It's going to be all right now."

Billy had gotten over his hurt and must have felt confident I wouldn't punish Marie because he climbed onto his chair and began working on a new picture.

I turned to Mrs. Riley, feeling embarrassed over the incident. "Sorry for the interruption. I guess the rainy weather is making the kids crabby. They do a lot better when they can run around outside and burn off excess energy."

She smiled like she understood. "My kids have been known to have a squabble or two."

At that moment I didn't care how she interpreted the incident. Marie was hurting and was more important than any inspection. No matter how many black marks it would cause, I realized Marie needed me to reassure her.

"If you don't mind, Mrs. Riley, I have to talk with Marie. It shouldn't take long. Maybe you can visit with Billy for a few minutes."

"I understand. Take your time. While you're gone, Billy can teach me how to draw such nice pictures."

When I entered Marie's room she was lying on the bed, hugging her Teddy Bear and staring at the ceiling.

"Are you going to send me away with that bitch?" she asked, her voice emotionless.

I sat on the edge of the bed. "Of course not. You shouldn't have hit Billy or used bad words, but you're my little girl now and I love you. I've told you before I won't ever send you away."

"You had that bitch come here to take us back," she insisted.

I didn't know whether Marie was still testing me or whether she actually believed Mrs. Riley was going to haul them off somewhere. There was so much I didn't understand about her fears. Somehow I had to make her realize she was secure and loved unconditionally.

"Bitch is a bad word," I said patiently. "The lady's name is Mrs. Riley and Child Protective Services sent her to see whether Mrs. Hall and I are taking good care of you and Billy."

"I don't believe you." There was an undercurrent I didn't recognize. Was it hopelessness or a subtle plea for reassurance? "You're going to send us away because we're no fuckin' good."

"You and Billy are wonderful kids and I love you both very much. Do you think Mrs. Hall and I would have given you this nice room and bought new clothes if we didn't want you to stay here forever?"

Marie didn't say a word, but she turned her back to me and I think she was beginning to cry.

"Mrs. Riley is here because she wants you to be happy in your new home," I explained. "She's going to be asking questions, and you can tell her anything you want. If you don't feel like talking, you don't have to. No matter what, I won't let anyone take you away from me." I didn't know what else to say. "You think about it for a few minutes before she comes up."

When I returned to the dining room, Mrs. Riley was seated beside Billy, watching him make patterns on a sheet of paper. "How's it going?" I asked.

"We're having a great time," she said. "Billy is a sweet little boy, and a wonderful artist."

Billy was beaming from the praise. "Yes, he is," I agreed. "Did you have enough time with him?"

"We did beautifully for a first visit. Is Marie all right?" She sounded genuinely concerned.

"I think so. Considering the circumstances it might be better if you visited in her room."

"That would be perfect. Is she's ready to talk with me?"

"I don't think there'll be a problem. Marie gets over her anger very quickly." I crossed my fingers behind my back and offered a silent prayer that I was right.

"Good. Then I might as well talk with her right now."

"Billy, you show Mrs. Riley to Marie's room and then come right back downstairs. Remember to tell your sister you're sorry for breaking her crayon."

Billy ran ahead, tugging at Mrs. Riley's hand and I waited in the living room. In a moment Billy came downstairs and returned to his drawings.

The social worker's visit with Marie turned into more than half an hour, and I was a nervous wreck by the time they came down. Marie sat at the table and resumed drawing as if nothing had happened. I would have given a year's pay to know what they had talked about, or whether Marie had even talked.

"I had a very nice visit with the children," Mrs. Riley said. She sounded sincere, but I was pretty certain the first inspection had been a disaster. "They both seem to be adjusting quite well."

"I think they're doing great," I said trying to sound confident. "I couldn't have asked for better children. Is there anything else you want to see, or do you have any questions?"

"No, I believe we've covered everything. I must compliment you on your housekeeping. You have a much neater home than mine. Of course my children are younger, but it seems I can never keep up with them. Sometimes I believe floors were invented so kids would have a place to put things."

"I can't take credit for the house. I wanted the children to have a positive female role model and we needed a woman's touch around here, so I hired a housekeeper who comes every weekday from two until nine. I'm sorry you missed meeting her. Mrs. Hall has raised five children of her own, and has been a great help taking care of Marie and Billy."

"Yes, I'd have loved to meet her. Maybe next time. Goodbye,

Marie. Billy." Mrs. Riley called.

Billy looked up from his picture and called, "Goodbye." Marie didn't respond.

I helped Mrs. Riley with her coat and watched her back to her car. The rain had let up some, but it still wasn't a fit day to be outside.

I had wanted to ask about her report, but decided what I didn't know wouldn't hurt me. There was nothing I could do to improve her impressions or how she treated the crayon incident. Since she had children of her own, I hoped she understood about sibling flare-ups. If this inspection came back to haunt me, I would simply have to deal with it at the appropriate time.

It was that night Marie had her first nightmare.

# CHAPTER TWENTY-FIVE

I was in my study at ten p.m. when Shadow came downstairs and nudged me a couple of times, making an urgent whining noise. He generally didn't disturb me unless there was something important in his dog world, like a pressing need to go outside. Since the rain had kept him indoors all day, I figured he probably did need to relieve himself.

"Just give me a minute, boy, and I'll let you out."

Shadow continued nudging and whining, which was unusual for such a patient dog. I finally gave up trying to concentrate, and pushed away from the computer. "Okay," I said. "One last trip outside before we go to bed."

Instead of his usual rush toward the back door, he took my hand in his mouth and gently, but insistently pulled me toward the stairs. Instantly I realized there must be something wrong with the kids. I took the stairs two at a time with Shadow leading the way directly into Marie's room.

Although the bathroom light was always left on so the kids could find their way if they got up during the night, the illumination didn't do much to brighten Marie's bedroom. I had to wait a moment for my eyes to adjust to the darkness.

Marie was crying softly, her face pressed against her Teddy Bear to muffle the sobs. Her forehead was hot and slick with perspiration. Had she caught some type of bug? Should I rush her to the emergency room? Should I call Emily and ask her advice? Maybe night sweats were normal for kids.

"What's wrong, sweetheart?" I asked sitting on the edge of the bed. Marie turned her back and curled into a fetal position. "What's wrong? I'm here to help."

Marie wasn't acting as if she were sick, but more like a frightened child. I gently stroked her damp hair. "I love you, Marie. Did you have a bad dream?"

She didn't answer, but her sobs were lessening, and I could feel her beginning to relax under my touch. "If you want to talk about the dream, I'm here."

After several minutes, her breathing assumed a regular rhythm and I knew she'd fallen asleep. There were so many things I didn't know, and children's bad dreams were one of them. I don't remember ever having a nightmare when I was a kid, but my bad dreams during the last couple of days had been terrifying. If I'd suffered nightmares just reading about her abuse, Marie's dreams must have been a hundred times worse. Maybe I couldn't control her fears, but if the nightmare returned, I could make certain she wouldn't wake up alone in the dark.

I tiptoed across the hall to Billy's room. He was breathing quietly and seemed at peace, although he had kicked off his covers. I pulled the blanket up to his chin and kissed him on the forehead. Then I carried Mom's old rocking chair from my bedroom and placed it beside Marie's bed. Shadow curled up at my feet; satisfied he had done his duty and could safely let me take over.

Once during the night Marie moaned softly and tossed under the covers, but when I stroked her head she quieted. No matter how much I wanted to ease her suffering, there was nothing I could do except rock and pray and hope her nightmare wouldn't return.

I will always believe Marie's bad dream saved our lives.

Although I tried to stay awake, I must have dozed because the faint sound of breaking glass woke me. Feeling groggy and disoriented, I wasn't sure whether I'd actually heard something or if the noise had been part of a dream. The bedside clock indicated it was a few minutes past two. I listened intently, but there was only the soft patter of rain against the window.

Satisfied the noise had been a dream, I had begun to nod off again when Shadow growled deep in his throat. I reached down to pet him when I heard a kitchen chair bumping the table. There was definitely someone in the house. Suddenly I was wide-awake. Pusher's thugs had come for the kids.

As I moved into the hallway, I cussed myself for being careless. I'd left the pistol and shotgun in my study when I'd rushed upstairs. Although it wasn't my weapon of choice, I tiptoed into my bedroom and grabbed the rifle from the closet.

My heart was pounding and I was breathing in shallow drafts. I'd never faced killers, and I was so frightened I was trembling. I forced myself to take a couple of deep, calming breaths.

As I passed the bathroom, I eased the door shut, figuring it wasn't a good idea to be silhouetted by a light behind me.

At the top of the stairs I paused and listened. I put my hand on Shadow to silence his growls, and heard the quiet sounds of two or more people moving cautiously through the house.

"Did you hear that?" a voice whispered from the living room.

"Hear what?" a deeper voice replied.

"Sounded like a dog growling. No one told us he had a goddamned dog."

"Shut up before you wake everyone."

I didn't have the courage to go downstairs, so I crouched on the top step and waited.

The street light in front of the house cast a soft glow through the living room windows, exposing a dark shadow as a man stepped into the vestibule. I levered a round into the rifle's chamber and called out.

"Who's there?"

A blinding flash and ear-shattering roar erupted from the foot of the stairs. I felt a stinging sensation as the bullet grazed my cheek and embedded in the wall behind me. If I'd been standing, it would have struck me in the chest.

With a fierce bark, Shadow bounded down the stairs. The intruder yelled and tried to back away, but the dog went for his throat and they both fell against the front door.

I cringed when two more gunshots came from the living

room, although I realized they weren't aimed at me. Shadow yelped and the intruder grunted.

"Damnit, you asshole, you shot me."

The wounded man pushed away from Shadow's limp form and staggered toward the living room. I fired two shots at the retreating figure, but knew I was shaking too badly to hit anything. Behind me both kids were screaming and sobbing. Billy ran across the hall to Marie's room.

"The sonofabitch has a gun," a voice moaned from the living room. "Let's get the fuck out of here."

Someone bumped into the dining room table and cursed. Then the back screen door slammed and there was silence.

My heart was pounding as I cautiously crept downstairs, all senses alert.

At the bottom of the steps Shadow was attempting to stand, whimpering in pain. When I touched him my hand came away sticky with blood. "It'll be okay, Shadow. You did good. You wait here now." I didn't want to leave him, but I had to make certain the intruders were gone.

I quickly moved through the house, snapping on lights as I went, nearly falling when I slipped in a small puddle of blood on the kitchen tiles. The back door was wide open and shards of glass were scattered on the floor from the broken pane the intruders had smashed to get at the lock.

Satisfied the invaders were no longer in the house, I closed and locked the door. In case the thugs returned, I wedged a kitchen chair under the doorknob. They could easily reach the lock through the broken window, but at least they would make noise moving the chair.

Then I went into the study and exchanged the rifle for the shotgun. I began shaking so violently from the adrenaline surge, I had to flop onto my desk chair and take several deep breaths.

There were too many things that needed to be done right away, and I couldn't afford to fall apart. Shadow had been badly wounded and might be dying. The kids had quieted, but needed to be reassured.

Taking care of Shadow and the kids would have to wait a minute. Still trembling, I reached for the phone and dialed 911. When the operator promised me the police were on the way, I called Emily. It was going to be hectic when the cops arrived, and Emily would be a stabilizing influence on Marie and Billy.

She sounded like she was half asleep, which was to be expected at two in the morning. She came awake quickly when I told her what had happened.

"Are the children all right," she asked, sounding calmer than I felt.

"Shadow was shot, but the kids are fine. I'll check them again as soon as I hang up."

"Did you call the police?"

"They're on the way."

"Then don't waste time on the phone," she scolded. "You take care of the children and I'll be there as soon as I can."

I felt a sense of relief and my shaking had settled to a slight tremor.

My heart nearly broke when I knelt beside Shadow and stroked his head. The fur on his neck and shoulder was saturated with blood and he looked at me with pleading eyes. There wasn't anything I could do to help, so I gave a gentle hug and hurried upstairs.

When I switched on the light, Marie and Billy were huddled together in the far corner of the room. They had the same wild animal look I'd seen when we found them in Jenny's apartment.

"It's okay now," I said in a soothing voice as I crouched in front of them. "The bad men are gone and you're safe." I reached out, gathered them into my arms and held them for a long minute.

"We have to go downstairs now," I explained as I heard the distant wail of approaching sirens. "Shadow saved our lives, but he's been hurt and we need to help him."

Marie held my hand in a tight grip as I carried Billy down the stairs.

Tears filled my eyes when Marie sat on the floor and took Shadow's head in her lap. She began sobbing and repeated over and over, "Poor Shadow".

"Will Shadow die?" Billy asked, tears streaming down his cheeks.

Concern about the dog had temporarily caused the kids to forget their own fears.

"I don't know," I said. "All we can do is pray for him."

Flashing lights flooded the living room as a squad car screeched to a halt in the driveway. Two officers, guns drawn, pushed open the front door and burst into the vestibule. The senior officer tapped his partner on the shoulder and pointed toward the dining room and kitchen. With his pistol at the ready, the second officer moved cautiously to search the house.

"I've already checked," I called. "The intruders are gone."

The senior officer turned his attention toward us. "Is everyone all right?" he asked.

"My dog's been shot," I said. "We need to get him to a vet right away."

"You're bleeding," he said, pointing at my cheek.

With everything that had happened, I'd completely forgotten about my wound. The blood was already crusting when I reached up and touched the cheek. "I'm all right," I said. "It's just a scratch."

"What about all that blood?" He indicated the trail of stains that led across the living room carpet.

"One of the intruders accidentally shot his accomplice," I explained. "Can't all this wait? I have to get my dog to the vet before he dies?"

"I'm sorry about your dog, but he's going to have to wait until we know what happened here."

Before I could reply the other officer returned. "The blood trail goes through the kitchen and out the back door," he said. "The rain's washed away everything outside, but I suspect the intruders went over the fence. At any rate, they're long gone."

At that moment Emily, wearing a robe, her hair up in curlers, pushed through the doorway.

"You can't come in here," the senior officer said, moving to block her.

"This is my family," Emily said firmly. "If you don't intend to shoot me, get your gun out of my face."

With an embarrassed expression he holstered his weapon and stepped aside.

She knelt and took Marie into her arms. As she hugged the sobbing girl she looked at me. "Are you certain the children aren't injured?"

"They're okay, but we have to get Shadow to the vet. The police won't let me leave."

"Please help Shadow," Marie pleaded. "He saved our lives."

"Of course I'll help." Emily stood and turned to the officers. "You can make yourselves useful by carrying this dog to my car."

I held Shadow's head as one of the cops helped me lift him into Emily's Ford van. "He'll get blood all over your seats," I said.

"After saving my babies, he can bleed wherever he wants." She laid her hand on my arm. "Don't worry," she said gently. "I've known Tom Kennedy all his life, and he'll get out of bed to take care of Shadow or I'll know the reason why."

"Can we go with him?" Marie pleaded.

I hugged her. "Not tonight. We'll see him tomorrow after the doctor fixes him." I sincerely hoped Shadow would be alive in the morning.

The police stayed for another half an hour, asking questions and taking blood samples from the kitchen floor. "If I were you, I'd have a doctor look at that cheek tomorrow," the senior officer suggested. "If we have any more questions, we'll get back to you."

The excitement must have drained the kids. Billy had fallen asleep in my arms and Marie could barely keep her eyes open. Billy woke briefly when I laid them in Marie's bed, but in a moment they were both asleep.

The scratch on my cheek had begun to sting, so I tiptoed into the bathroom. The bullet had barely creased my cheekbone, and there had been very little bleeding. I splashed water on my face and spread antibiotic cream on the wound. Then I began shaking when I realized the bullet had only missed killing me by an inch.

I returned to Marie's room and resumed my vigil in the rocker, the shotgun across my lap. With the adrenaline still pumping, I knew I wouldn't sleep any more that night.

# CHAPTER TWENTY-SIX

The faint sound of someone fumbling at the front door lock jolted me awake. I grabbed the shotgun before it fell off my lap and tried to clear sleep from my mind. The bedside clock indicated it was nearly eight. Marie and Billy were still asleep; looking so peaceful it was hard to recall the night's terror.

My heart was pounding as I gripped the shotgun and moved toward the hall.

"Jon, it's me," Emily called softly from the foot of the stairs.

In daylight the house was an even worse mess than I'd remembered. Shadow's blood was puddled in the vestibule, and bloody footprints were everywhere. The blood trail across the living room carpet had soaked in and I doubted whether even Emily would be able to clean away the stains.

"How are the children?" Emily asked. She looked as if she hadn't slept, but sometime during the night she'd gotten dressed and brushed her hair.

"They're still sleeping," I said.

"Would you please put down that shotgun?" Emily complained. "Never did feel comfortable around loaded guns."

"Sorry." I felt sheepish as I put the gun in the hall closet and followed Emily into the living room.

"This house is a mess," she said, plopping down on the sofa. "I won't ever get it clean again."

"What about Shadow?" I asked. "Is he going to be okay?"

"We won't know until later this morning. I rousted Tom Kennedy out of bed and he operated right away. He had the gall to chase me out of the surgery, telling me to check back around ten this morning? To think I used to wipe his snotty nose and now he's ordering me around."

"Damn, I nearly forgot, the kids have a ten o'clock appointment with Dr. Scott. I'd better call and cancel it."

"You'll do no such thing. After last night those children will need to see their psychologist. I'm sure Shadow won't be able to come home this morning. I'll call Tom Kennedy and have a report when you get back from Campbell."

As usual Emily was right. After last night's excitement, the kids undoubtedly needed counseling, and I wanted to talk with Dr. Scott. We had been lucky this time, but I doubted whether we'd survive another attack. The good doctor was going to allow the children to be questioned or I'd find another psychologist.

"If we're going to keep the appointment, I'd better get the kids up," I agreed. "We'll have to be on the road in an hour."

"I'll get started with breakfast. They're going to need something nourishing this morning." When I was halfway up the stairs, Emily called after me. "And you take a shower. You don't look like you slept a wink last night."

Although Emily and I had talked quietly, we must have awakened the kids. They were both sitting in the middle of Marie's bed looking frightened and anxious.

"Did Shadow die?" Marie asked.

"No, he didn't," I reassured them. "I think he's going to be all right, but we won't know for certain until later today. Mrs. Hall said the doctor is taking good care of him."

"Would God help Shadow if I prayed?" Marie asked in a quiet, timid voice, like she needed reassurance. "Does God care about dogs?"

Marie's offer to give God another chance surprised me and made me happy at the same time. I wanted her to trust again, but what if Shadow died? Would that totally destroy her faith in God?

I reached out and swept Marie into a hug. "Of course God cares about dogs, and He'll listen to your prayer." Maybe I should have prepared her for the worst, telling her God doesn't always answer prayers the way we want, but that would put limits on Marie's emerging faith. If Shadow died we'd just have to deal with that when it happened.

"Can I pray for Shadow, too?" Billy asked.

"God would like that." I included him in the hug. "He loves to hear prayers from children."

We all knelt beside the bed. Marie made the sign of the cross, clasped her hands, and closed her eyes. "Please, God, make Shadow well again. He's the best dog in the world, and he saved our lives. We love him and want him to come back."

"Make Shadow okay," Billy echoed.

"Is that a good enough prayer?" Marie asked, like she lacked confidence.

"It's a great prayer, and I know God heard it." I stood and gave the kids another hug. "Now you guys get downstairs. Mrs. Hall is fixing something special for breakfast."

Billy raced ahead and I could hear the excitement in his voice. "Mrs. Hall, Shadow is going to be all better, 'cause Marie and me asked God to fix him."

\* \* \*

When we arrived at Psychological Associates, I explained to the receptionist that I urgently needed to talk with Dr. Scott before she saw the kids. The young girl escorted me into a counseling room and I waited ten anxious minutes, worried about leaving Marie and Billy unprotected.

"Nancy said you have something urgent to discuss." Dr. Scott was frowning, as if she were displeased because I was using the children's time.

Without preamble, I said, "Pusher came after the kids last night."

Her attitude immediately changed. "What happened? Were the children injured?"

"Not physically, but they were scared to death." I gave her a synopsis of the events. "Next time we might not be so lucky."

"Maybe there won't be a next time," she said, attempting to calm me. "You frightened the intruders last night. Since they know you're ready for them, they'll probably give up."

"That's not likely. There's too much money involved for Pusher to just forget about it. The next time they'll be better prepared." I took a deep breath. "Dr. Scott, I need your permission for the police to question Marie and Billy."

"I know you're frightened for the children, but I really don't believe they're ready for the trauma of a police interrogation. Revisiting their mother's death could destroy whatever progress we've already made."

I had anticipated Dr. Scott's cooperation, and her reply angered me. "Don't you think it would be better to take a step backward then have them tortured to death?" I snapped.

"You may be over estimating the danger," she said, remaining clinically calm. "You don't know for certain Pusher's gang will come back, or that the men last night even had anything to do with the drugs."

"Do you see this?" I pointed at the scratch on my cheek. "If that bullet had been an inch to the left, I'd be dead. If it hadn't been for my dog we might all be dead. This won't end until the drugs and money are found. Do you want to bet our lives that those hoodlums won't be coming back?"

"Even though last night was a terrible ordeal, you aren't looking at it rationally. Those men may have been a couple of burglars with no connection to this sordid drug problem. If that's the case I'm sure they've been frightened off and the children aren't in any further danger. If you stopped to think about it, you'd realize last night may have had positive consequences for the children."

"You've got to be kidding," I snapped. "Being frightened half to death, with bullets flying everywhere, couldn't have been a positive experience."

"Don't you think you're exaggerating just a bit?" she asked with professional patience. "Marie and Billy have always had bad experiences with adults. Every adult they've known, even their mother, has hurt and abused them. Last night, perhaps for the first time in their lives, an adult stood up and risked death to keep them from being harmed. It would have taken months of counseling for us to have achieved the same results."

"I can't believe you're spouting psychological mumbo jumbo when the kids were nearly killed." I was angry, on the verge of losing my temper. "Maybe I need to find a psychologist whose first priority is saving their lives."

"Of course I'm concerned about any threat to the children, but when this is over, we still have to heal their mental scars," she insisted.

"We can't heal scars if they're dead," I snapped.

"I assure you it won't come to that. When I talk with Marie and Billy this morning I'll be able to evaluate whether they're ready for police interrogation."

"Okay, you can talk with them," I agreed. "Just remember, I'm not going to risk their lives for the sake of psychological counseling."

While Dr. Scott visited with the children I paced the waiting area and sat and paced again, never taking my hand off the pistol in my jacket pocket. Not knowing what else to do, I used my cell phone to contact Detective Kincaid.

"We've got to do something about Pusher before we're all dead," I said after telling him about the home invasion.

"Short of putting the kids in protective custody, we're doing everything we can."

"Well, it's not enough. Not by a damned sight. One of those guys was wounded badly enough to need medical attention. You should be able to arrest him when he goes to a doctor. I'll bet he gives you enough information to put Pusher away."

"I'm afraid that isn't going to help."

"And why not?"

"I think we've already found your wounded man. He was dead. Instead of taking him to a doctor, Pusher silenced him."

"Are you sure it was the same guy?"

"Pretty sure. He had a bullet wound in his side that had been bleeding for a while, and a bullet in the back of the head that shut his mouth for good."

"Damnit, we can't let this go on forever."

"I still think one of the kids is the key to this whole thing. We need to question them—and the sooner the better."

"I'm working on that."

"Good. You keep pushing from your end, and I'll keep jogging the system from my end."

Kincaid hadn't done much to relieve my anxiety, and my nerves were stretched to the breaking point by the time Dr. Scott was ready to see me again.

"As I understand the situation," she said, "the police want to talk with Marie and Billy to learn whether they know where their mother hid the drugs and money."

"That's the whole point," I grumbled. "If the cops can recover the stuff, Pusher won't have any reason to come after them."

"Marie and Billy are both handling last night's episode better than I would have anticipated," she continued, maintaining a professional calm. "They seem to be more concerned about your dog then the danger to themselves. However, I'm still convinced a police interrogation would definitely be harmful at this time." She held up her hand to prevent my interruption. "I realize you want the police involved immediately because you believe the children's lives may be in danger. There is another way to handle the situation."

"What did you have in mind?" I knew there was no solution other than finding Jenny's loot.

"With your permission, I would like to try hypnosis on Marie. Delving into her subconscious would not only determine whether she knows anything, it would also give me deeper insights into her mind. Hypnosis would definitely be less traumatic than an interrogation."

"Hypnosis sounds like a great idea. Let's do it."

"It isn't that simple. I believe Marie will be a good subject, but if we're going to achieve meaningful results, I'll need to condition her for deep relaxation."

"What does that mean?" I felt like she was offering a carrot and then taking it away.

"I know you want immediate resolution, but it may be a week or two before Marie is ready to be hypnotized."

"We can't wait a week or two," I protested.

"You're in a hurry because you think Marie will have the answers you want. Have you considered the consequences if she doesn't know where her mother hid the drugs and money?"

That brought me up short. Pusher wouldn't believe us if we put out the word that Marie didn't know anything. He would still have to try his methods. "We won't be any worse off then we are now," I finally decided. "We have to try something. I'm afraid of what might happen if we wait too long."

"We need to take this one day at a time and do what's best for Marie no matter how long it takes," Dr. Scott insisted. "I'll begin the conditioning at our Monday appointment. We have to assume the children will survive the current situation, which means you still need to work with their other problems."

"I realize that."

"Right now it's important that you consider their education," Dr. Scott said. "Marie and I talked about school during this session and she had a very angry reaction. Apparently, when she turned six, Jennifer was still functioning as a mother—at least on a part-time basis—and made arrangements for Marie to attend school. As you know, children can be very cruel to each other. The well-dressed, well provided for children teased her and laughed at her dirty, ragged clothing and stringy hair. Obviously Marie was crushed. She ran from the school building and never returned. Then the system let her down again when the authorities failed to follow-up."

"That's terrible," I agreed, "but it's part of her past, and we have to look toward the future."

"That's why you have to be thinking about her education. Marie would normally enter the fifth grade this year. Although she's very intelligent, she can't even read at a beginner's level. If you enroll her in school, the administration will place her with a class of slow learners and it would destroy what little self-esteem she has."

"What do you suggest?" I felt like I was caught in a maze with booby traps at every turn. With so much on my plate, schooling Marie and Billy had never entered my mind. I certainly didn't want to compound Marie's problems, but the law and Child Protective Services would require me to send the kids to school.

"There's still time before school begins, so you'll be able to begin some pre-school training. First, I suggest you obtain materials and teach Marie to read. It may not be easy, but there are books and programs available in bookstores or Wal-Mart. If a tutor is available in Westport, you might consider hiring someone. It's extremely important that Marie learns to read as soon as possible."

"Between Mrs. Hall and me, I'm sure we can handle the reading. But that doesn't solve the schooling problem. Even if Marie learns to read, there isn't enough time to bring her up to age level."

"I suggest you home school her."

"I don't know anything about teaching," I protested. "I wouldn't have the first idea how to home school anyone."

"I've got contact information for you to get started. I don't believe the papers for home schooling have to be filed until October, so you have time to think about it. The important agenda now is to begin teaching Marie to read. Learning will do wonders for her self-esteem."

"Okay, I'll work on Marie's reading, but we have to move forward with the hypnosis. I'll give you one week to prepare her, and if you aren't ready by then, I'll find someone who will do the job."

I stormed out of Dr. Scott's office, grabbed the kids, and headed for the parking lot. There weren't any suspicious characters in sight, but I didn't feel comfortable until the kids were safely secured in the car.

I decided to stop at Wal-Mart to see what educational

materials were available. After looking through all the choices, I was impressed by a LeapPad program designed to teach beginning readers. An appropriate book was placed on the program's platform, and when a word was pressed with the pointing device, a recording pronounced the word. Since Marie couldn't read at all, I didn't think it would insult her intelligence.

Then we stopped at the bookstore in the mall. They had a large selection of beginner's books. As a starter, I selected several Dr. Seuss Read Along books.

When we got home, Emily had good news.

"I talked with Dr. Kennedy, and he said Shadow is going to be as good as new."

Billy clapped his hands and laughed. Marie was more subdued, but a genuine smile lit her eyes. "I knew he would get better," she said softly.

"Can we pick him up today?" I asked.

"No, he'll have to stay at the vet's office for a couple of days," Emily explained. "Then when he comes home, he'll have to take it easy for a few weeks. So you kids can't have him chasing sticks until he's strong again."

"Can we visit him in the hospital?" Billy asked.

"Bless your heart," Emily said. "Dr. Kennedy won't let Shadow have any visitors right now."

It was obvious Marie was pleased, and I knew why. "See, God answered your prayer," I said, giving her a big hug. "He does listen to you."

She didn't say anything, but I felt a reassuring pressure as she returned my hug.

\* \* \*

That evening while Emily was preparing supper, I got out the reading program. Although Marie was less than enthusiastic, we began our first lesson.

"I don't want to read this book," Marie stated emphatically. "It's for babies."

"You don't have any choice." She had probably been let down so many times in life, by so many people, she didn't want to risk another failure. "Learning to read is something you have to do. I'll bet you'll enjoy it once we get going."

"I'll hate it," she said just as firmly.

I slowly read the first page of a talking book, showing her how to get the pronunciation by pressing the pointer against the word. Marie wanted to resist, but the process fascinated her. After she read the first page, it was like a light went on in her eyes and she was suddenly enthusiastic. We went through the book several times, and with each reading Marie remembered more of the words and relied less on the book's recording. Her excitement made me feel like we had accomplished something wonderful.

"I think that's enough for now," I suggested after the fourth go through. "We don't want to wear you out."

"Please, let me read it one more time," she pleaded.

This was the first time she'd been truly enthusiastic about anything, and I didn't have the heart to refuse. "Okay, but only once more. Then we have to get washed up for supper."

I felt a warm glow as Marie read the story again. For her it was like a drink of water to someone dying of thirst. Reading was obviously going to be fun and rewarding.

After we ate, she was just about bursting with pride when she read the book for Mrs. Hall. Emily had raised enough kids of her own that she knew how to heap on the praise without overdoing it.

Before Marie would agree to take her bath and go to bed, I had to promise we would tackle another book first thing in the morning.

Marie's accomplishments gave me a sense of pride. Even though we still had a myriad of problems, and Pusher's shadow hovered over us, I decided watching part of her mind awaken made all of our efforts worthwhile.

# CHAPTER TWENTY-SEVEN

I doubt whether I relaxed for a single minute during the next week, although for the sake of the children, I attempted to make life appear normal. I patched three bullet holes in the walls and replaced the windowpane in the back door. Although she grumbled the whole time, Emily cleaned up the mess from the break-in until you couldn't tell it had ever happened. By some magic formula known only to her, she even managed to remove the bloodstains from the living room carpet.

Monday, Wednesday, and Thursday, at staggered times, we drove into Campbell for our sessions with Dr. Scott, who worked on conditioning Marie to hypnosis. She assured me Marie was making progress and would be ready very soon. Since there hadn't been any further incidents concerning Pusher, I didn't pressure her as much as I should have.

The kids and I were eagerly waiting Tuesday morning when Emily brought Shadow home. A large area on his right side had been shaved and a bandage protected stitches. Even though the wound obviously hurt, Shadow couldn't restrain his excitement when he burst into the house. I was concerned he might pull the stitches, but there was no curbing his joy at being reunited with his family. He licked everyone's face a hundred times, and his tail was sweeping hard enough to nearly knock Billy off his feet.

Marie looked like she would burst with pride and happiness. "God heard my prayer," she said, a big grin lighting her face. "He saved Shadow's life, just like I asked."

"Why bless your heart," Emily said. "Of course he heard your prayers. God always listens to you." She took a tissue from her apron pocket and blew her nose.

"Take it easy with Shadow," I cautioned. "He isn't completely healed and you don't want to hurt him."

"Why don't you kids take Shadow into the back yard, while I fix lunch," Emily suggested. "Just remember, the doctor said he shouldn't be running, so don't have him chasing sticks."

After the Tuesday evening catechism lesson Sister Joan approached me, wearing a huge smile. "Marie is suddenly taking an interest in our lessons, and she's even participating. I wouldn't have expected progress so soon. Without a doubt God is smiling on both children. You don't know how happy that makes me."

Whether it was learning to read, or the knowledge God had answered her prayers, or a new sense of security, or a combination of everything, Marie's entire attitude changed. Although a haunted look lingered deep in her eyes, it was overlaid by an expression of peace I'd never seen before. She had begun joining Billy and me for prayers and never once retreated into her shell. Twice I heard her giggle. It was the sweetest sound in the world.

As I watched her beginning to open up, I decided Dr. Scott must have been right. Pusher might actually have done us a favor. His attack had gone a long way toward convincing Marie there were adults who would protect her.

It was impossible to keep Marie away from her books, and she made remarkable progress. She took to reading like Shadow devoured doggie treats. In a few days she nearly wore out the LeapPad books and even began reading the Dr. Seuss stories. Discovering words had obviously opened the world for her and she couldn't explore new dimensions quickly enough. If I hadn't been so proud, I might have become annoyed by her constant demands to decipher traffic signs and cereal boxes and anything else containing words.

I tried to interest Billy in the LeapPad kindergarten books, but he never made the connection between playing and learning. For a short time he enjoyed pressing the words and hearing the pronunciations, but quickly lost interest. When he became restless, I let him go back to his toy cars and trucks.

Marie's interest in reading made me seriously consider the problem of schooling.  The first day of classes, scheduled for the Wednesday before Labor Day, was only three weeks away. My decision would have been easier if I had known for certain I would obtain permanent custody.

"Isn't it just like a man to worry about something that won't ever happen," Emily said.  "You know we aren't going to let anyone take our kids.  You have to make decisions believing our children will be with us forever."

Billy lacked some social skills, but both Emily and I were certain he was ready for public school kindergarten.  Although I was pleased with Marie's achievements, she was still a long way behind her age level.  Placing her in public school would be a mistake.  Dr. Scott's suggestion about home schooling seemed the only viable option.

I went on the Internet and looked up the State's home schooling guidelines.  According to the statute, the Home Based Private Educational Program required "at least 875 hours of instruction, including a sequentially progressive curriculum of fundamental instruction in reading, language arts, mathematics, social studies, science, and health".  Five hours of instruction per day for about thirty-five weeks sounded intimidating, but I figured Emily and I could handle it.  If it became necessary, there was always the option of hiring a tutor. There were probably retired schoolteachers in Westport who would be willing to take on a student.

I phoned the State Department of Public Instruction and asked them to mail the required enrollment forms.
When I explained my decision to the kids, Billy was excited at the prospect of school. Marie was less than enthusiastic.

"Billy will hate school," she stated emphatically.  "Why can't he stay home with me?"

Was she remembering her own cruel experiences in first grade, or was she afraid if Billy went to school he wouldn't need her anymore?  For most of her life Marie had believed her only worth was in caring for and protecting her brother. My heart ached for her, but I knew it was time to begin reducing their dependence on each other.

"The law says I have to send Billy to school," I explained.

"Then I have to go too," she insisted. "He's such a baby. He'll be scared all by himself."

I wrapped my arms around Marie and she snuggled against me. "I know you're worried about Billy, but he'll be just fine. Kindergarten is only for half a day."

"But he'll need me," she said, sounding frightened.

"I need you to stay here with me. Think of how I'd feel if you both were gone all day. Trust me. This will be best for all of us."

Marie wasn't pleased with my decision, but at least for the moment she accepted what she couldn't change. I would have given a year's pay to be able to read her mind.

I frequently wondered how much we would have accomplished without Emily. She was like a mother hen with two new chicks, and had taken it upon herself to come in at eleven every day so she would have more time with the children. When I suggested raising her pay, she acted as if I had insulted her.

Although both kids had been helping with the dishes from their first day, Emily began teaching Marie how to prepare meals.

"Everyone needs to know how to cook their own food—even boys," Emily said. "Your Uncle Jon knows how to cook, doesn't he?"

"He doesn't cook as good as you," Marie suggested.

"Bless your heart." Emily gave her a warm hug. "Men are never as good in the kitchen as us girls, but they need to know how to cook so they won't starve when we aren't around to take care of them. I'll teach Billy when he's tall enough to work on the counter, but right now it's your turn."

She took Marie grocery shopping, helped her select menus for each day, and assigned her the tasks of preparing lunch and helping with supper. Along with her success at reading, learning to cook made Marie feel a new sense of pride.

Emily didn't forget me when she scheduled jobs. I was

assigned the duty of making breakfast, and wasn't allowed to get away with preparing cold cereal.

"The children need something warm in their bellies to start the day," Emily insisted. "If you can't figure out meals for yourself, I'll plan menus and expect you to follow them."

* * *

There were so many things to consider in the few weeks remaining before the court hearing. Marie's birthday was just around the corner, and it was time to plan a celebration.

"I doubt if the kids ever celebrated a birthday," I told Emily. "Why don't we surprise Marie with a party?"

"It always amazes me when you have a good idea," Emily agreed. "Kids need birthday parties, with cake and balloons and presents. I can't imagine a ten-year-old who never celebrated her birthday."

"Marie loves chicken," I suggested. "Why don't we plan on a chicken dinner, with a party right after supper?"

"I never heard such foolishness in all my life." Emily frowned at my stupidity. "It's a birthday party, not a holiday dinner. Birthdays need to be in the afternoon with chocolate cake and white icing decorated with red candles."

I laughed. "Okay, I bow to your vast experience. But if it's going to be a surprise we can't tell Billy until the last minute. There's no way he could keep a secret."

"First you surprise me with a good idea, and then you make a dumb comment," Emily scolded. "Billy will have to know so he can buy a present for his sister. Life isn't only about getting things, you know. Kids have to learn to give."

"You're right. If we can keep Marie away while we're decorating, I can take Billy shopping the day of the party."

"I can handle Marie," Emily suggested. "I'll begin teaching her to sew, and our first project will be making a pretty dress. On her birthday we'll go upstairs for a final fitting. I'll be able to keep her busy long enough for you to take Billy shopping and set up the decorations."

"Perfect," I agreed. "You know, I'm getting excited about this myself."

"Well, don't get carried away like men always do," Emily warned. "If she's never had a birthday party, she's probably never received presents. A birthday isn't Christmas, and a whole pile of gifts would be overwhelming. We certainly don't want to spoil her."

"Maybe she deserves to be spoiled a little."

"Of course she does. All kids need to be spoiled once in a while—to be the center of attention. That's why we have birthday parties. But we still don't need to go overboard. One or two presents will be more than enough."

"Okay. Once again I bow to your wisdom," I agreed. "On her birthday, Marie will get one present from each of us."

"We'll have to have at least one present for Billy," Emily said. "He's never had a party of his own either, and he's too young to understand it isn't his birthday. He'll be crushed if he doesn't have at least one gift to open."

I was more than willing to let Emily set the ground rules and make all the preparations because finding the perfect present for my little girl would keep my mind occupied for the next several days.

# CHAPTER TWENTY-EIGHT

O n the day of Marie's surprise party Emily arrived at noon and hustled Marie upstairs to make the final alterations on the new dress.

"While you girls are busy, Billy and I have to run to the store," I announced.

"Then you can pick up a loaf of bread," Emily called down.

I had ordered helium filled birthday balloons from Hillman's Florist, and we picked them up first. Billy was riding in the front seat with me so I put the balloons in the back where they were bouncing against the roof of the car.

"Can I have a balloon?" Billy asked, fascinated by the bright colors and the way the balloons floated free.

"Maybe later," I explained. "These are for you sister's party. Did you know today is Marie's birthday?"

"No." He looked confused. "What's a birthday?"

It broke my heart that so many things normal youngsters took for granted were foreign to my kids. It had never occurred to me that Billy wouldn't even know what a birthday was. I didn't know when I'd learned about birthdays because they had always been there, even before my first memories.

"Every year, on the anniversary of the day you were born, you are one year older, and that's your birthday." I wasn't sure I could explain the concept to a five-year-old. "It's ten years today since Marie was born and we're going to celebrate her special day. We're going to have a party with presents and cake and ice cream."

"Is it my birthday too?" he asked.

I didn't think he was getting the idea. "No, you were born in

January, so your birthday won't be for a couple of months yet."

"Oh," he said, sounding disappointed. "I want a birthday."

"We'll have a party for you in January, but Marie is older and her birthday comes first. We're going to stop at the Dollar Store so you can buy her a present. Everyone gets gifts on their birthday."

"Will I get presents on my birthday?" Billy asked.

"Of course, you will," I said, praying he would be with me in January. "Marie doesn't know we're having a party, so it's going to be a big surprise. Doesn't that sound like fun?"

Billy was obviously disappointed until we were in the toy section and he enthusiastically began looking for Marie's gift. He wanted to get her a big, red fire truck until I convinced him Marie would rather have something more suited for a girl. We finally selected a coloring book and a small set of watercolors.

When we got home, I told him we had to sneak into the house so Marie wouldn't know we were back. Apparently Billy knew about sneaking because he tiptoed and whispered as we carried in the cake and present Emily had left in her car, put them on the dining room table, arranged the party plates, and tied the balloons to the back of the chairs. Then I brought out the extra large gift I'd hidden in my study and helped Billy wrap the coloring book and watercolors in birthday paper. After one last look around, I decided we were ready.

"I'm going to call Mrs. Hall and Marie now. When they come into the dining room, we'll yell, 'surprise'. Okay?"

Billy was so excited I thought he was going to wet his pants. "This is fun!"

"Mrs. Hall. Marie. We're home."

"Just in time," Emily said as they came down the stairs. "What do you think of Marie's new dress?"

The dress was a light flowered print with short sleeves and lace around the collar. Emily had arranged Marie's hair in a ponytail, and she looked like an angel. It was hard to tell whether she was embarrassed or pleased to be the center of attention.

"The dress is fantastic, but Marie looks even prettier," I said. "Why don't you come into the dining room where the light's better so I can really see it?"

"Surprise!" Billy shouted.

"Not yet," I said in a stage whisper. "I'll let you know when it's time."

Marie stepped into the dining room, astonished at the sight of the cake and balloons and gaily-wrapped presents. She had obviously never seen anything like it in her life.

We all shouted, "Surprise!" Billy clapped his hands and jumped up and down in excitement.

"Happy Birthday, Marie," Emily said, stooping to give her a big hug. "This is all for you because you're such a special little girl."

When I hugged Marie she was trembling. "Happy Birthday, Sweetheart."

"Is this really and truly for me?" There was awe in her voice, as if she were dreaming.

"It's your birthday party, but I hope you'll let the rest of us have some cake," I joked.

Marie tapped a balloon, testing to see if it was real, and watched in amazement as it bounced back and forth.

"Well, don't just stand there, Uncle Jon, light the birthday candles." Emily took Marie's hand and led her to the head of the table where I normally sat. "The birthday girl gets the seat of honor."

When I lit the candles Marie was completely overwhelmed by the spectacle. She still looked tentative; as if she were afraid someone would take everything away. My heart ached to realize no one had ever given her a special day. Tears welled in my eyes and I had to blink to clear my vision.

"Happy Birthday, Angel," I said. "Close your eyes, make a wish, and blow out the candles. If you blow them all out, your wish will come true."

Marie hesitated as if she wanted the candles to burn forever. "Will my wish really come true?" she asked, finding it difficult to believe wishes were ever fulfilled.

"Bless your heart." Emily laid her hand on Marie's arm. "If you blow out the candles, and don't tell anyone what you wished for, it has to come true. That's the birthday rule."

Marie leaned over the cake, took a deep breath and blew. It took two tries, but she managed to extinguish all the candles. She clapped her hands. "Now my wish will come true!"

"It certainly will," Emily assured her. "Birthday wishes always come true."

Billy was jumping up and down in excitement. He gave Marie a big hug, nearly knocking her off the chair. "Can I blow out candles and get a wish?" he squealed.

"Not today," Emily said. "You get to have a cake and blow out candles on your birthday."

"I want to blow out the candles," he complained.

"Is it alright if Billy blows out some candles?" I asked Marie.

Apparently she had already shared so much with her brother, she readily agreed. I relit five candles and Billy puffed at each one, blowing them out individually. "I did it!" he shouted, jumping up and down. "I get my very own wish. I'm going to get a fire truck."

"You aren't supposed to tell anyone what you wished for," Emily scolded.

Billy's excitement deflated like a punctured balloon. "I'm sorry," he said, beginning to cry. "I forgot."

He looked so comically dejected, I nearly laughed when I gave him a hug. "It's okay. You're allowed to forget one time."

He perked up when Mrs. Hall also hugged him. "No sad faces today," she said. "I'm sure your wish will come true anyway."

Emily handed Marie a package. "Let's get on with the party. It's time for you to open your gifts."

Marie took the gift and held it as if she didn't know what to do. If the candles and decorations were overwhelming, the though of getting presents was almost more than she could comprehend.

"You have to take off the wrapping paper to see what's

inside," I said. "Go ahead. Just tear it off."

Marie's eyes sparkled and she had a smile that nearly split her face as she ripped off the paper. Mrs. Hall's gift was a jewelry box with a heart shaped necklace resting on the red velvet lining. Emily placed the necklace around Marie's neck and received a hug in return.

"The box plays music." Emily showed her how to wind the key on the bottom of the box, and when she lifted the lid, we all listened to 'When You Wish Upon A Star'.

"Oh, I love it," Marie squealed. "Do I get to keep it? Is it really mine?"

"Of course," Emily said. "Every time you look at it, I want you to remember your tenth birthday."

"There's more," I said, prompting Billy to hand over his gift.

"I chosed this myself," he bragged, jumping up and down with excitement.

Marie tore off the wrappings and hugged the coloring book and watercolors. She wanted to immediately paint a picture, but I convinced her it would be better to wait until after the party.

Finally I handed her the largest box on the table. "This is from me, for the prettiest little girl in the world."

Marie ripped off the wrappings, revealing a beautiful doll with golden hair and eyes that opened when she picked it up. She hugged the doll, tears streaming down her cheeks.

"What's wrong?" I asked, afraid I had inadvertently touched some unknown pain.

"I've always wanted my very own doll," she said. "Can I really keep her?"

I wrapped my arms around both Marie and the doll. "Yes, it's yours forever. I'm glad you like it."

"Can I give her a name?" she asked tentatively, as if naming the doll would really make it hers.

"I think that would be a wonderful idea," I agreed.

"Is it all right if I call her Suzy?" she asked.

"That's a perfect name," Emily said. "I couldn't have picked a better one myself."

I was proud of the way Billy had been enjoying Marie's party, but I knew he didn't understand this wasn't also his celebration.

"Normally on your birthday you would be the only one getting presents," I said to Marie. "But Billy's just a little boy and he doesn't understand about birthdays. Would you mind if we gave him a present too?"

Marie hesitated. I could see she was trying to decide which of her gifts she was willing to give her brother.

"You don't have to give Billy one of your presents, Sweetheart." Damn, it broke my heart to realize Marie thought she would have to sacrifice one of her treasures. "We have a gift here just for him."

I picked up the last present and handed it to Billy. "This is for you."

He ripped open the gift, which was the fire truck he had wanted to buy for Marie. He laughed and hugged the truck. "My wish did comed true," he squealed.

"Yes, it did," I agreed.

"You can play with your presents later," Emily said, wiping tears from her eyes. "Let's eat the cake and ice cream while it's still fresh." She quickly cleared away the pile of wrapping paper and brought in the chocolate sundaes she had prepared. Then we cut the cake and all sang "Happy Birthday" as Marie took the first slice.

The kids were too excited to eat much, and for the first time since I'd known them, they left food on their plates.

I had found an old 'Pin The Tail On The Donkey' game and we played it after we'd eaten. By the time all four of us had attempted to pin the tail, we were laughing so hard I had tears in my eyes. I'd picked up some party favors and awarded everyone a prize.

Then, while Emily and I cleaned up, Billy played with his fire truck and Marie painted a picture in her coloring book, hugging her doll the whole time. She played the music box so often I was afraid it would break.

That evening after our nighttime prayers, Marie lingered a

moment.

"Is it all right if I add something of my own?" she asked.

"Of course."

"Thank you God for my birthday party." She looked at me with a question in her eyes. "Was that okay?"

"It was perfect." It made me feel warm and happy. I had to swallow against the lump in my throat. I hoped God was as pleased with Marie's prayer as I was.

"I like birthday's," Billy said as I was tucking him in. "Can we have a party for me?"

"When it's your birthday, I promise we'll have a big party."

"Tomorrow?" he asked tentatively.

I laughed. "Not tomorrow, but soon." I leaned over and kissed his forehead.

When Marie climbed into bed, she clung to her doll. "Can Suzy sleep with me?" she asked, hugging the doll as if she were afraid I would take it away. "Just for tonight. I don't want her to be lonely."

"I think that would be nice," I agreed. "This is Suzy's first night in a new house, and she'd feel safer sleeping with her best friend."

"And can I play my music box?"

"Of course." I wound the key and let Marie open the lid. "Just don't play it so often it wears out."

"I won't," she said, very seriously. "I promise."

When I leaned over to kiss her forehead, Marie reached up and hugged me with her free arm. "Thank you, Uncle Jon. This is the best day ever."

I wasn't ashamed of the tears that came to my eyes as I left the room. It had also been my best day ever.

# CHAPTER TWENTY-NINE

Sometimes life is going so smoothly it's hard to remember the bumps in the road. I had to constantly remind myself the threat from the drug gang was very real, and it didn't seem possible the court hearing was approaching at breakneck speed.

Both Marie and Billy were adjusting better than anticipated. There was no longer any doubt that seeking custody was the best decision I'd ever made. The kids and Emily made my life full and satisfying. The emptiness of my existence before they entered my life was a rapidly fading memory.

Emily was a stabilizing force, the glue that held the family together. Marie had moved beyond the talking books and spent hours reading to her doll, Suzy. Billy was getting so excited about the prospect of kindergarten that he began showing an interest in the talking books. The software program I'd completed for Lee's Manufacturing was performing beautifully, and Henry Jerrold had been so pleased he offered a contract to design software for Lee's sister company.

Everything was so perfect, I knew it couldn't last. In the back of my mind I was waiting for something to go wrong.

Then Marie had another nightmare.

I had gone to bed around ten-thirty and was in a deep sleep when Shadow put his cold, wet nose against my back. The bedside clock indicated it was only a little past one—not nearly Shadow's morning time. He never disturbed me in the middle of the night. I came awake instantly, knowing something was wrong.

The dog whined softly while I fumbled for my robe and

slippers. I banged my knee on the dresser and limped behind as he led me to Marie's bedroom.

In the dim light I could see she had kicked off her covers and was moaning as she tossed from side to side. When I touched her sweat damp forehead she awakened with a whimper, looking frightened and disoriented.

"It's all right," I soothed, sitting on the bed. "It was just a bad dream. I'm here now."

She began crying softly and snuggled against me. I lay on the bed and held her, stroking her back until she fell asleep.

Gently untangling, I pulled the covers up to her chin and kissed her forehead. I tiptoed across the hall to Billy's room. He was sleeping peacefully as I straightened his covers and quietly went downstairs.

This time I wasn't going to be caught without my weapons. After double-checking the locks on the doors and windows, I got the shotgun from my study and went back upstairs. Shadow curled at my feet when I moved the rocking chair into Marie's bedroom, and settled for an all night vigil.

In the quiet of the night a million thoughts raced through my mind. Those thugs had invaded our house the only other time Marie experienced a bad dream. It made me wonder if Marie's nightmares were triggered by some psychic sense that warned of approaching danger.

It was a long five hours before the sky began to lighten with false dawn. Marie and Billy were still sleeping peacefully when I went downstairs and let Shadow out. The night had passed without incident, but I was still nervous, like I knew something frightening was still coming.

About nine o'clock Detective Kincaid phoned.

"We found Pusher's body last night," he said, sounding like I wasn't the only one who had been awake all night.

"What happened?" I asked, overwhelmed with a sense of relief.

"It looked like a gangland execution," he said. "Someone had worked him over pretty good before firing a single bullet into the back of his head."

The knot that had been in my stomach since Marie's nightmare began to unravel. "Then it's over," I said.

"Maybe not." Kincaid paused and it sounded like he was sipping coffee. "Although it might be totally unrelated, we think Pusher's suppliers killed him because he hadn't recovered the money and drugs. These people are not a forgiving group."

"If Pusher's dead, it should be finished," I insisted.

"I wish it were true," Kincaid said. "Street gossip suggests your kids are in more danger than ever. Whoever wasted Pusher wants the drugs and money so badly they've offered to split the merchandise and cash fifty-fifty with anyone who can recover it. Believe me, that's enough of an incentive to get every scumbag in Campbell looking."

"Are you saying that anyone we meet on the street could be a threat to my kids?" My stomach was knotting again and I felt like screaming into the phone. "Damn it, can't you do something to protect us? Isn't that why we have police?"

"I'm open to suggestions," Kincaid grumbled. "We can't keep an eye on all the creeps in town. Our best bet is to locate the loot so we can take it out of circulation. We've torn Jennifer's apartment apart and didn't find a clue. At the moment, your kids are the only possible lead. I'm going to pressure Children's Court again for permission to question them, but I doubt whether the Judge will be sympathetic. In the meantime, I've alerted the Westport police to increase surveillance around your house."

"That isn't going to help, and you know it. Unless the Westport cops park a squad car in my driveway, they aren't going to do any better than last time."

"There isn't anything else I can do. Maybe you could take the kids on a vacation where no one will be able to find you."

I immediately thought of, and then rejected, Ralph Hensley's fishing cabin. Too many people knew Ralph and I sometimes spent weekends there and it was too isolated a location. If some hoodlums learned I had the kids there, we would be easy targets.

"That's no solution," I said. "Even if we had a place to hide, we'd have to come back some time and they'd still be looking for the kids."

"I don't know what else to suggest. It might only be a temporary fix, but at least you'd be safe until we're able to locate the cache."

"No matter where we ran, I'd be watching our backs every minute, just waiting for some creep to show up on our doorstep. This has to end right now before I have a nervous breakdown."

"Yeah, I'd like this finished, too, but until the loot is found, your kids will be a target. Believe me, these scumbags have long memories."

I was sweating and my heart was pounding so hard my chest hurt. There was only one solution. We would have to find out if Marie knew what Jenny had done with the drugs and money. Dr. Scott no longer had the luxury of taking her time. She would either try the hypnosis today or I would find someone who would.

"Will the court allow that?" Kincaid asked when I explained about hypnotizing Marie.

"I don't give a damn what the court will allow. We're talking about my kids, and I'll do whatever is necessary to protect them. We have an appointment this afternoon, and I'll make damned sure the doctor cooperates. Will you meet us at Psychological Associates at one?"

"I'll be there," he promised.

Maybe I was overreacting, but for this trip to Campbell I carried the pistol in my jacket pocket and also took the shotgun, leaning it against the front passenger seat.

Marie and Billy must have sensed the tension because they were even quieter than usual. My nerves were stretched to the breaking point as I constantly monitored the rear view mirror for sinister cars although I wouldn't have recognized a tail if we'd had one. Each time we stopped for a red light, I kept my hand on the pistol and suspiciously examined every pedestrian. Even with my senses at full alert, I never saw the car waiting in ambush at Psychological Associates.

We were nearly to the front of the parking lot when a green sedan suddenly backed into the lane in front of us. I stood on my brakes and screeched to a halt only inches from a collision.

I was ready to jump out and cuss a careless driver when two Hispanic men appeared on the far side of the sedan. They took positions behind the hood and trunk, leveling assault rifles at us.

"Get down," I shouted as I slammed the gearshift into reverse and tramped on the gas pedal.

This time I did slam into the car that had pulled behind us to cut off our retreat. I was leaning over to grab the shotgun when the windshield disintegrated from a hail of automatic rifle fire. If I'd been sitting behind the steering wheel, the bullets would have taken off my head.

There was no way anyone could have known we'd be at Psychological Associates at this time unless there was an inside source. It could have been someone from the police or even someone in Dr. Scott's office. There was enough money involved to tempt a saint. But I had other things to worry about at the moment.

Rising only high enough to see over the dash, I poked the shotgun through the shattered windshield and fired twice in the general direction of the front car. I don't know whether the buckshot hit anyone, but there was a lull in the firing.

Suddenly my car began to rock as a man from the second vehicle tried to pull open the locked back door. He had raised a rifle to smash the rear window when I twisted in the seat and fired. The glass shattered and a full load of buckshot caught him in the face and chest.

Marie and Billy were crouched on the backseat floor, whimpering in terror. I was afraid they might have been injured, but there wasn't time to check.

I ducked at the sound of another flurry of gunshots, but quickly realized no bullets were striking the car. When I peeked over the dash, I saw a uniformed police officer and Detective Kincaid advancing on the two blocking cars. There was no sign of the gunmen.

"Mr. Wilson," Kincaid shouted. "Are you and the kids all right?"

"I think so," I called back.

"Don't shoot," Kincaid warned. "It's over."

There was a wail of distant sirens when I opened the back door and gathered Marie and Billy in a protective hug.

"It's okay. You're safe now."

Kincaid approached, holstering his pistol. "An ambulance is on the way. Are you sure no one's hurt?"

"I don't think so." Although the kids were badly frightened, it didn't appear as if the bullets or glass had hit them.

"You're bleeding," Kincaid observed.

I had forgotten about the shattered windshield. "It's only a few scratches. They aren't serious." I was too happy to be alive to worry about minor cuts.

It was only seconds before an ambulance and two more squad cars arrived. Almost as quickly a mob of spectators appeared.

A paramedic treated my cuts while another examined Marie and Billy. My knees felt as if they had become unhinged and I was trembling. I leaned against the front fender, taking deep breaths. The man I had shot was sprawled on his back, his face and chest a mass of blood. I felt my lunch coming up when I realized I had killed a man. Leaning over the front of my car, I emptied my stomach.

"Don't be ashamed," Kincaid said. "I did that the first time I was in a fire fight."

I nodded. "Did any of them get away?"

"Near as I could tell there were only the three and they're all dead."

"You know someone had to tell them we would be here at this time. There's no other way they could have known."

"Figured that out myself," Kincaid said. "I guarantee you I'll find out who has a loose tongue and I'll come down hard on them."

When the paramedic assured me Marie and Billy weren't injured, I crouched and opened my arms for the kids.

"It's okay," I said. "You're safe now. No one is going to hurt you."

"It would have been a different story if you hadn't asked me to be here," Kincaid said. "You were damned lucky this time."

"There won't be a next time," I said. "One way or another, this is going to be finished today."

# CHAPTER THIRTY

Since I'd never killed anyone before, I was afraid I might be arrested, or at least taken to the police station to file reports or something of that sort. Detective Kincaid did confiscate my shotgun, but he must have been eager to get on with Marie's hypnosis, because he allowed a uniformed officer to take my statement. He made me promise to stop at the police station on my way home to file a more formal report.

When the tow truck arrived for my bullet riddled car we tried the engine and it started immediately. No warning lights came on, but I wasn't going to drive far without a windshield. I paid the driver with a credit card and directed him to haul the wreck to the GM dealer where I could rent a vehicle while mine was being repaired.

By the time everything was settled with the police and the wrecker, we were more than an hour late for our appointment, but I doubt whether anyone noticed. The Psychological Associates' staff must have been part of the spectator mob, because we had to wait another ten minutes for them to begin straggling in.

The delay allowed me to recover from the adrenaline rush and get my blood pressure back to normal. Marie and Billy had stopped crying, but they both clung to me like I was the only stable point in their world.

Kincaid had come into the waiting room with us, looking like he needed something to settle his nerves. He probably didn't kill gunmen everyday.

"I hope this doesn't take all afternoon," he grumbled. "I haven't closed my eyes since yesterday morning, and I'm going to have hours of paperwork before I go home. On top of that, I'll have to face Internal Affairs for a shooting board."

"What's that?" I asked.

Kincaid gave a big sigh. "Every time a cop fires his gun outside the pistol range, Internal Affairs convenes a board of inquiry to determine if the shooting was justified. Since we've got three dead perps, they'll check ballistics to see who actually wasted the scumbags."

"After saving our lives, you should get a medal rather than a board of inquiry," I said. "Those bastards were shooting at you."

"Oh, the board will rule the shooting justified. It's their job to make certain we didn't violate the perp's civil rights."

The receptionist stepped into the waiting area. "Mr. Wilson, Dr. Scott will see Marie and Billy now."

I untangled myself from the children. "You guys wait here with Detective Kincaid for a few minutes." I turned toward the receptionist. "I want to talk with Dr. Scott before she sees the kids."

I hadn't seen Dr. Scott in the parking lot, but she must have heard about the gun battle, so I didn't bother explaining or waste time with pleasantries.

"I want you to hypnotize Marie today," I stated firmly. "We can't wait any longer to find out whether she knows what her mother did with the drugs and money."

Even though Dr. Scott was attempting to look and sound professional, I could see she was still shaken from the shooting outside her office. "I understand your concern," she said. "All of the excitement must have been traumatic for you and the children. However, particularly after today's events, I don't believe Marie is ready to revisit her mother's death."

"You don't even begin to understand my concern," I said, vainly attempting to remain calm. "My car windows have been shot out by automatic rifle fire. The kids and I were within an inch of being killed. Every creep in Campbell is trying to kidnap Marie and Billy so they can be tortured for information. This is going to end today. Marie may be traumatized, but she'll get over it. She won't recover from a bullet in the head."

"Please calm down, Mr. Wilson," she said. "Don't you think it would be best to discuss this with Children's Court and Child Protective Services before we attempt to hypnotize Marie?"

"I don't give a damn about Children's Court or CPS. I'm paying the bills, not the county. None of those people are getting shot at. You may believe Marie's mental health is your top priority, but I think keeping her alive rates number one. If you won't hypnotize Marie, I'll find someone who will." I stood and prepared to stalk out of the room.

"Please sit down," she said, trying to calm me. "I realize the shooting was traumatic for you, but just consider how frightening it was for Marie. She needs a few days to settle down before we can safely explore her subconscious."

"Are you living on some other planet?" I asked, beginning to lose my temper. "We don't have a few days. Do you think those scumbags were playing games in the parking lot? I want Marie hypnotized today."

Scott sighed and had a martyred expression. "If you insist, I can attempt to hypnotize her as long as you clearly understood hypnosis at this time is against my professional judgment."

"You can make any protest you want, but this is going to end today," I insisted. "If you want me to sign a paper saying I take full responsibility, I'll do it. We're wasting time arguing."

"Okay, bring Marie in," she said, obviously unhappy with my decision. "I'll see if I can relax her enough to reach a hypnotic state."

"Detective Kincaid of the Campbell police is here. I want him to sit in on the session."

"Absolutely not," Dr. Scott said vehemently. "Marie is under a great deal of stress and I may not be able to put her under as it is. Having a stranger in the room will make it impossible."

For a moment I was going to object, but quickly decided Dr. Scott needed to have her small victory. "I'll accept that," I agreed. "But I intend to remain and I insist on taping the session."

"Of course," Dr. Scott snapped. "I always record hypnosis

sessions."

When I went to get Marie, I explained the situation to Kincaid.

"I'll wait here with Billy," he reluctantly agreed, "but only with the stipulation that I get a copy of the tape."

Dr. Scott greeted Marie as if there had never been an argument, although she ignored me.

"We're going to do the relaxation exercise we've been practicing," she said in a quiet, soothing voice. "You're perfectly safe. There's a policemen in the waiting room and your Uncle Jon is here to make certain no one hurts you. Do you think you can relax?"

Marie nodded, but looked tense. She glanced at me and I gave her a reassuring smile.

Dr. Scott placed a metronome on the table in front of Marie and pushed the baton to begin the measured cadence. "We've done this before, and you know it makes you feel very rested. Concentrate on the moving pointer as it goes back and forth. Back and forth. Relax. All the tension is oozing from your body. You're feeling peaceful and more and more relaxed. Your eyelids are growing heavy. You want to close your eyes, but you keep watching the pointer moving back and forth, back and forth. With each beat you're becoming more and more relaxed. Your eyelids are getting heavier and heavier. You're feeling very drowsy. You're completely relaxed and can't keep your eyes open any longer. Let them close as you go deeper and deeper into relaxation. You feel peaceful and the only sound you hear is my voice."

Marie's chin dropped against her chest and she was breathing rhythmically, as if she'd actually fallen asleep.

"You're in a garden surrounded by beautiful flowers," Scott continued. "There's a soft breeze and you can hear the restful sounds of running water. Uncle Jon is in the garden with you, holding your hand. You feel completely safe and at peace, happy and contented."

Dr. Scott nodded at me and I gently gripped Marie's hand. It felt warm and relaxed.

"Do you see the garden and smell the flowers?"

"Yes." Marie's voice had a dreamy quality.

"Good. You're going to leave the garden for a few minutes, but you can come back whenever you want. No matter what happens, you'll be safe as long as you hold Uncle Jon's hand. He'll protect you."

Dr. Scott took a deep breath. "You're traveling back in time, back to the apartment where you lived with your mother. Are you in the apartment?"

Marie squeezed my hand hard and she wrinkled her nose at the remembered odors. She was frowning and tears began to seep from under her eyelids. "Yes."

"Tell me what you see," Dr. Scott said in a soothing voice.

"Mommy is asleep and she won't wake up." Marie sounded agitated. "Billy and I are both shaking her, but she won't wake up."

"It's alright, Marie. Just relax. Uncle Jon is with you, and you're back in the beautiful garden. Remember, no matter what you see, you'll be safe."

Marie relaxed her grip and the frown disappeared. She instantly looked very peaceful.

"You're going back in time again, back to the apartment before your mother goes to sleep. You and Billy are waiting for her to come home. You're both happy because you hear her opening the door. Tell me what is happening."

Marie's look of contentment vanished and I could feel the tension in her grip. "Mommy brought us a big box of chicken" she murmured. "Billy and I are hungry because she was gone a long time."

"You're doing very well. Relax. Uncle Jon has your hand and you know you're safe. Your mother gives you and Billy the chicken. Does she have anything else with her?"

Marie frowned. "She has a bag of heroin." Her voice sounded angry. "I hate it when she has drugs because she always goes to sleep."

"Relax. Hold Uncle Jon's hand and everything will be all right. Does your mother have anything else?"

"Mommy has a key." Marie squinted with closed eyes, as if she were attempting to see clearly.

"Is it the apartment key?"

"No."

"What is the key for?"

"I don't know."

"Do you see where your mother puts the key?"

"No. Mommy goes into the bedroom while Billy and I eat the chicken."

"You know your mother is hiding the key. Where does she put it?"

"I hear Mommy putting the key where she hides her money."

"Where does she hide her money?"

"I'm not supposed to ever tell anyone."

"It's alright to tell us," Dr. Scott suggested. "Your mother would want Uncle Jon to know. Tell him where she puts the key."

"Behind the board in the closet."

"Which board does she hide it behind?"

"The one along the wall where she keeps her money."

"Relax. You have left the apartment and are back in the beautiful garden. You feel happy and peaceful. You're completely rested and I'm going to wake you. You won't remember going back to the apartment. You'll only remember the beautiful garden. I will count to five, and when I say five, your eyes will open. You'll feel refreshed and happy. One. Two. Three. Four. Five. You're awake. Open your eyes."

Marie's eyes popped open and she stretched like she'd just awakened from sleep.

"Are you okay, Honey?" I asked.

She nodded and smiled. "I feel good. I was in a beautiful garden and you were there with me. It was like a wonderful dream."

"I know, Sweetheart." I turned to Dr. Scott. "I want a copy of that tape."

She placed another cassette in the recorder and made a copy. "I hope you're satisfied," she said as she gave me the tape. "Now please leave me alone with Marie for a few minutes."

Billy was playing with some toy cars when I returned to the waiting area. Detective Kincaid looked eager to be somewhere else.

"I don't know whether this will help or not," I said handing him the tape. "Jenny had a key on that last day, and Marie thinks she knows where her mother hid it."

"Yeah, a key. That might be it." Kincaid looked excited. "Jennifer must have realized the loot wouldn't be safe in the apartment. All that money and China White would have been too tempting to leave with a friend. It would make sense for her to stash it somewhere, like in a public locker. I'll get on this right away."

"Could you please wait and give us a ride to the GM dealer where the wrecker towed my car. I could call a cab, but I'd feel a lot safer with a police officer."

Kincaid glanced at his watch. "Okay, if it isn't too much longer."

"I'd appreciate it."

"Let's hope this tape tells us what we need to know. Once we find the drugs and money, I'll make certain the word is put out on the streets. Then this whole mess should be over for good."

I wanted to feel a sense of relief, but the tension didn't ease. Until I knew for certain Jenny's loot had been located, I was going to lose a lot of sleep.

# CHAPTER THIRTY-ONE

Detective Kincaid phoned at eleven o'clock that night."I hope I didn't wake you," he said, sounding as if he still hadn't gotten enough sleep. "I knew you'd want to know we found the drugs and money. We made certain the right people heard about it so I'm pretty sure the word is already on the streets. I'd be careful for a day or two, but the kids should be out of it now."

The knot in my stomach began to unravel and I discovered my hands were trembling. "Where did Jenny hide the stuff?" I asked.

"We found the key behind a loose baseboard in the closet where Marie said it would be. The key fit a locker at the Greyhound bus station. As far as we know the loot was all there, minus the single bag of China White Jennifer had taken. We also discovered over five thousand dollars cash hidden in the closet wall. There's no way we can connect that money to the drug deal, so we're treating it as Jennifer's personal property. With Jennifer dead, the money rightfully belongs to Marie and Billy. After the dust settles, you should be able to claim it for them."

"It isn't likely Jenny was putting away cash for her old age. Any money you found must be part of the drug deal and I don't want anything to do with it."

"That's your call, but if it were up to me, I'd grab the cash and run," Kincaid said. "You could always put it away for the kids. Five thousand bucks would be a nice nest egg for college. At least think about it. I'll give a call when the money is released and you can decide whether or not you want to claim it."

\* \* \*

Over the next several days the constant fear of intruders faded and we resumed a fairly normal life. I probably would have been happier if the court date, less than a month away, wasn't hanging over my head. Uncertainty about permanent custody made it difficult to plan for the future.

The school year was nearly on us and I worried about how my schooling decisions would affect the kids. If Billy started kindergarten and had to change schools after a couple of weeks, would the adjustment be more difficult for him? If I began home schooling Marie and new foster parents enrolled her in public school, would it destroy the progress she had made during the last two months?

Emily argued that we should think positively and assume I would gain permanent custody. I knew she was right, but it didn't ease the worry eating away at my gut.

Although Billy was excited about the prospect of a new adventure I don't think he really understood what kindergarten meant. It was Marie who realized how much Billy attending school would impact her life. As the fateful day approached, she became more withdrawn. Taking care of her brother had been the foundation of her self image and she must have been terrified her value as a person would be destroyed. Somehow I had to reassure her.

Emily had raised five children of her own and had enough experience so she could probably help Marie over the traumatic shift in her life, but I couldn't abdicate my obligations. If I were going to be a responsible parent it was my duty to deal with Marie's problem.

The day before school opened was one of those perfect late August days that signal the fading of summer. The kids had been in the backyard nearly all afternoon playing with Shadow. The dog, almost completely recovered from his wound, was running himself ragged retrieving sticks for Billy. When I stepped outside Marie was sitting on the porch steps watching.

I sat on the top step beside her. "Why aren't you playing with Billy and Shadow?" I asked. "Are you worried about tomorrow when Billy goes to school?"

She didn't respond, turning her back toward me.

"It must be hard, knowing Billy will be going to school by himself. You probably think when he begins kindergarten he won't need you any longer. That isn't true. You're both part of a family now and we'll always need each other."

By remaining mute Marie wasn't making this easy for me.

"You know, in a lot of ways a family is like that big oak tree in the corner of the yard. Did you ever wonder why the tree never falls down, even when we have a strong wind storm?"

Marie shook her head, which was encouraging. At least it indicated she hadn't tuned me out.

"The tree's roots reach deep into the ground and keep the tree from blowing away or falling down. No matter how big a storm or how hard the wind blows, that old tree just stands there."

"The wind blows off limbs," Marie said.

"Yes, the wind can break some of the branches, but the roots support the rest of the tree. That's the way it is with families. Everyone in the family is like a root, giving each of us strength and security."

Even in the city I knew Marie must have seen trees shedding their leaves in autumn and budding with new life in spring. I hoped I could draw an understandable parallel between the tree's seasons and Billy going to school.

"In a few more weeks, when the weather is colder, all the leaves will turn a beautiful golden color and begin falling off the tree. Then next spring fresh green leaves will grow on the branches. The tree has gone through those changes every season since before I was born. Families also change every year as we each grow older and stronger. But even when the family changes we still need each other, just like trees need their roots and leaves.

"It'll be a big change for all of us when Billy starts

kindergarten tomorrow. You and I and Mrs. Hall will each have to make an adjustment. You have to understand he'll still be your brother and part of our family—just that he's beginning to grow up."

"He needs me," Marie said so softly I almost didn't hear. "He's just a baby."

"Of course he needs you, just like Mrs. Hall and Billy and I will always need you and you'll always need us. We're family."

I was afraid I was doing a lousy job of reaching Marie. "Do you understand what I'm trying to tell you?" I asked.

When Marie didn't respond for a very long minute, I thought I'd completely lost her. "I've always taken care of Billy," she finally said. "I don't want anything to change. I don't want him to go to school."

"I know some changes are scary. You've done a wonderful job protecting Billy, but it's time to let him go for a few hours a day."

"When Billy goes to school, he'll meet other people. He won't need me anymore. I'll be alone." There was a catch in Marie's voice and I could see she was trying very hard not to cry. She must have realized she needed Billy even more than he needed her. He had been her anchor, the only thing that had enabled her to endure, and if she lost him, she would lose her value as a person.

"You won't ever be alone, Sweetheart. Mrs. Hall and I love you and need you. We are your roots, just like you're part of our roots. We'll always be here for you."

"But Billy's such a baby. He'll be scared and I'm the only one who knows how to make him stop crying."

I moved closer to Marie and put my arm around her. She turned her face into my side and began crying softly.

"Deep down in your heart you always knew Billy would grow up one day. Right now he's still a little boy, and needs you to be strong for him, like the roots are strong for the oak tree. But you don't have to take care of him by yourself any longer. Now you can let Mrs. Hall and me help you. It's time for you to begin letting go and starting to take care of yourself."

Marie's frail body was shaking with silent sobs. "I'm afraid," she whispered.

"I know. I'm afraid too. But as long as we have each other, we can face anything."

We sat for a long time as I hugged Marie and let her cry out the fear and grief and loneliness bottled up inside. Even after she had emptied all the tears from her heart, we remained there until Mrs. Hall called us for supper.

# CHAPTER THIRTY-TWO

Emily insisted on arriving early Wednesday morning to get Billy ready for his first day of school. I'd told her Marie and I could handle the job, but there was no denying Emily when she made up her mind.

"What do you know about a child's first day in kindergarten?" she scolded. "If I know men, you wouldn't even remember to give him a good breakfast."

Unexpectedly Marie took a vigorous role in the morning's activities. While Emily was fussing over breakfast, Marie helped dress Billy and combed his hair, doing a surprisingly good job. I knew how brave she was in spite of a broken heart. A mother could not have been more concerned about her child's first excursion away from home.

"You be good and pay attention," she cautioned. "If any of those kids give you shit, let me know and I'll take care of them."

Was she remembering her own unhappy school experience when there was no one to support her? Considering what the effort was costing her emotionally, I didn't have the heart to correct her language.

After being the center of attention at home, Billy was bubbling over with enthusiasm until we arrived at the school and he saw the mob of mothers and youngsters crowded into the school hallway. He ducked behind my leg and held on. I was happy to see he wasn't the only timid child, and he did better than some.

A little girl burst into tears, and as if tears were contagious, about half the kids began wailing. I felt sorry for the teacher, Jessica Lappin, who would have to deal with all these frightened, unhappy youngsters when the parents left. I figured the first day of kindergarten must have been scheduled for only one hour because that was about how long she would be able to tolerate the misery.

"You be a good boy, Billy," I said, seating him at one of the little tables. "I'll be back in an hour. Do whatever Miss Lappin tells you and you'll have a lot of fun."

If I thought he would have fun, Billy had no such confidence. He couldn't have looked more miserable if I'd abandoned him on some lonely country road.

Miss Lappin shooed the last heart-broken parent from the room and firmly shut the door. Some of the mothers lingered in the hallway, taking occasional peeks through the door's little window.

I realized the hour would drag if I waited outside the classroom, so I walked around the block a couple of times. When I returned a small group of mothers had gathered near the drinking fountain, talking quietly. I glanced through the door's window and saw Billy sitting on the floor with the other children, finger-painting on large sheets of paper. Satisfied everything was going to be all right, I waited the rest of the hour in the car.

Five minutes before the scheduled end of class I joined the mothers who began entering the building. We waited in the hallway until Miss Lappin opened the door and a gaggle of excited kids burst out, pairing with their mothers. Billy wasn't among them.

I stepped into the nearly empty room and saw him sitting against the wall staring at the floor, like he didn't believe I would return.

"Hey, Billy, aren't you coming home?" I called.

When he heard my voice his face brightened and he ran to me, wrapping his arms around my leg. "Come on, big guy," I said, untangling his arms. "We have to get home so you can tell Marie and Mrs. Hall about your first day in school."

Once we were in the car's familiar environment, Billy began

talking non-stop, continuing the chatter when we arrived home. Marie listened for a few minutes, then went to her room and closed the door. I considered going upstairs to be with her, but decided there was nothing I could say to comfort her. She would have to accept things that couldn't be changed—that her brother was beginning to move away from her and live his own life.

After I had heard about his first day in kindergarten for the third time, I left Billy with Mrs. Hall and went into my study to work on a new program. I could hear Emily moving around the kitchen with Billy dogging her footsteps, keeping up a rapid-fire recital. She must have learned patience from her own children because she seemed to enjoy the chatter.

Taking Billy to kindergarten turned out to be easier than home schooling Marie. Using a book from the "Learn at Home" series, I began teaching her to write. She didn't tackle the first lessons with her usual enthusiasm, but when she realized writing would allow her to create her own stories, she became excited about learning.

I was feeling pleased with both kid's progress until Friday, when I picked up Billy from his class.

Miss Lappin intercepted me. "Mr. Wilson, may I speak with you a moment?"

"Sure." She didn't appear to have good news.

"Billy, go over and play with the blocks," she instructed. "See if you can build a big house while I talk with your uncle."

He handed me his backpack and went to the far end of the room where there were shelves with toys on them.

"Mr. Wilson, we have a serious problem with Billy," she said quietly. "His behavior is totally unacceptable."

"In what way?" I was surprised, thinking he had become a pretty normal five-year-old. From Miss Lappin's tone, I figured he must have done something serious.

"Billy uses language better suited to a drunken longshoreman. In just this one class he used the 'F' word several times." She looked at me with an accusing expression as if I were the source of Billy's grammar. "I certainly hope you don't allow that sort of language at home."

"Of course not." Billy hadn't used street language for weeks, and I was surprised he had been cussing in school. Was he attempting to gain attention?

"I won't be able to allow him in class if his language doesn't improve. I'm sure you realize how impressionable five-year-olds can be. He uses words he shouldn't even know, and some of the other children are already beginning to copy him."

"I'm not making excuses for Billy, but it might help if I explain a little about his background," I said. "I've only had custody since his mother died from a drug overdose about two months ago. Both Billy and his sister had been physically and sexually abused and were living in conditions you would have to see to believe. The only language he knew was what he heard from alcoholics and drug addicts. We've been working to improve his vocabulary and I thought he was making great progress. I'll talk to him about his language, but I'd appreciate your help." I briefly explained our good word, bad word strategy. "Whenever he uses an unacceptable word, if you tell him it's a bad word, I'm sure the problem will disappear."

"I didn't know about his background." Miss Lappin looked sympathetic, but I could tell she didn't intend to lose control. "Of course I'll make some allowances, but we can't have him using gutter language around the other children. I hope you can appreciate my position. It won't be long before the parents begin complaining."

"I understand," I agreed. "Billy is really a sweet little boy and I know he wants to do what's right. If we both point out unacceptable words, I'm certain his language will improve immediately."

"We can try, but there will have to be a modification in his vocabulary." She didn't sound convinced. "However, bad language isn't the only problem. It isn't unusual for kindergarteners to have difficulty learning to share, but Billy is more aggressive than normal. He bullies everyone, and if he wants a toy, he just takes it. When I correct him, he doesn't listen."

"I promise to talk with Billy and make certain he behaves in class," I said. "He isn't aggressive at home. I'll explain about sharing and that he has to follow your instructions. I'd appreciate your patience. He's really a good kid. He just doesn't understand."

"I don't want to sound as if I'm not willing to work with him. The other children aren't perfect angels, but Billy has been the most disruptive. I thought it would be easier to solve the problems if we attacked them early."

"I appreciate you bringing this to my attention. I promise a big improvement in Billy's behavior when he comes back after Labor Day."

When we got home I asked Emily to supervise Marie's lessons while I took Billy into my study and closed the door.

"Miss Lappin told me you're using bad words at school. You know better than that. I want you to use good words so people will know you're a good boy. Will you do that for me?"

Billy looked like he was going to cry. "Sometimes I forget."

"I know everyone can forget once in a while, but you're going to have to try harder. Miss Lappin also told me you aren't sharing toys. You can't take things away from other kids just because you want to play with them. You know how to share. I've never seen you take any of Marie's things."

"If I took her stuff she'd hit me," he said. "The kids at school are babies. They know if they mess with me I'll punch 'em."

"Billy, I'm ashamed of you. You can't go around hitting people to get the things you want. It wouldn't be a very nice world if everyone did that, would it?"

Now Billy was crying. "I'm sorry," he sobbed.

I felt terrible. Being a parent was not going to be easy.

Emily must have been eavesdropping on our conversation because she opened the door and stuck her head in the room. "Uncle Jon, I've run into this problem with my own kids. Let me talk with Billy."

I don't know what Emily said, but it must have hit home.

Miss Lappin never mentioned Billy's behavior again.

\* \* \*

Tuesday morning after the Labor Day weekend, Emily took Marie and Billy upstairs to inspect their rooms and to get Billy dressed for kindergarten. I was feeling content and happy as I booted the computer to check my email. Billy was going to do very well in school, and Marie was beginning to enjoy her home study lessons. The world was a good place and things simply couldn't have been going any smoother.

Suddenly Shadow barked and bolted from the study. Marie screamed, and I heard something heavy tumbling down the stairs.

# CHAPTER THIRTY-THREE

**B**illy lay in a twisted heap at the bottom of the stairs, copious amounts of blood flowing from a large gash on his forehead. My first impulse was to sweep him into my arms, but I realized if he had a back or neck injury, moving him might cause further damage.

Marie stood frozen at the top of the stairs, making a low moaning sound. "Marie, I need your help," I called. "Bring some towels from the bathroom. Hurry."

My urgent appeal broke through her paralysis, and she hurried toward the bathroom.

Hampered by her arthritis, Emily was hobbling down the stairs. "Is he all right?" she asked, a hint of panic in her voice.

"I don't know." I felt helpless. "He's breathing, but he's unconscious."

Marie was sobbing, on the verge of hysteria when she rushed past Emily and handed me several towels. I pressed one against the head wound to stop the bleeding.

"Calm down, Sweetheart," I said, trying to sound reassuring. "Billy's going to be all right, but we need to call for help. Go to the phone and dial 911. When someone answers, ask them to send an ambulance. Be sure to tell them our address. Can you do that?"

It took a moment for the request to penetrate Marie's panic. Then she ran into the kitchen and I heard her dialing. "My brother fell down the stairs and he's bleeding," she sobbed into the phone. After giving the operator our address, she hung up, and hurried back.

Emily finally reached the bottom of the stairs and took

charge of Marie, holding the girl while she wept. "There, there, Honey. It'll be all right."

When we heard the ambulance siren turn into our street, Emily held the door until two paramedics rushed into the vestibule.

"We'll take over." A burley paramedic gently pushed me aside.

While he checked vital signs, the other paramedic inserted an IV into Billy's arm and placed a dressing on the head wound.

"Ed, get the gurney," the second paramedic ordered. "And bring the backboard."

"How is he?" I asked, feeling helpless.

"Looks like a broken arm and a head injury." He was applying a temporary splint to Billy's left arm. "We'll use the backboard as a precaution, but that doesn't mean there are any neck or back injuries."

The burley paramedic wheeled in the gurney, crowding Emily, Marie, and me into the living room.

It was the injustice of the accident that twisted my gut. Billy had survived a lifetime of abuse and threats from the drug gang, only to be injured when he should have been safe. I felt an unreasoning anger against God for continuing to torment such an innocent child.

After gently placing a backboard under the unconscious boy, the paramedics lifted Billy onto the gurney, covered him with a blanket, and strapped him securely in place.

"Can I ride with Billy?" I asked.

The paramedic hesitated. "Nothing you can do now. Why don't you follow in your car?"

Emily helped Marie into her coat as we rushed out the door. We were in my car and backing out of the driveway as the paramedics took off with sirens wailing. I ignored the speed limit, hugging the ambulance's rear bumper until it screeched to a halt at the emergency entrance of the Westport Hospital. Billy had already been wheeled inside when we hurried through the pedestrian entrance.

Emily led Marie to the plastic chairs in the waiting area while I went directly to the reception desk, identified myself, and asked about Billy.

"He's in a treatment room with Dr. Hill," the young, efficient nurse said. "Are you his father?"

"I'm his legal guardian."

"Then you need to sign a permission form so Dr. Hill can treat him."

I filled in the required blanks, signed where required, and handed her the document. She passed over another that asked for pertinent information such as name, address, phone number, and medical history.

"Is William allergic to any medications?" she asked as she scanned the information I had provided.

"Not that I'm aware of."

She handed the form back. "You didn't fill in the insurance information."

"Billy isn't covered by insurance," I explained. "I'll be paying the bill."

She looked at me like not having insurance created unnecessary paperwork. She selected another form from the file cabinet and passed it to me. I signed, agreeing to accept financial responsibility.

"Do you need treatment?" she asked after I'd completed the last form.

I was momentarily puzzled before realizing my shirt was covered with blood. "No, I'm okay. It's Billy's blood."

Satisfied that she wasn't going to need any further paperwork, the nurse waved toward the waiting area. "Please have a seat. You can talk to Dr. Hill after he's examined William."

"May I see Billy?" I asked.

"Not until the doctor completes his examination. It shouldn't be long."

There were four other people scattered around the waiting room, studiously avoiding looking at each other. A TV, suspended from the ceiling was playing, but no one appeared to be watching.

Marie was still sobbing and Emily hugged her, stroking her head, softly repeating, "There, there, Honey. It'll be all right." When I joined them, Emily turned to me. "The poor thing thinks it's her fault."

"It is my fault," Marie sobbed.

"I'm sure it was an accident," I assured her before questioning Emily. "How did Billy fall?" I asked.

"It happened so fast," Emily explained. "He was horsing around and was too close to the top step when he stumbled."

"See, it was an accident." I put my hand on Marie's arm. "You didn't do anything wrong."

"I'm supposed to take care of Billy," she sobbed. "I should have been watching him."

"Mrs. Hall and I are supposed to take care of Billy, too. Sometimes accidents happen and they aren't anyone's fault."

"You don't understand," Marie sobbed. "I was angry because Billy was so happy about going to school. I should have been watching and kept him away from the stairs. Now he's going to die."

"Billy isn't going to die," Emily insisted. "He's a tough little boy. You wait and see. He'll be just fine."

Marie continued sobbing as if her heart would break. I felt the same pain and fear and sense of helplessness.

"The best thing we can do now is say a prayer for Billy and ask God to heal him," Emily suggested. "God heard your prayer for Shadow, and he'll listen when we pray for Billy."

The other people in the waiting area looked uncomfortable and turned away when Emily, Marie, and I knelt on the tile floor and quietly prayed an 'Our Father' and a 'Hail Mary'.

"Please, God, make Billy well again," Marie added. There was still fear and guilt in her eyes, but the prayers appeared to have calmed her.

It was nearly thirty minutes before a doctor came out of the treatment area and approached us. "Are you the boy's father," he asked.

"I'm Billy's uncle and guardian."

The doctor nodded. "I'm Dr. Hill. Billy regained consciousness a few minutes ago. He has a simple fracture of both the ulna and radius. Those are the two bones that run the length of the forearm. He may also have a concussion, but we won't know for certain until we see the X-rays."

Dr. Hill seemed nervous and I didn't take that as a good sign. "Will he be all right?" I asked.

"A child that young heals rapidly with proper treatment." Dr. Hill was behaving strangely, as if he were uncomfortable talking with me.

"Can I see him?" I asked, suspicious there was something he was keeping from us.

"You can see William after he's moved into a room. If he only had a broken arm, he could go home today, but with a head injury, he should remain overnight for observation."

While we were talking, a police officer entered the emergency room and visited briefly with the receptionist, who pointed in our direction. The officer looked angry as he approached. He was a tall, burly man with a crew cut and a military bearing. It wasn't likely many people would choose to argue with him.

Dr. Hill seemed relieved by the policeman's presence. "Excuse me," he said, hurriedly departing. "I have to get back to my patient."

"Hello, David," Emily said, apparently recognizing the officer.

He nodded curtly toward her and then addressed me. "Mr. Wilson?" he asked.

"Yes."

"I understand your son was supposedly injured falling down the stairs," he said gruffly.

"Billy is my nephew," I said. "I didn't see the accident, but as far as I know, that's what happened." The officer's aggressive attitude puzzled me.

"Is your nephew prone to accidents?"

"No more than any other five-year-old. Why are you asking

all these questions?"

It was embarrassing to have everyone in the room staring at us.

"There's some doubt whether the fall was accidental, or even whether the injuries were the result of a fall," the cop stated.

"Of course it was an accident. What else could it be? Why is it necessary for the police to be here?"

"Dr. Hill reported suspected child abuse and that's a police matter."

I sighed and relaxed. "I can explain that," I said. There was no reason Dr. Hill would be aware of Billy's history, and the scars from his previous trauma must have looked suspicious.

"I'm sure you can explain, but before you say anything else, I'm going to read your Miranda rights." He pulled a small card from his pocket and began to read. "You have the right to remain silent…"

"What is this?" I interrupted, feeling angry and confused. "Are you arresting me?"

"David Henderson, don't make an ass of yourself," Emily scolded. "Mr. Wilson has never mistreated these children."

"Stay out of this, Mrs. Hall," he said, obviously irritated. "Child abuse is a serious charge and it's my duty to investigate."

"Then investigate and don't do something stupid. Instead of running in here and trying to arrest innocent people, why don't you find out the facts?"

Officer Henderson looked embarrassed. "Mrs. Hall, please don't interfere with official police business."

"Don't talk to me in that tone of voice, David Henderson. You're not so big I can't turn you over my knee." Emily's voice had risen until she was almost shouting. Her emotional outburst frightened Marie and she huddled against Mrs. Hall, crying again. "Mr. Wilson wasn't even there when Billy fell. But I was. Are you going to arrest me?"

"Please keep your voice down, Mrs. Hall," Officer Henderson cautioned. "You're scaring the little girl."

"You're the one frightening Marie," Emily said, lowering her voice. "If you'd bothered to check the facts, the doctor would have told you Billy's scars are months old. The boy was abused before he came to live with Mr. Wilson, which is why Mr. Wilson has custody. Before you make a complete fool of yourself, why don't you make a couple of phone calls? Ruth Greco is our family doctor and can verify what I've told you. If you can't get hold of Dr. Greco, the Campbell police have all the facts."

There was no denying Emily when her temper was triggered. It was the first time I'd ever seen a policeman intimidated. "Just calm down, Mrs. Hall. I'll make the phone calls," Officer Henderson agreed. He pointed a finger at me. "Mr. Wilson, you remain here. Don't try to leave the building."

"I'm not going anywhere." I snapped.

"I've known David all his life," Emily said when the policeman walked to the reception desk. "He used to be best friends with my son, Wayne. He's a good man, but was always on the impetuous side."

Officer Henderson was on the phone for about ten minutes before he returned, looking embarrassed. "The Campbell police confirmed your story," he said. "I'm sorry to have been so gruff, but allegations of child abuse are serious."

"Next time don't be in such a hurry to arrest someone," Emily said with an 'I-told-you-so' tone.

He ignored her and spoke to me. "Please accept my apology."

"I understand you were doing your job. No harm done."

Marie, Emily and I resumed our seats and watched Officer Henderson stop at the reception desk and speak with the nurse before leaving.

After another stressful twenty minutes trying to comfort each other Dr. Hill came out of the treatment room. "I apologize for my earlier suspicions," he said. "But I'm required by law to report evidence of child abuse."

"How's Billy?" I asked, ignoring his apology.

"Other than the broken arm and the cut on his forehead—that required twenty stitches— he should be alright. I don't believe his head injury is serious, but I'd like to keep him overnight for observation. He's already been moved to a room."

"Can we see him?" I asked.

"Certainly, but only for a few minutes."

Billy was the only patient in a semi-private room directly across from the nurse's station. Except for a night-light and the illumination from the hallway, the room was dark. A nurse was arranging Billy's blankets when we entered.

The small boy looked lost in the hospital bed, his face as pale as the large bandage on his forehead. His left arm was in a cast elevated over his head by a system of wires and pulleys. I felt like crying. Nothing but bad things had happened to the kids all their lives. When they should have been safe and secure, this had to happen.

"You can only stay a few minutes," the nurse said. "He needs his rest."

"I want to remain with him tonight," I said.

"Are you his father?"

"I'm his guardian."

The nurse considered for a moment. "All right, you can stay, but the others will have to leave."

Marie went to the bed and tried to hug her brother. "I'm sorry," she said, beginning to cry again.

"Mrs. Hall, would you take my car and drive Marie home?" I handed her my keys. "I'd appreciate it if you'd stay with her tonight."

"You didn't think I'd go home when I'm needed, did you?" She sounded like I'd hurt her feeling. "You be sure to phone if anything happens."

"I want to stay," Marie pleaded.

"There's nothing more you can do here, Honey," Emily said.

"You go home and get a good night's sleep." I hugged her. "You can visit Billy tomorrow when he's feeling better."

Emily took Marie's hand and led the reluctant girl from the room. I sat in the bedside chair, prepared for an all night vigil.

Billy woke once during the night. Still half asleep, he looked around, fear in his eyes. I leaned over the bed and kissed his cheek.  He settled then, and I held his hand until he dropped off to sleep.

# CHAPTER THIRTY-FOUR

When Dr. Greco made morning rounds, Billy was sitting on the edge of the bed, enjoying a hospital breakfast of scrambled eggs, toast, milk, orange juice, and a large cinnamon roll. The nurse had removed his arm from the pulley device, arranging a sling around his neck to support the cast.

"How are you doing this morning, Billy?" she asked, removing the bandage and examining the stitches in his forehead.

"I felled down the stairs and broked my arm," Billy exclaimed.

"Yes, I know." She put a fresh, smaller dressing over the stitches. "You aren't going to do that again, are you?"

"I'm going to be real careful," Billy said, looking so serious I nearly laughed.

"So, what's the prognosis?" I asked. "Will he be going home today?"

"I don't see why not. Let him rest today, and unless something unexpected comes up, he should be able to go to school Thursday. Schedule an appointment at the clinic for Monday and we'll remove the stitches. The nurse will give you instructions for taking care of the arm and cast." She made a notation on the chart. "I hear there was a little excitement in the emergency room last night."

I assumed she was referring to Officer Henderson's visit. "Nothing serious. Just a little misunderstanding."

"It must have been awkward for you, but we can't be too careful where children are concerned. Dr. Hill was only doing his duty."

"I'd probably have done the same thing in his place," I agreed. "Maybe if someone had called the police when the kids were younger they would have been spared a lot of pain."

"I'm glad you understand," she said, heading for the door. "See you Monday, Billy. And no more falling down stairs."

I phoned Emily and asked her to pick us up and bring clean clothes for Billy. While we waited, I did the necessary paperwork at the nurse's station and collected the plastic bag containing his bloodstained clothing.

"I felled down the stairs and broked my arm," Billy exclaimed as soon as Emily and Marie walked into the room. He waved his cast like it was a trophy.

"Yes, you did," Emily said, giving him a hug. "And don't you ever do that again. Why, you nearly scared me to death."

Billy giggled. "I sure won't do that again."

A short, chubby candy striper pushed a wheelchair into the room. "Hop on Billy," she said. "It's time to go home."

"We don't need a wheelchair," I protested.

"Hospital policy. We have to give discharged patients a ride to the entrance."

Billy thoroughly enjoyed the wheelchair ride and would have preferred being pushed across the parking lot, but reluctantly got off at the entrance and walked with us to the car. He kept up a constant chatter all the way home, and I was grateful Emily was there to listen to his monologue.

For my part, I prayed silently that we wouldn't have any more excitement.

* * *

By Monday morning life was back to normal—at least as normal as it ever got.

Billy had been something of a celebrity in the Thursday and Friday afternoon kindergarten classes when he told everyone about his adventures. All the children drew little pictures on his cast, which he displayed to us over and over until we cringed inwardly every time he took the cast from its sling.

Marie still amazed me with her intelligence. She had quickly grasped the fundamentals of writing, and her penmanship was improving daily. Even though I was concerned we might be doing too much too soon, we had begun simple addition problems. As with everything else, she relished the opportunity to learn a new skill and was doing better than I expected.

She was working on a math lesson and Billy was busy cutting out pictures on the dining room table when I glanced at the clock and saw it was nearly eleven.

"Time to take a break, Marie," I said. "Finish the problem you're working on, and then wash up. We have to start lunch before Mrs. Hall gets here."

The floor around the dining room table was littered with scraps from Billy's cutting. "You'd better clean up that mess before Mrs. Hall gets here," I suggested.

He picked up the larger scraps and put them in the kitchen trash. He was having such a hard time with the little pieces I suggested he use the vacuum cleaner even though it would be awkward with his left arm in the sling. I was tempted to vacuum for him, but Emily insisted he clean up his own messes. I wasn't in the mood for a scolding if she walked in while I let Billy play the invalid.

I almost didn't hear the doorbell over the noise of the vacuum, and was surprised to find Ann Riley at the door.
"Sorry to just show up on your doorstep," she said. "I hope this isn't an inconvenient time. I was in the area and thought we could get the monthly inspection out of the way."

"Not a problem," I said, suspecting she had purposefully come unannounced just to catch us doing something negative. I was convinced Child Protective Services was looking for evidence of my incompetence.

"This'll be the last inspection before the court hearing," she said. "I'll miss visiting with Marie and Billy."

I laughed. "Not that we haven't enjoyed your visits, but I'll be glad to be done with this whole routine."

We stepped into the dining room just as Billy turned off the vacuum cleaner. Mrs. Riley frowned when she saw the cast and the bandage on his forehead.

"My goodness, Billy, what happened to you?"

"I felled down the stairs," he exclaimed, overjoyed to have a new audience for his story. "I went to the hospital and rode in a wheelchair. I broked my arm and everyone drew pictures on my cast. Do you want to put your name on it?"

"Of course I do," she said, scribbling a signature on the cast.

Mrs. Riley glanced into the kitchen where Marie was gathering the ingredients for grilled cheese sandwiches and chicken noodle soup. "Good morning, Marie."

"Hi." She smiled and continued with her preparations.

The social worker looked at me with a question in her eyes. "Shouldn't Marie be in school at this time of day?"

"She's home-schooling and doing extremely well," I explained. "I've never met a smarter little girl. You might want to see some of her completed lessons."

"I'd like that," she said, stepping into the kitchen. "I see you're also learning to be a cook, Marie. Do you prepare many meals?"

"I always make lunch," Marie boasted. "Mrs. Hall usually lets me help with supper. Uncle Jon says I'm already a better cook than he is."

"Would you like to join us for lunch?" I asked. "It wouldn't be a problem to put on one more plate."

"That would be very nice."

At that moment Emily came bursting into the front room. "What a crummy day. At least it's not snowing yet. But you mark my words. We're going to have snow before Halloween." Then she noticed Mrs. Riley. "Oh, hello."

I introduced the women. "Mrs. Hall has been a wonderful help with the house and the children."

"I'd love to show you how much progress the kids have made during the last two months," Emily grumbled, more curtly than normal. "But I know you're not here to listen to me ramble. You just forget I'm around and get on with your inspection. I'll be in the kitchen if you need me."

By the time Mrs. Riley had completed her walk through of the house, Emily and Marie had lunch on the table.

"This is an excellent grilled cheese sandwich," Mrs. Riley said. "It's been a long, long time since I've had one this good."

Marie was nearly bursting with pride. "Thank you."

As soon as everyone had finished eating, I stood up. "You're going to have to excuse us. It's time to get Billy ready for school. Marie, you help him put away the vacuum cleaner and then give him a hand getting dressed. We can do the dishes later."

"He took the cleaner out," Marie complained. "He should put it away."

"Don't argue. You know Billy gets the cord all goofed up. Just be a good girl and help him."

"I really wanted to talk with both children," Mrs. Riley said.

"I wish there was more time, but Billy missed two school days last week because of the accident, and really can't afford to be absent again. You can visit with Marie, and she'll show you her schoolwork. Feel free to check out anything in the house. Mrs. Hall can answer your questions. I should be back in ten minutes or so."

When I returned, Marie was showing Mrs. Riley some of the math lessons we'd already done and corrected.

"Wouldn't you like to go to school where you can meet new friends?" Mrs. Riley asked.

"Uncle Jon says if I work hard and learn my lessons really well this year, I might go to school next year."

"Marie, you've been visiting long enough," Emily said, standing in the kitchen doorway, hands on hips. "You've got dirty dishes to wash before you get back to your lessons."

"The dishes can wait a minute, Mrs. Hall," I said, irritated by Emily's attitude. It wasn't like her to be rude.

"That's all right, Mr. Wilson," Mrs. Riley said, glancing at her watch. "Marie and I were finished and I have to be going."

I walked her to the door and helped with her coat. "It's only a couple of weeks until the custody hearing," I said.   "I was wondering what sort of report you'll be giving the judge."

"I'm afraid I'm not at liberty to discuss that.  You can ask Mrs. Henderson to show you the reports, but I doubt whether she'll release the information.  Our evaluations are confidential unless Judge Monroe decides you should have access.  If you insist on reading them, your attorney will have to petition the court."

"I don't think that will be necessary.  I was just curious." Going to the trouble of petitioning the court didn't seem worth the effort, but I'd ask Jim Stanley what he thought and go by his advice.

I escorted Mrs. Riley to her car, and then waited until Emily and Marie had finished the dishes. Marie was struggling over her math assignment when I confronted Emily.

"I didn't appreciate you interrupting Mrs. Riley.  You know the reports from Child Protective Services could make the difference between whether or not I get custody."

"Maybe I should have tiptoed around while she was here, but the way she was asking questions about Marie's schooling raised my hackles.  You mark my words.  She's going to cause trouble."

"Well, you didn't help matters any."

I called Jim Stanley to remind him about our scheduled court date on the twenty-first.  He promised to contact everyone involved, from the doctors to the lawyers, to Child Protective Services and obtain copies of their reports.

"What do you want me to do in the meantime?" I asked.

"There isn't anything you can do.  I'll call when I've got everything together and I've talked with the CPS attorney."

"I feel like I should be doing something.  I really want permanent custody."

"Don't worry about it. Judge Monroe obviously leans toward kids staying with family.  If Child Protective Services wants to fight custody, they'll need a damned good reason.  You aren't keeping anything from me, are you?"

"No.  Everything is going better than I expected.  No offense to your profession, but I always worry that the legal system isn't going to do the logical thing."

"Hey, I've got a client waiting for me," Jim said. "I'll have Madge set up an appointment after I get the paperwork together. Meanwhile, stop worrying."

There was no way I could stop worrying. Marie and Billy had become an important part of my life, and I had no desire to become a bachelor again. More than anything, I wanted the kids to be with me for Thanksgiving and Christmas and Billy's January birthday.

I was not going to allow the court to take away my children.

# CHAPTER THIRTY-FIVE

My anxiety level peaked as the date for the court hearing approached. I couldn't concentrate on work and didn't have an appetite, even when Emily and Marie prepared a particularly delicious meal. Every morning when I looked at the sleeping children, I wondered whether I was one day closer to losing them forever. They had become such an integral part of my existence; I knew life would be hollow without them.

Madge called on Thursday to schedule a Friday morning appointment for my final consultation with Jim Stanley before the Tuesday morning court date. It wasn't her fault, but I had to bite my tongue to keep from snapping at her for waiting until nearly the last minute.

When I got to Jim's office, I wasn't in a very good mood, and his opening remarks didn't help my attitude.

"First, Child Protective Services still intends to fight custody," he said.

"Damn it, that's BS and you know it. The kids are doing great and they're happy with me. CPS should have backed off after the fiasco with the Blackmans. If they'd had their way, Marie and Billy would be dead now."

"Hey, I'm on your side, remember. Maybe someone in the bureaucracy doesn't like you. Any way, they're going to contest, and I don't have any idea what their argument will be."

"Don't they have to abide by a disclosure rule or something of that sort?"

"Not in civil actions like this. CPS isn't under any obligation to divulge their case prior to the hearing. The court only requires them to make their monthly reports available to us."

"At least that's something. Shouldn't the reports give us a clue?"

"Here, read them for yourself." He handed me a sheaf of papers. "As you can see, they're just check boxes that don't tell us a damned thing. Explanations must have been verbal or CPS conveniently forgot to include them."

"Damn it, we can't go into this blind. Don't they have to give the judge a brief or something?"

"They probably have, but CPS knows how to play the game. They waited until the last minute to send the reports, knowing I wouldn't be able to reach Judge Monroe. Apparently she's taking a long weekend. All we're going to have before the hearing is what's in your hands."

"So, where do we go from here?" I asked. "Jim, I don't have to tell you that winning permanent custody means everything to me and the kids."

"I'll do the best I can. We know they'll make an issue out of the attacks by the drug people. Since the kids were nearly killed, they'll argue that you put them in harm's way—that you didn't exercise sufficient caution. I have enough information about what happened to make a convincing rebuttal. I suspect CPS will also have updated psychological reports."

"Damn it, I pay Dr. Scott's bills. Isn't it a violation of confidentiality or something for her to give information without my permission?"

"Priests and lawyers have confidentiality, but doctors are still a murky legal question. The psychological reports are important to the court, and most likely Dr. Scott will voluntarily cooperate. You might have grounds for a lawsuit against Psychological Associates, but that's another can of worms. For now, let's assume she makes her evaluations available to CPS or the court. Is she likely to say anything that would cause a problem?"

I shook my head. "I don't see how. She wasn't too thrilled about hypnotizing Marie, but since Marie wasn't traumatized and her information removed the drug threat, Scott's objections shouldn't be a problem. Both kids have been making great progress. She even suggested cutting Marie's sessions to twice a week and Billy to once a week."

"Good. That sounds like there shouldn't be any surprises from the good doctor. From what you've told me, it isn't likely CPS will have any aces up their sleeves that could hurt us. Just relax and enjoy the weekend. Everything will work out fine."

"I'm not going to be able to relax until this is over."

Jim came around the desk and shook my hand. "I want you to know I was wrong. When you first suggested seeking custody, I was certain it was a huge mistake. Well, I've changed my mind. Now I think you're doing absolutely the right thing."

\* \* \*

I told Emily about my appointment with Jim Stanley and she agreed CPS couldn't have any surprises for us.

"The Judge is going to see how well the children are doing and won't have any choice but to rule in our favor."

"I hope you're right."

"What time is the court hearing?" she asked.

"You don't have to come with us."

Emily put her fists on her hips and leaned toward me. "Jonathon Wilson, if you think I'm going to sit around here while some judge in Campbell decides where our kids are going to live, then you have another think coming!"

"I just thought you'd have better things to do than sit in court."

"Well, you thought wrong. No matter what happens, those kids will need me, and I'm going to be there for them."

"Now comes the hardest part," I said. "I've never told the kids that custody was only temporary."

"Then we'll tell them together," Emily said firmly.

That evening after the dishes were washed and put away, Emily and I gathered the kids for a family conference. I didn't have any idea how I was going to explain custody so they would understand, but I had to try.

"Do you remember after your mother died, when Mrs. Henderson and Child Protective Services took care of you for several days before you came to live with me?" I asked.

"I remember," Billy said. "I didn't like it. They didn't have any toys and Marie wasn't with me."

Marie simply nodded, looking suspicious, as if she already realized she wouldn't enjoy this discussion.

"Before I could bring you home, I had to get permission from Children's Court because Child Protective Services was worried about whether I would take proper care of you guys. They wanted you to live with a foster family where you would have a mother and father."

"We have you and Mrs. Hall," Marie said. "We like you better than any old foster parents."

"Bless your heart." Emily gathered both kids into a hug.

"Anyway, the judge decided to give me a chance to see if we could be a family," I continued. "She said you could come to live with me for three months, and then the court would decide whether you had a good home."

"I want to stay here," Billy said.

"Both Mrs. Hall and I want you to live here," I agreed. "But we have to go to court Tuesday morning so the judge can decide if you'll be here forever."

"Are you going to send us away?" Marie asked, with the same detached look she had when she came to live with me. There was a pain in her eyes that suggested she should have known better than to trust anyone. I was afraid she would tune out so that whatever I said couldn't hurt.

"Of course I'm not going to send you away," I said as positively as I could. "I'm going to fight with everything I have to keep you with me. I just want you to understand that the judge might decide I haven't done a good job."

"I don't want to go away," Billy said, beginning to cry.

"Don't worry. Mrs. Hall and I love you kids and we won't let anyone take you from us."

"Can we stay if we're good and don't eat so much?" Billy

asked.

"You can stay even if you eat every bit of food in the house, including Shadow's dog food," I promised.

Marie tried to pretend it didn't matter, but her emotions were too close to the surface. Tears were caught in the corners of her eyes. "I don't believe you. You're going to send us away because you don't want us anymore."

"Hogwash," Emily said, sweeping Marie into her arms. "You know that isn't true. I don't want to hear such foolish talk. Uncle Jon is going to fight to keep you with us, and I'll be standing right at his side."

"Remember we're a family now—you, me, and Mrs. Hall. But I'll need your help. We all have to pray very hard and ask God to keep us together."

That night when I tucked Marie into bed, she reached out to hug me and began crying softly. "Please don't send me away," she whimpered. "I'll be good. I promise."

"I won't ever send you away. You're my little girl now and I love you very much. I'll fight the court just as hard as I fought those bad men."

I held her until she fell asleep. Then I went into my room and lay on the bed, staring at the ceiling, feeling frightened and helpless.

# CHAPTER THIRTY-SIX

When Emily arrived at seven o'clock Tuesday morning, I was up, dressed, and had just awakened the kids. Marie and Billy breakfasted on French toast and sausage links while still in their pajamas. I was too nervous to eat anything.

"You get Billy dressed while I wash the dishes," Emily ordered. "Marie, I laid out your new dress. Don't dawdle. We have to be on our way in a few minutes."

I helped Billy into his dark blue slacks and a short sleeve blue shirt that would slip over his cast. Marie was monopolizing the bathroom, so I took Billy downstairs to comb his unruly hair.

"My, don't you look handsome, this morning," Emily said as she adjusted his sling.

"I'm handsome this morning," Billy agreed. "Will the Judge like me?"

"Of course she will."

We all had our jackets on and Marie was still upstairs. "Hurry up, Marie," I called. "We don't want to be late."

"I'm coming," she replied.

I must have looked startled when Marie came down the stairs. She was wearing a new red dress with white trim. Her hair was perfectly brushed and secured with a barrette on each side. It was her make-up that caught my attention.

Somewhere Marie had found a tube of crimson lipstick and applied it liberally. The coloring had smeared at the corners of her mouth and when she smiled lipstick stains were visible on her teeth.

Emily must have known I was going to say something

because she jabbed a sharp elbow into my ribs and stepped in front of me. "My, don't you look pretty," she said, holding Marie at arm's length and smiling at her.

Marie looked so proud and happy my heart melted. She smiled expectantly at me. "You look great, Sweetheart," I said. "But..."

"No but about it, Marie, you look beautiful," Emily said. "You kids get in the car. Uncle Jon and I will be out in a minute."

"We can't let Marie go to court looking like that," I said when the kids were outside.

"Jonathon Wilson, if you say one word to Marie about her lipstick, I'll never forgive you."

"But what will Judge Monroe think?"

"I don't care what the judge thinks. Why don't you stop worrying about making an impression and consider Marie? It's the most important day of her life and she's trying to look her best in the only way she knows. Think what it'll do to her self-esteem if you criticize her. Child abuse isn't only about hitting and torturing kids, you know. If you criticize the lipstick, it'll leave a scar on her heart that won't ever heal."

"Maybe you could help her fix it properly," I suggested.

"I'll do no such thing. That child is wearing lipstick to please us, and I won't do a single, solitary thing to make her think we aren't thrilled with what she's done."

During the drive to Campbell, I watched Marie in the rear view mirror. She looked prouder and happier than I'd ever seen her. Emily had been right. Nothing, not even a court appearance, was so important that I would chance taking that sparkle from her eyes. Damn it, if Judge Monroe didn't like the lipstick, maybe she didn't have any business being a judge in Children's Court.

# CHAPTER THIRTY-SEVEN

J im Stanley was shuffling papers at the defense table when we arrived in the courtroom. As Emily and the two kids slid onto the front row of spectator seats, I introduced them. Jim smiled and shook hands, looking at me with a raised eyebrow when he greeted Marie. I frowned at him, and with a slight shrug, he acted as if nothing were unusual.

We had barely settled when Frank Johnson entered and walked directly to the other table, doing a double take as he glanced at Marie. I quickly stepped across the aisle and whispered to him. "If you say one word, or make one comment about Marie's lipstick, I'll break your face."

He took a step backward and looked startled. "Are you threatening me?" he asked.

"Keep your voice down," I hissed. "You can take it any way you want."

Before he could respond, the stenographer took her seat, followed immediately by Judge Monroe. Everyone stood, but she waved us down while she studied the folder on her desk.

Johnson stood. "Your Honor, may I approach the bench?"

She motioned him forward. They talked in low voices for a moment before she looked up. "Mr. Wilson, would you and Mr. Stanley please approach the bench."

Jim and I walked to the front of the room and Judge Monroe addressed me in a quiet voice. "Mr. Johnson has just informed me that you threatened him."

"It was more in the nature of a warning," I explained.

"And what was the nature of this warning?" she asked sternly.

"I told him if he made any reference to Marie's lipstick I would break his face."

Judge Monroe looked past us to where the children were sitting and suppressed a smile. "Mr. Wilson, do you realize threatening an officer of the court is a serious offense? I could hold you in contempt."

"Yes, Your Honor." I tried to sound contrite, but knew it didn't come off.

"I'm sure Mr. Wilson didn't mean it, Your Honor," Jim said.

"No offense intended to the court, Your Honor, but I meant every word," I affirmed.

Judge Monroe put on a serious face and leaned closer to the CPS attorney. "Mr. Johnson, apparently Mr. Wilson is serious about punching you in the nose if you mention the lipstick. If he hit you I would have him arrested, but that wouldn't save your nose, would it? It might be better for all concerned if you take Mr. Wilson's warning seriously and refrain from mentioning the lipstick." She sat back in her chair and spoke in a normal voice. "Now, let's get on with this hearing."

Johnson looked disappointed as we returned to our places.

"The matter before us is the final custody hearing for Marie and William Wilson," Judge Monroe said to the stenographer. "Let the record show Child Protective Services is represented by Frank Johnson, and James Stanley is representing Jonathon Wilson."

She opened another folder. "Mr. Johnson, you may proceed."

"Your Honor, Child Protective Services believes Mr. Wilson has demonstrated an inability to properly supervise Marie and William," he began. "As we stated at the previous hearing, we believe the children's best interests will be served in our foster care program."

"I have the most recent psychological reports from Dr. Deana Scott," Judge Monroe said indicating a sheaf of papers. "They suggest the children are making excellent progress. I'd be interested in hearing why Child Protective Services believes the children should not remain with Mr. Wilson."

"Yes, Your Honor.  During the last three months there have been several examples illustrating Mr. Wilson's inability to properly care for the children."

Jim leaned over and whispered in my ear.  "It sounds like you may have pissed him off."

"I'm sure the court is aware of two highly publicized incidents where Mr. Wilson actually endangered the children's lives," Johnson continued.  "Apparently Mr. Wilson's neighborhood isn't as safe an environment as we had assumed.  Mr. Wilson has found it necessary to have several loaded weapons, without the protection of trigger locks, where they are accessible to the children.  Several weeks ago there was a home invasion with shots fired by Mr. Wilson, without regard to the children's safety.  Then, just three weeks ago, Mr. Wilson had Marie and William with him during a gun battle where three men were killed.  It was only by the Grace of God that the children weren't injured."

"He's twisting it all around," I whispered to Jim.

"Keep cool.  We'll have a chance to tell our story."

Johnson pointed to where the children sat.  "I would like to draw the court's attention to William's broken left arm, which was reportedly caused by an accidental fall down a flight of stairs.  Although abuse was not proven, the attending physician considered the alleged accident suspicious and requested an investigation by the Westport police.  Whether or not the incident was an accident, it clearly demonstrates a lack of adequate supervision.

"Last week when Mrs. Riley conducted an unannounced, court ordered inspection, she found William with his arm in a cast, being forced to vacuum the carpet.  She also observed Marie preparing a meal for the entire family.  We believe this strongly suggests Mr. Wilson is using the children to maintain his household in a manner inappropriate to their ages, without consideration of their handicaps."

I leaned close to Jim.  "He's making it sound as if I'm some sort of monster, abusing the kids."

"As indicated in Dr. Scott's report, Mr. Wilson insisted, against the psychologist's professional advice, that Marie be hypnotized.  This is another clear example of Mr. Wilson considering his own agenda more important than the state of Marie's mental health.

"Finally, there is the matter of the children's education. Mr. Wilson has elected to home school Marie while enrolling William in a public kindergarten class. Child Protective Services has no objection to home schooling, although we question whether Mr. Wilson has credentials qualifying him to teach. CPS would provide a tutor to work with both children until they are ready to attend public educational facilities."

"The statute regarding home schooling doesn't require parents or guardians to have teaching certification before they enroll in the program," Judge Monroe noted.

"We understand that, Your Honor.  However, Mr. Wilson has demonstrated poor judgment in his educational choices. William's social skills are obviously not up to normal standards, and we believe he should also be home schooled until such time as he is able to interact properly with other children.  His kindergarten teacher reported frequent vulgar language in class, and on more than one occasion Billy has struck other children without provocation.

"There may be further instances of custodial abuse we aren't aware of, but even so, Mr. Wilson has clearly racked up an impressive list during only three months.  Therefore we ask the court to grant custody to Child Protective Services."

Johnson sat down and Judge Monroe turned to Jim.  "Mr. Stanley, do you have a response?"

"Yes, Your Honor," Jim said. "May I consult with my client for a moment?"

"Make it brief."

"What about Billy's problems in kindergarten?" he whispered.

"It isn't a problem," I said.  "He had some adjustment difficulties the first few days, but we've addressed the situation and it's not an issue."

Jim stood. "Thank you, Your Honor. We categorically deny Mr. Johnson's allegations, and contend he distorted the facts to present a prejudiced viewpoint. Rather than simply refute his arguments point by point, with your permission, I would like to call a witness who can give evidence in our behalf."

Judge Monroe nodded. "Call your witness."

"Mrs. Emily Hall, would you please take the witness stand?"

Johnson jumped to his feet. "Objection!"

"To what are you objecting, Mr. Johnson?"

"Mrs. Hall is not an impartial witness. She's employed by Mr. Wilson and has a financial interest in supporting his position."

"Objection overruled. I would assume, Mr. Johnson, you are sufficiently proficient in the art of cross-examination to expose prejudicial testimony. Besides, I'm interested in hearing what Mrs. Hall has to say."

Emily came to the front of the courtroom, swore the oath, and sat in the witness chair.

Jim walked around the table and approached her. "Mrs. Hall, how long have you been employed as a housekeeper for Mr. Wilson?"

"Just about three months. I started a few days after Marie and Billy came to live with him."

"I understand you raised several children of your own."

"Three boys and two girls," Emily proudly announced.

"So, would it be correct to state you've had extensive experience with children?"

"Over thirty years."

"Then, as an expert, would you say Marie and Billy are happy and being properly cared for?"

"Objection!" Johnson said.

"What is your objection this time?" Judge Monroe asked, frowning.

"Just because Mrs. Hall raised five children doesn't qualify her as an expert."

"Objection overruled. Mr. Johnson, this is an informal

hearing. Unless you have a point of law, please refrain from delaying the proceedings with frivolous objections. I'm not certain there is such a thing as an expert on raising children, but Mrs. Hall's experience certainly qualifies her to give an opinion." She turned to Emily. "You may answer the question."

"Yes, Your Honor." She turned to Jim. "Would you repeat the question?"

"Do you believe Marie and Billy are happy and properly cared for?"

"Of course. Mr. Wilson treats those children better than I treated mine. They're as happy as any youngsters I've ever known."

"Were you present when Billy had his accident?"

"Yes."

"Would you please tell the court what happened?"

"It all happened so fast," Emily said. "Billy was horsing around, like a five-year-old will, when he stumbled and fell down the stairs."

"Was Mr. Wilson present at the time?"

"He was downstairs in his study."

"In your opinion, was the accident the result of inadequate supervision?"

"Certainly not." Emily sounded indignant. "I was only a couple of feet away. You can't supervise children any closer than that. As I said, it happened so fast, I doubt whether anyone could have prevented the fall."

"Were you aware of the children being required to do household chores?"

"It was my idea, and I wouldn't want it any other way," Emily stated. "It gives children a sense of belonging when they're given responsibilities around the house. Marie and Billy are proud of their accomplishments."

"Thank you, Mrs. Hall." Jim turned to Johnson. "Your witness."

Johnson rose from his chair. "Mrs. Hall, don't you agree these children are performing chores inappropriate for their ages?"

"I don't know what you consider inappropriate."

"For example, don't you agree it was inappropriate for William to be forced to vacuum the carpet in spite of his age and his broken arm?"

"Billy was perfectly capable of handling the vacuum cleaner. Don't you require your children to clean up a mess they've made?"

"I'm the one asking questions," Johnson said.

"Then don't ask such foolish ones," Emily snapped.

Johnson looked embarrassed when he turned to Judge Monroe who was attempting to suppress a smile. "I have no further questions for this witness, Your Honor."

"You are excused, Mrs. Hall," Judge Monroe said. "Do you have anything further, Mr. Stanley?"

"Yes, Your Honor." Jim stood and paused while Emily returned to her seat with the children. "Although I'm sure the court is aware of the facts, I would like to address the issue of the shootings." He briefly explained the situation with Pusher and Jenny's involvement with the drugs and money.

"It was Detective Kincaid who suggested Mr. Wilson have one or more guns in the house. Mr. Wilson carefully instructed the children about the dangers of loaded weapons, and as much as possible, kept them away from the children. Considering the nature of the threat against them, the weapons were essential. If Mr. Wilson's guns had not been handy, it's very likely we wouldn't be in court today because the children would be dead. Unless Child Protective Services could have arranged twenty-four hour police protection, foster parents would not have been able to protect the children as well as Mr. Wilson did."

"Objection," Johnson said. "Counsel is speculating."

"Objection sustained. Please stick to the facts, Mr. Stanley."

"Yes, Your Honor. We admit that Dr. Scott strenuously objected to hypnotizing Marie, and only proceeded because of Mr. Wilson's insistence. However, he was convinced any temporary setback to her treatment was far outweighed by the threat to both Marie and Billy's lives. As it turned out, there were no adverse effects to Marie, and subsequently the hypnosis resulted in locating the drugs and money, which removed the children from danger.

"The last three months have presented unique problems no one could have anticipated. We believe Mr. Wilson handled the situation better than most people in similar circumstances. Marie and Billy have not only survived the threat to their lives, but are happy in their new home. We believe it would border on criminal to remove them from Mr. Wilson's care."

When Jim sat, I stood. "Your Honor, may I make a statement?"

"Do you have facts bearing on a decision in this matter?"

"No, Your Honor. I would like to state my opinion for your consideration."

"You may make your statement, but please be brief."

"Thank you." I said, attempting to organize my thoughts. "When I requested custody of Marie and Billy three months ago, I did it from a sense of obligation and perhaps more than a little guilt. I'll be the first to admit I didn't know what I was getting into. They have suffered abuse, lived in conditions I still cannot imagine, and have problems beyond comprehension. Yet in just three short months they've begun to adjust to their new life. I've come to love them as if they were my own children.

"If they are placed with Child Protective Services, I realize every effort will be made to find foster homes for them, but there is no guarantee they'll remain together. Your Honor, from the time Billy was born, these children have been forced to depend on each other. I firmly believe it was this bonding that allowed them to survive.

"Marie and Billy must be allowed to remain with me as they learn to reach out to other people, such as myself and Mrs. Hall. Three months is not long enough to erase the effects of years of misery, but it has been a start. They have begun to establish a firm foundation with their own family. Some day both Marie and Billy will spread their wings and soar into the future, but before children can have wings they must have strong roots. I sincerely believe I can provide those roots."

I sat down, and for a moment the courtroom was silent. "Thank you, Mr. Wilson. Does Child Protective Services have anything further to present?"

"No, Your Honor."

"Then court will recess for one hour while I consider my decision."

Marie, Billy, Mrs. Hall, and I went out into the hallway. I was pretty sure Billy had no idea what was happening in the courtroom, but Marie understood.

"Will they take us away?" she asked, looking lonely and frightened.

"I don't know, but if the judge says you have to go with Child Protective Services, it won't be over. I'll fight to keep you— whatever it takes—even if we have to run away. I love you both. You're my children now, no matter what the judge decides."

"I don't want to go away," Billy said, beginning to cry. "I want to stay with you and Mrs. Hall."

"Bless your heart," Emily said, taking Billy into her arms. "You don't have to cry. Everything will be okay.

"I promise you, one way or another, we'll all stay together," I said.

Emily and I took the children to the café across the street and bought them ice cream. Apparently Billy was convinced he was safe because he attacked his treat with an appetite. Marie only nibbled, and there was a worried look in her eyes.

After the longest hour in my life, we went back into the courtroom and took our seats.

Judge Monroe consulted her notes and looked up. "As I've stated on numerous occasions, I believe Child Protective Services and our foster care system is second to none. They perform an invaluable service to our community and to children in need of protection and security. However, Mr. Johnson, after consulting my notes and your own brief, I've concluded you twisted the facts to support your position. That sort of tactic might work with a jury, but it insulted my intelligence. If you ever do that in my courtroom again, I will cite you for contempt."

She smiled at me. "Mr. Wilson, it has been a very difficult three months. It is my opinion few people could have handled the situation as well. Obviously you have demonstrated a high degree of love and dedication. It's my decision that permanent custody of Marie and William Wilson be granted to Jonathon Wilson."

It was as if a great weight had been lifted from my shoulders.

Before I could thank Jim Stanley, Marie was hugging me around the waist and crying. "Are we going to stay with you forever?"

"Yes. We're now officially a family." I knelt to hug her and she kissed me on the cheek. Then Billy was there trying to hug both of us and Emily attempted to wrap all of us in her embrace.

When we stepped out of the courthouse I had never been prouder of anything in my life than the lipstick smear on my cheek. We all stood for a moment on the steps, holding hands and breathing the clean, crisp air.

Leading the way, I started down the courthouse steps. "Let's go home," I said. "Shadow is waiting for his family."

## Suffer The Children

If you enjoyed this book, please consider posting a review on Amazon. Even if it's only a few sentences, it would be a huge help for other readers when making a decision whether a book is worth reading. This link will take you directly to the Amazon book page: http://amzn.to/35QERzN